THE LAST
AVATAR

VISHWAS MUDAGAL is a best-selling author, serial entrepreneur, CEO, angel investor and a motivational speaker. An alumnus of RV College of Engineering, Bengaluru, he is currently the CEO & co-founder of GoodWorkLabs and the co-founder of GoodWorks CoWork.

Writing is his passion, and he has embraced storytelling as his parallel career. He is the author of the best-selling novel, *Losing My Religion*.

Mudagal is a widely followed social media influencer with more than 60 million views on his web series called *AskVishwas*. To know more, visit: www.vishwasmudagal. com

THE LAST
AVATAR

AGE OF KALKI 1

VISHWAS MUDAGAL

HarperCollins *Publishers* India

First published in India by
HarperCollins *Publishers* in 2018
A-75, Sector 57, Noida, Uttar Pradesh 201301, India
www.harpercollins.co.in

2 4 6 8 10 9 7 5 3 1

P-ISBN: 978-93-5302-466-6
E-ISBN: 978-93-5302-467-3

Typeset in 11/14 ITC New Baskerville Std at
Manipal Digital Systems, Manipal

Printed and bound at
Thomson Press (India) Ltd

Dedicated
to the brave soldiers of India and to their families.

Whenever there is decay of righteousness and there is rise of unrighteousness, then I manifest myself;

For the protection of the good, for the destruction of evil and for the sake of firmly establishing righteousness, I am born from age to age.

Bhagavad Gita, Chapter 4, Verse: 7-8

In the near future...

PROLOGUE

Professor Haridas and his associate ran for their lives. 'We don't have time. The package cannot fall into their wicked hands,' shouted Haridas, gasping for breath as they treaded a treacherous terrain in the dead of the night. The fact that it was a moonless night didn't help.

Deep inside the excavation site at Mohenjo-daro in the Sindh province of Pakistan, Haridas was part of an elite team of scholars and archaeologists gathered by the dreaded extremist group, Invisible Hand, to unearth the treasures of the ancient Indus Valley Civilization. The package he held in his hand was the prize of their two years of struggle. He had managed to steal it and escape as instructed by the Rudras, to whom he owed his allegiance as an undercover operative, and under no circumstances was he supposed to let it fall into the wrong hands.

'What have you found? What does the package contain?' asked Haridas's associate, a trained agent sent to extract the professor from the excavation site.

They heard dogs barking and a chopper thundering to life at a distance.

'This can't be good. They know we are on the run! We have to hurry,' Haridas said, struggling to see through the darkness. 'Listen to me carefully,' he continued. 'It is, in fact, what we were hoping to find. It's one of the original scripts of the Scripture of Gods. In the wrong hands, the Scripture possesses enough knowledge to destroy our planet.'

Since 316 BC, when Emperor Chandragupta Maurya and his Chief Advisor Chanakya first regrouped the ancient secret society called the Rudras, different people in power had tried to get access to the nine sets of scriptures that were believed to hold 'absolute' knowledge. They were collectively called the Scripture of Gods and had been protected by the Rudras since ancient times. But a few centuries ago, the Rudras had lost some of the scripts, and now that they had finally reclaimed at least one of them, they had to take it to safety—even if it meant giving up their lives in the process.

Haridas and his associate reached a steep slope that led to the river. It looked like a death trap. The current was too powerful, and with the dogs chasing them and the vehicles approaching with search lights, they had no time to think. The choppers were still relentlessly trying to locate them.

'We have to jump,' the associate said, and held the professor tightly as they slid down the slope.

By the time they reached the riverside, they were bruised and bleeding. To their horror, a chopper caught them in the spotlight and they were soon surrounded by mercenary trucks.

'Professor Haridas! You turned out to be a clever little mouse,' spoke a cold voice on the loudspeaker. He was the commander of the mercenaries and incharge of the expedition to unearth the scriptures. He stood at the top of the slope with a gun in his hand and cut a terrifying figure. 'But if you thought I didn't have my eyes on you, you were mistaken.'

Haridas and his associate tried to run but were outnumbered and surrounded.

'Give me the scripture and I will consider sparing your life.'

'Never. Not even if I have to die today,' Haridas yelled.

'I will not ask again,' the commander said as he fired a bullet between Haridas's associate's eyes. His skull burst open and Haridas watched in horror as he collapsed to the ground.

'You monster! This is exactly why you are not worthy of the knowledge this scripture possesses,' Haridas roared.

Losing his patience, the commander fired another shot. It hit Haridas's right knee; he screamed in pain as he fell to the ground but held the scripture close to his chest.

'You and your secret society, the so-called Rudras.' He laughed. 'You're nothing but a bunch of idiots. You don't know how to wield power. The destruction of India is inevitable but with the help of this scripture, we will ensure that an age of slavery is cast upon you from which you will never rise again.'

'Dear God,' Haridas prayed as he raised his arm to throw the scripture into the river. 'Protect this scripture. Protect it for the sake of the human race.' But before he could move further, two quick bullets hit his hands and the scripture fell to the ground. He shrieked in pain.

'Pray as much as you want but your gods cannot protect you or your country. This is the beginning of India's end.' The commander started to move towards Haridas; his men closed in from every direction.

But suddenly, a distant sound rang through the skies and began to grow steadily. Everyone looked around. It sounded as if a supersonic jet was approaching with breathtaking speed. Lightning lit up the sky, accompanied by thunder that shook the ground.

'Something's coming,' one of the men said. They checked the radar but there was nothing on the screen.

'That's impossible!' the commander yelled. By then the sound had become a deafening thunder clap. They clutched their ears in pain just as a lightning bolt struck the earth, sending ripples through the ground and throwing everyone and everything up in the air. The trucks turned upside down, the machines stopped working and the choppers fell to the ground, exploding on impact.

'Everybody take cover,' the commander said loudly. Most of his men were dead, or too wounded to move, but the remaining ones did as ordered and held their guns ready to fire. The stench of their fear spread through the air.

'Commander, what is happening?' asked one of the men.

'I have no freaking clue. But that was one hell of an entry … Hit the spotlights,' he ordered when he saw that the lights were still focused on where Haridas was lying motionless, holding the scripture close to his heart. There was too much dust in the air, making it impossible to get clear visuals.

There was a hush on the ground when the dust settled.

'I can see its eyes,' said a fearful soldier.

'Eyes of a giant …' the commander gaped, then yelled, 'Fire!'

The men immediately started firing bullets, missiles and rockets. A huge plume of dust, fire and smoke rose through the air. They stopped after a while to see if they had succeeded in destroying whatever the hell had landed amidst them.

'Is that all you've got?' asked a powerful voice. Startled, the mercenaries involuntarily flung back a few steps. The voice was so potent that it sounded like God himself. His laser eyes became bigger as he walked forward through the fire and, as he became visible, they saw something they had never in their wildest dreams.

'That's not possible,' said the commander again in disbelief.

'Am I hallucinating?' asked a soldier, rubbing his eyes. Several of the men ran for their lives.

Through the fire, they could see a giant walking closer to them. His tail moved slowly, like a snake with its hood up. His towering structure and the mace in his hand sent shivers down the spines of the men who surrounded him. A variety of guns and swords hung all over his body and the lightning sword in his other hand gleamed in the darkness. But it was his face that was the most terrifying of all.

'What is that?!'

'Hanuman … Lord Hanuman,' the commander stammered, horrified beyond his wits. He tried to report to his headquarters but all communications were jammed.

The soldier then saw the face of the giant. Powerful, fearless and awe-inspiring, the face of Lord Hanuman had a grandeur that was other-worldly.

'How is this even possible?'

'I have no clue,' the commander whispered.

The massive figure moved towards Professor Haridas and turned him around. The old man had bled profusely; there was no way he was going to make it. He looked up at Lord Hanuman with prayers in his mind and smiled.

'Jai Bajrang Bali …' he breathed his last and closed his eyes.

The giant took the scripture from him. A compartment opened up in his chest and he placed it inside. Then he turned towards the rest of the men.

'He's a machine! A cyborg! We can take him down,' screamed the commander. 'Attack him!'

Thousands of miles away in India, in a secret facility called the Garuda, a deep voice spoke on the transmitter to the Vanaroid, a next-generation combat machine built in the shape of Lord Hanuman.

'Give them hell,' he said in a measured tone.

'Affirmative,' responded the Vanaroid at Mohenjo-daro. Swinging his lightning sword in one hand and his mace, the gada, in the other, he pounced on his enemies.

ONE

'Where is Kalki?' asked the prime minster.
'Still incommunicado,' answered General Ramsey over the secure phone line. 'The last communication we had from him was a month ago in Amsterdam, when our covert mission went bust.'

There was a brief pause.

'Any news from Tiger? Or anyone from his team?' PM Subhash Acharya, one of the most loved Indian prime ministers in history, asked further, getting up from his chair in his office situated at 7, Lok Kalyan Marg, New Delhi.

'None. Tiger cannot be traced either. Something unexpected has happened, that's for sure.' Ramsey sighed.

'I'm beginning to worry now, especially when the Invisible Hand has upped its ante. We need him here,' Acharya stressed.

'He's your protégé more than mine. You know he'll come back; he always does.'

'I can't help but feel guilty. I sent him on that mission … We all got played,' he said, rubbing the bridge of his nose.

'He will return. Give him some time,' Ramsey assured.

'Find him. Wherever he is on Earth, bring him back and fast.'

'Yes, sir.'

Acharya hung up the phone and Defence Minister Jagan Singh was sent in. The two had been as thick as thieves for decades and had climbed the political ladder together.

'Acharya, I think we have underestimated what the Invisible Hand has been up to for the last decade,' Jagan said as they took their seats.

'I'm afraid you're right. Any new information?'

'Yes. After the debriefing of our undercover assets, we have concluded that they have been working on a grand plan of sorts.' Jagan handed Acharya the reports.

'What sort of plan?'

'While people think the Invisible Hand has become a mere terrorist group operating mainly in Pakistan, Afghanistan, Iraq and Syria, we know that deep down their core philosophy to enslave the world has not died. Under the patronage of General Jian of China, they now have access to unlimited resources and are working on destabilizing several governments across the world.

'They're instating key assets in the governments and military ranks of several countries where democracy is either weak or non-existent. This includes Pakistan, Iran and various north African and south-east Asian countries.'

'Pakistan?'

'Yes, and it gets worse. There are reports that they have infested the Indian army.'

Acharya got up from his seat, shocked. 'What are you saying? Are you sure?'

'There is no concrete evidence, if you ask me, but it's a strong theory. It's very likely that it has already happened and there are one or more moles, deployed a long time ago, high up in our army ranks. They play their cards over decades.'

'If they get to the top, they will become dictators and destroy our democratic system,' said Acharya, worried.

Jagan took a deep breath and said, 'No matter what, we need to find out who they are and weed them out … I wonder what the Invisible Hand's end goal is.'

'Destruction. Slavery. Total control of the world. Think of your worst nightmares,' Acharya said. 'I have to alert the Rudras. It's time we destroy them from their roots.'

'Before we end this meeting, I want to understand one thing. Have we uncovered the nexus between General Jian and the Invisible Hand?' asked Acharya.

'Theories suggest that Jian was brainwashed by the Invisible Hand when he was young and inducted into their cult. Since then, he has been secretly supporting and funding their agenda, against the wishes of Chinese President Wang. He is acting independent of the Chinese government and President Wang hasn't been able to reign him in. Because of all his connections and insane ambition, Jian has become the Invisible Hand's most powerful weapon.'

'A powerful, rogue general in the Chinese army in bed with the most dreadful terrorist organisation. God save this planet!'

❖

General Jian was in a security review meeting at his office in Beijing when he got a call on his private number. He excused himself and swiftly moved out.

'General, this is Zar,' spoke a grave voice. The most-wanted terrorist mastermind on the planet, Master Zar was the head of the Invisible Hand's military wing. 'I have good news. Our mole in the Rudras has agreed to help us fast-track decrypting the map of Shambala.'

'That's brilliant! I'm sure they have no clue that we found two more scriptures at Mohenjo-daro after Haridas's death. We were lucky that those scriptures contain the map of Shambala ... If the Rudras think that sending some mystery squad to kill our excavation party will make us give up, they're wrong. They clearly underestimate us,' Jian enthused.

'We still don't know what they sent to Mohenjo-daro that day. I lost a trusted lieutenant and an entire crew. I will avenge them,' growled Zar.

'Indeed, we will. For now, do whatever it takes to decode the map so we can find the *Weapons of Gods* buried in Shambala. Those ancient weapons would make a nuke look like a toy. Don't forget that it was one of their scriptures that led to our technological prowess.'

'How can I forget? My own powers come from the Scripture of Gods,' admitted Zar. Master Zar's extraordinary powers were both a myth and a legend; people spoke about them but no one knew for certain what they were.

'Imagine if we could get hold of all their scriptures. We will be invincible—perhaps even immortal. That's what I want; to rule the world,' said Jian.

'And together, we will, god willing … I will ensure we break the code and get you the map of Shambala. We will possess those weapons at any cost.'

'Excellent! I cannot wait. Before you leave, when is our prisoner Kalki being shipped to China?' asked Jian.

'He is en route. Our men should hand him over to your intelligence wing today.'

Jian chuckled. 'I want him crawling at my feet. He's ruined our party too many times. But not anymore. I will have him begging for mercy before I cut his head off.'

TWO

'Neel … Neel, wake up,' she said softly, running her fingers through his hair. He breathed in her fragrance when the ends of her long tresses tickled his face.

'I don't want to wake up. Come back here,' he whispered.

She planted a kiss on his forehead. 'It's time.'

He smiled and took a deep breath, reaching out for her as he lazily opened his eyes. His smile died instantly when he encountered only darkness. He looked around, trying to find a ray of light, but it was pitch-black. The floor felt hard and cold as ice.

He closed his eyes and saw her beautiful face again, smiling brightly at him.

It was morning and the summer breeze was hopelessly romantic. It felt like heaven.

'I have to go,' she whispered, getting up.

'What's the hurry?' he said, holding her hand.

She escaped his grip. 'You know I have to.'

'Arya … No. Stay with me.' But she was gone.

He reopened his eyes and came back to reality. This was a new room—he always woke up in a different setting—and his head felt heavy with sedatives. He cursed himself for getting into this situation. *Don't trust anyone; that was the one rule and you broke it ...* He knew he had been betrayed in the worst possible way, handed over to the enemy on a silver platter. It hurt that his countrymen had done it but it was not the first time he had been betrayed by someone he trusted.

His last known location was Amsterdam in the Netherlands. He didn't know where he was now; they hadn't provided him a view of the outside world. For all he knew, he could be halfway across the globe right now.

He couldn't say who his captors were with certainty. They could be the Chinese, Pakistanis or any of India's enemies or friends. It could also very well be the Invisible Hand. All he knew was they wanted the information he possessed. He was a catch; the biggest catch. At the same time, he was surprised to be alive for he was worth more dead than alive to his enemies.

In Amsterdam, he had been beaten, tortured, starved, questioned under a truth serum and subjected to every trick you could find in the torture rulebook but had still kept his mouth shut.

His left arm hurt intolerably and his skull seemed ready to burst open at the slightest movement. He couldn't move much; he was tied to the walls with what seemed like magnetic chains, which were impossible to escape.

Blood dripped from his arms and legs, running out of sutures and bandages. *They can break my body, but they can't break my mind.*

'Water,' he croaked out loud, mustering the energy left in him. His voice echoed in the silent room. He shivered as the chill from the floor and the walls seeped into his bones. *It's a freakin' mortuary.*

The lights suddenly came on and he cried out as they hit his dilated pupils. He squeezed his eyes shut and his hands jerked in their bonds, trying to cover his eyes.

Two men came inside and removed the chains from the wall, leaving the magnetic handcuffs on so he couldn't move his limbs. They dragged him outside to an interrogation room and pushed him to the floor. He tried to place who they were.

'Chinese?' Neel mumbled to himself.

'Yes, you piece of shit,' yelled one guard in a heavy Chinese accent before they pulled him up, tied him to the table and left the room.

The room had an earthy feel, with an eerie chill in the air. He sensed that he was somewhere up in the mountains. The place looked at least a few hundred years old but was obviously renovated. The furniture in the room looked old and somewhat Tibetan. *Could be the Himalayas,* he deduced.

'Give me some water, you scumbags,' he growled.

There was no glass wall or window but he knew they were monitoring him. A minute or two later, another Chinese officer walked in with a water bottle in one hand and a laptop in the other.

'Good morning, Mr Kalki. How are you feeling today?' he asked.

'Just terrific. Your hospitality is out of this world,' said Neel, eyeing the bottle of water.

'You have a sense of humour; I like that. Now, we can do this in two ways. First, we continue the way it has been going. You refuse to cooperate and you don't speak. You can expect a lot of pain, should you choose this path, until we get the information we need from you. Your second option is to tell us everything and you will be free to go.'

Neel laughed.

'You know why you have been brought to this facility?'

'I don't give a tiny rat's ass,' he snarled and jerked in an attempt to free himself from the chains. The officer stepped back reflexively.

Neel laughed again. 'Where do they find chickens like you to join this "elite" intelligence wing of yours?'

The officer slapped Neel across his face.

'Behave, Mr Kalki. I don't want to slap you again. You are the pride of your nation. The avenger of the righteous. That's what they call you right? The saviour, the protector!' He laughed. 'What would they say if they knew you were getting slapped and beaten like a dog by Chinese intelligence agents?'

'Chinese intelligence agents, you say? You clown; you slap like a two-year-old.'

The officer slapped him with more force this time.

Neel continued to laugh. 'Is that your best?'

'So what they say about you is true. You are a maniac; a dog that needs to be put down. Do you know why your own people betrayed you? Because you are a pain in the ass for a lot of important people and they decided to remove you from the equation.'

Well, I can't disagree with that, Neel thought.

'You're wasting your time. Shoot me right now and get it over with. I'm not telling you jack shit,' Neel growled.

The officer opened his laptop and pulled up an Indian television news clip on the screen.

'It's quite impressive, what your country thinks about you,' he said.

'Hero of a billion,' read the news ticker at the bottom of the screen. The anchor said, 'No one knows who Kalki is! Where was he born and who is his family?' Rare pictures and video clips of Kalki in his trademark mask followed.

'He likes to operate in the shadows, never showing his real face. It's clear that he wants no fame or credit for his deeds; he only wants to destroy India's enemies … He shows no mercy to anyone who hurts our country. Who could this guardian angel be?

'The only thing we know about him is that he is the man behind the Astras group, who supply futuristic weapons and technology to the Indian defence forces. How does he manage to do business with the government yet remain invisible? That's the billion-dollar question. Either no one in the government has any answer or they are covering it up.'

The next clip showed hundreds of people wearing his mask marching on the streets, chanting his name and thanking him.

'This footage was taken five years ago when Kalki saved 236 passengers on the Air India plane that was hijacked over the Indian ocean.

'In another story, some believe he was the one who undertook the mission to kidnap the most-wanted terrorist Ali Haider from Karachi, a task no one thought was possible. The stories of Kalki's heroics are numerous yet no one has any clue who he is,' the anchor said.

'That's enough,' said Neel. 'Where are you going with this?'

'Mr Kalki, your company Astras is the largest defence equipment manufacturer for the Indian defence forces. Your firm created the ultra-drones that man the Indian borders right now. And no one knows how you build such advance weapons. Perhaps that is the reason every country wants you dead. Be happy that we have kept you alive—the orders were to shoot you on sight. The only reason you are alive is because you can help us.'

'Help you? Don't you get it? No matter what you do, I won't say a word.'

The officer gave him a third whack across the face.

'Listen to me carefully if you want to stay alive … First, we want to know what you are planning next for the Indian army. Next, we need the details of your cyber warfare division. You are the only external agency guarding Indian cyber assets and I want to know how you do it.'

Neel just chuckled.

'What is The Vanar Sena?' the officer pressed.

'The what?' Neel asked in disbelief.

'The army of ape-shaped robots. Does it really exist?' he held up a blurry picture of what looked like Lord Hanuman.

'Seriously, officer, are you high?' Neel said, getting annoyed.

'Who are the council members of the Rudras?' the officer moved on.

'The Rudras? I have no idea what you're talking about.'

The officer punched his stomach. 'Mr Kalki, either you give me the information I need in the next twenty-four hours or you die. It's your choice.'

'The only person I will talk to is your boss. Otherwise, you're not getting anything!'

'I'm the boss around here,' the officer shouted.

'I'm talking about your real boss: General Jian,' Neel stressed in fluent Mandarin. Among several other languages, he could read and write Mandarin effectively.

The officer called the guards inside. 'Don't give him any food or water. Before you throw him back in that dark room, torture him to the brink of death. Do that every day till he's ready to speak to me. I want him begging for mercy,' he ordered.

He then looked at Neel. 'I'll make you talk, Kalki.'

'Good luck,' said Neel, before he was dragged out.

A week later, the officer, who was called Agent Chow, along with the deputy chief of the Chinese intelligence wing entered the cell where Neel was lying unconscious on the floor.

'Sir, he is impossible. I have never seen anyone like him before,' the guard said in Mandarin.

'No one could possibly take this torture for so long. He doesn't even talk under the truth serum. You must report this to General Jian before Kalki dies,' Agent Chow muttered.

'General Jian is occupied with something critical at the moment; but I will leave him a message … He won't be happy that we weren't able to break Kalki,' the deputy chief said, calling Jian's office.

THREE

There was a knock on the door of the most powerful man on earth at the White House, Washington, D.C., USA.

'Mr President … Mr President, sir,' the voice behind the door said loudly.

'What time is it?' President Cooper asked his wife, who had woken up in surprise.

She looked at the clock with blurred vision. 'It's 2.05 a.m.'

Cooper hurried to the door. He knew it must be a matter of great urgency if he was being woken up at this hour.

Another terrorist attack? He worried internally.

'What is it, Michael?' he asked, opening the door.

'Mr President, there is a situation. You are needed in the situation room immediately,' he said, even as the president grabbed his overcoat.

They started walking hurriedly. 'For the love of God, what is the emergency? Tell me before I get a heart attack.'

'China is being nuked, sir.'

'What?!'

'The prime minister is in an important meeting. We cannot disturb him,' said the secretary in New Delhi.

'Trust me, Ritesh, he would want to be disturbed with the kind of news we have. I'm not going to repeat myself,' warned Defence Minister Jagan Singh.

Ritesh ran into the meeting, looking visibly worried.

'Sir, Defence Minister Jagan Singh is on the phone.'

'What's the matter, Jagan?' asked Prime Minister Acharya.

'We're tracking a nuclear missile right now. The trajectory shows it's going to hit Beijing in fifteen minutes.'

'What? Are you sure?' Acharya gasped. A nuclear strike was nearly impossible in today's times unless the weapons got into terrorist hands because the nuclear strike codes were only accessible to the heads of the state.

'Yes, we are one hundred per cent sure.'

'How is this possible?'

'We don't know yet. It originated somewhere in the Pacific Ocean. Come to the war room; I'm waiting.'

'Right away.'

'What's the origin?' asked President Cooper. All the key members of the defence council and his cabinet were gathered in the situation room at the White House.

'Sir, we are tracing it as we speak. You will have the answer in two minutes,' said his Chief of Staff.

'Did you alert the Chinese?'

'They already know, sir. They can't possibly evacuate a city of thirty million people in ten minutes,' added the Chief of Staff.

'Sir, we traced the origin and you are not going to believe it,' said the defence secretary, walking in through the door.

'Where?'

'It was shot from a Chinese warship cruising in the north Pacific Ocean near Papua New Guinea!'

There was a stunned silence in the room.

'What is going on here?! Why would China bomb itself with a nuclear missile? Is it a coup? What are the possibilities?' Cooper asked.

'It could be a coup or it could be militants. There is no guarantee; it could be anyone,' the defence secretary said.

'The missile will enter the Chinese airspace in five minutes, sir.'

'Do we have a visual?'

'Yes, sir. Coming on-screen now. It's a direct feed from our satellites.'

They waited with baited breath. Although Beijing had deployed the missile defence system, there was no guarantee that it would work as advanced missiles tech could outsmart anything.

Thirty million people could die today, bringing one of the most powerful countries on Earth to its knees. It would be a blow that the human race would never recover from.

'Sir, Chinese media have a visual from the ground. It's live on TV.'

'Coming on screen two now.'

They could see alarm bells ringing in all parts of Beijing. Mass evacuation was being undertaken with whatever time they had on their hands. It was chaos—

stampedes on the streets, looting in shops, burglaries in houses.

They saw the missile enter the Chinese airspace over their waters and got their second shock. The missile, which was supposed to travel all the way to Beijing, blasted mid-way in the air as soon as it entered their airspace.

'What stopped it?' asked Cooper, mouth wide open.

No one had the answer.

The blast shook the earth below with shockwaves. This was followed by a brilliant flash of light and a loud booming sound. A firestorm raged on all sides.

Any human who might have seen the blast with naked eyes was sure to have lost their vision to the intensity of the light. A blast such as this one had not been seen by humanity since the atomic blast at Nagasaki in 1945.

'Mother of God! That was at least a five-megaton yield nuclear warhead. It would have been enough to annihilate Beijing,' said the defence secretary.

Suddenly, it looked as though the firestorm was contained in a giant invisible dome spanning a radius of two kilometres. The massive ripples in the sea created by the blast didn't escape the dome either.

'What is that dome? How did it appear out of thin air?' Cooper asked in disbelief. Beads of sweat had appeared on his forehead.

An invisible shield seemed to be preventing the blast from spreading into the airspace by creating an impenetrable dome. The water directly below had risen due to the blast, but only inside the dome. The sea outside it was calm, as though nothing had happened. This technology was unheard of. History was being made.

Within minutes, the blast was diffused and the dome disappeared.

'What just happened?' Cooper asked. They stared at each other in silence.

'It looked like a shield, sir. A nuclear shield,' breathed out General Smith, the head of the US Army.

The sea and the sky were once again calm and clear.

'General, did we just witness a demonstration of the Chinese nuclear shield?'

'I'm afraid that seems to be the case, sir. That's the reason Chinese media had cameras set up ahead of time to showcase it to the world,' said Smith.

'An invisible shield that can diffuse a nuclear explosion mid-air?' he yelled and threw a chair at the screen. Everyone sat silently as it broke into pieces. 'Would any of you say my reaction is uncalled for? Tell me!' He banged his fists on the table.

'No, sir.'

'Do you know what this means? It means China can screw us at will.'

Prime Minister Acharya drank a glass of water as the occupants of the room looked at him, dumbstruck. No one had seen the PM sweat before but, then, no one had witnessed such an event either.

'What was that, Jagan?' he asked, trying to digest the gravity of what had unfolded in front of them.

'Looks like some defence shield that can absorb blasts and diffuse the radiations.' The Chinese media were playing the news in a loop, claiming the shield absorbs even the nuclear radiation after diffusing any fission or fusion particles; there was no trace of radiation whatsoever.

'What do we know about this?'

'It's codenamed the Great Shield of China. We have no knowledge about the technology behind it but we know they have been experimenting for the last three decades. No one knew how far they had reached and whether it was feasible to deploy it on the field, but today we saw a demonstration,' said Jagan.

'So, we can't strike back in case a war emerges with China?'

'With such technology in their hands, no one can. We have very few options remaining against China now and they can strike us anytime.'

'Do we have anything close to their shield technology?' Acharya asked. 'I know your ministry always has classified projects going on.'

'Not that I know of. The Chinese have huge funding and a great determination for getting results in their advanced weaponry programme. Not to mention the success they had in their super-soldier programme.'

Acharya removed his spectacles and rubbed his face. The event was a game changer; it would totally shift the power balance in the world and could take Earth back to the dark ages.

'Any reports on who authorized it?'

'It cannot be a planned strike. Something's cooking on the Chinese side. It was probably General Jian who orchestrated this. It's not the typical Chinese way of operating; it's too dramatic. The demonstration must have shaken the entire country; there was panic everywhere in Beijing.'

'In that case, the situation is much worse than one could possibly imagine. It was very irresponsible of China to allow this. They have played a practical joke on themselves and the world ... It couldn't have been worse for us; the Invisible Hand is raising its hood again and we know Jian is in bed with them. If he gets to power in China, it's the end of peace in this world,' Acharya said.

There was a long silence.

'Let's call an emergency meeting of the defence forces and the Security Council,' he spoke after some time. 'Next, let's speak with the US President and the allies. In parallel, start discussions with the Chinese and the UN to bring peace to the region.'

The mood in the room was grim and it was not without reason.

'Prepare for war without triggering any panic. It's only a matter of time.'

FOUR

President Wang looked at General Jian, furious. Wang was the head of China's communist party and the commander of the defence forces of the country. He was pushing seventy-nine and never before had he let such a grave event happen under his rule; he held himself responsible for every bit of it.

They had assembled in the government headquarters at Beijing for an emergency meeting. The national security advisors and the heads of the three defence forces were all present in the room.

'Did you just launch a nuclear missile on your own country?' Wang yelled in Mandarin. There was no regret on General Jian's face, only pride.

'Who authorized the launch?' he asked angrily.

'I did, sir,' said General Jian.

'I'm the commander of the nation and the nuclear button can be pushed only by me. How did this happen?'

'You should ask General Jian that question, sir,' said Defence Minister Yang Shu, who was known as the hard taskmaster of the party. He was seething with anger.

'It's not important to know how I launched the missile,' barked Jian. 'What's important to note is that this was the only way we could demonstrate the nuclear shield technology to the world. The people in this room don't have the guts to do what is necessary to protect this country. I wouldn't have taken such drastic steps if you had allowed me to demonstrate it peacefully. You deployed the shields only when you saw a real nuclear weapon coming our way. You should thank me for this.'

'General, I'm this close to putting you on a death sentence. Watch your every word. What you have done is called treason,' the president lashed out.

'Treason? Are you all out of your minds? Am I the only one here who feels this was the right step? You left me no option, sir.'

'You compromised the national security, put thirty million lives at risk and brought shame to our country with this irresponsible act; yet you have the audacity to talk in such a fashion? You will not be spared after this,' Yang said in anger.

'I didn't put anyone at risk; practically no one realized the nuclear warhead was approaching and the shield didn't let the missile pass through.'

'Nearly 340 people are dead in Beijing. Do you know what people went through in those twenty minutes?'

'A necessary sacrifice and a small price for a greater cause, I suppose,' Jian quipped.

'Those 340 lives mean nothing to you? Tell me this, what if the shield had failed?' Wang questioned.

'Sir, let's not discuss hypothetical scenarios.'

'General Jian, what will we tell the world now? It's an embarrassment to our government and our people

… Moreover, this can push the world on the brink of a world war,' Yang said.

'Tell them it was a planned activity to demonstrate our technology to the world. Tell them that we can deploy the shield to all our allies; roll out a new allies' programme, where we get paid for the national security of our allies. Are you fine gentlemen actually asking me such trivial questions? We have finally put an end to the US dominance over the world with this move. Am I the only one with the brains to realize this?'

'Stop it, Jian!' shouted President Wang. 'This is not how I had planned it. This event will trigger panic and chaos across the world, the ramifications of which will be felt by tens of generations after us. We have to be a responsible superpower, not act on the whims of one man. The country is in a mess right now. There will be unrest and we already had enough on our plates in China.'

Jian laughed. 'This is hilarious. Don't you get it? This event will push all other problems into oblivion. People will hail us because we have deployed the Great Shield of China! I have solved a great problem for you.'

'The fact is that you acted on your sole discretion without consulting anyone in this room. You illegally obtained access to the nuclear codes and put millions of lives at risk; you have embarrassed this office in the eyes of the world. You have established the fact that China doesn't have control over its assets. You must be punished.'

They looked silently at President Wang.

'I hereby strip you of all your powers and sentence you to life in prison,' he declared.

'Everyone in this room has lost their balls,' Jian lashed out angrily.

'Jian!' yelled Wang.

'Yes, Father. Yes. You have no fire left in you anymore.'

'Do *not* call me Father.'

'Gladly. I am ashamed to call a coward my father. You have forgotten who you are and it's because of who you are surrounding yourself with.' He looked at Nushen.

She looked back, unblinking.

'All right. Put me in jail,' he shouted. 'Tell the world I have done it. You will only encourage your enemies to stand up to you when they know the dragon of China has been subdued. They don't fear you; they fear me. The world fears me!'

'That's enough. Get out of my sight before I hang you to death. Out!'

General Jian gazed around the room. 'This is not over. Everyone here will pay,' he said, then looked at Nushen. 'Especially you.' He was handcuffed and taken out of the room by the guards.

Everyone waited silently for Wang to talk. He took some time to regain his composure. 'We can't tell the world that we had a rogue in our top ranks. Let's prepare a brief to showcase the technology in a better way. We will control the situation at home and now that the cat is out of the bag, let's draft a new allies' policy to make the most of the shield. We need to work with the UN to assure China is no threat to any country and that this is a technology for peace and protection.'

He drank a glass of water and cleared his throat.

'I never wanted this to happen again; this unrest, this climate of violence that we last saw during the cold war … But what's done is done. Let's assure every country that we have a no first-strike policy. China won't use nuclear weapons against any country, unless provoked, and we will protect our allies, opening our doors to any country that wants to become our ally.'

He sighed. 'I need some time alone. I will see you all in a while to discuss this further.'

'Yes, sir,' they said and started filing out.

'Nushen, a word please.'

She sat back down. Nushen was the key security advisor to the president and a former Chinese intelligence wing hero. Wang trusted her more than anyone else.

When everyone left, he said, 'I should have listened to you and cut his powers long ago. He used my weakness as his strength.'

She was silent.

'I failed this country.'

'Sir, don't be so hard on yourself. It is not your fault,' she said.

'Yes, it is. It is all my fault! The duty of the president is to protect the country first; personal emotions come later. And I failed.'

'Like you said, sir, what's done is done. I'm sure we can handle the situation. On the brighter side, it will clearly establish China as the biggest military power in the world.'

'Perhaps, yes, but this is not the way …' he said painfully.

There was silence for a while.

'Do you remember when I had asked you who the biggest threat to China was?' asked Wang.

'Yes, sir, I had replied with Americans or Indians,' she replied. 'I was obviously wrong.'

'Remember, no country or state can be bad. The populace of a country is always good, because it's simple economics. People need good conditions for their families; peace and prosperity are what civilization moves towards, no matter what. But it's the individuals who rule the countries that make the difference and the individual experiences of these rulers that ultimately lead to a country's actions and the future of its populace.'

Nushen nodded. 'You're right. Hitler made Germans the villains; had he not hated the Jews, things would have been different right now. Had Gandhi believed in violence, things would have been different now ... History is, to a great degree, made by the rulers.'

Wang sipped his tea. 'Jian was one of the biggest potential threats to China and it became a reality,' he confided. 'His connections run deep around the globe, especially because of his allegiance to the Invisible Hand.'

He looked at Nushen. 'I will not be here forever to make the right decisions ... Succession plans are in place but anything can happen. With Jian in prison, we don't have an immediate threat but I'm counting on you to do the right things when it really matters. Even if it means you have to act against my family.'

'Yes, sir, you can count on me.'

'I know there is much you need to do here in Beijing, especially during this unprecedented crisis, but I need you to do something for me,' he said.

'Anything, sir. You only have to command.'

'This morning, I heard from my sources that Jian had managed to get his hands on Kalki, one of the most influential men in the Indian defence sector. I'm sure you've heard of him.'

'Of course, who hasn't? He is a legend, a ghost, a vigilante. He is the leader of the Astras group and rumoured to be a core member of the Rudras. No one knows his true identity. This is huge. How did it happen?'

'We don't know yet. Jian managed to keep it under wraps and hid him in a secret facility near the Indian border. Apparently, Jian was headed there himself when he was summoned here ... The interrogations with Kalki have revealed nothing till now. Hardly anyone survives the tortures beyond a couple of days, yet it's been two weeks and he has said nothing.'

'Nothing?'

'No. Seems like he enjoys pain. They give him truth serum and instead of telling the truth, he shuts himself down. Doesn't speak a word. I have been told that he wishes to speak only with Jian. I need you to interrogate him and figure out what the hell is going on.'

'Sure, sir, but don't you need me here to hold your fort by your side?' She asked, concerned. Babysitting an interrogation near the Indian border cut off from the rest of the world didn't seem like a priority.

'Nushen, I have a feeling this is important. He is one of the most dangerous men in the world. Moreover, we

need to know what the Indians are doing. The ultra-
drones they deployed to guard their borders were the
best in the world and Kalki was the mastermind behind
it. He is our key. Especially after today's demonstration,
it becomes critical to know India's plans. I know you
want to be here, so wrap it up in a few days and get back
soon.'

'Yes, sir,' she said, worried. *I hope Kalki talks soon …*

'One last thing … you need to know that his death
means more to us than the information he possesses.
You will personally execute him before you return. The
information he possesses is important but he could
become a major liability if he remains alive.'

'Understood, sir,' Nushen said and closed the door
behind her.

FIVE

❋

The eerie mountain cold bit her face but she liked the crispness of the air. Nushen alighted the chopper that landed in the secret facility on top of a mammoth mountain. Hidden deep inside the Himalayas near the India–China border, the place was an abandoned ancient Tibetan monastery. *It would have been a good getaway from the hustle-bustle of Beijing if the situation wasn't so screwed up,* she thought, looking at the snow-clad mountains in front of her. The view took her breath away and she watched the majestic mountains for a long time.

She was already thinking about Kalki. Nobody had ever withstood the torture as he had but no person had withstood the pain she inflicted during her intelligence days either. *He will break,* she thought. She had once been the decorated top agent of the wing, running covert operations for the Chinese, before she was called to Beijing by President Wang to join his elite security advisory committee. She was even code-named the 'Super-Agent' by her agency.

There was not a single day when she didn't miss the missions, the guns, the gadgets and the danger. She liked to challenge her mind and body; Beijing had taken away all her fun.

Two personal guards accompanied her. From hiding her identity to ensuring everyone she met was checked, they took care of every detail. She was one of China's biggest assets and President Wang had ensured no one could reach her.

When she entered the facility, she was impressed by the ancient Tibetan architecture and how well it had been renovated.

'Welcome, Madam Nushen,' Agent Chow greeted in Mandarin and saluted her.

'Agent Chow.' She saluted back.

'It's an honour to meet a legend like you. A dream come true,' Chow said in awe.

She nodded in acknowledgment.

To Chow, she appeared to be strong and in total control of herself. Someone who cannot be messed around with.

'Let's get to work, Chow. I don't plan to stay here for more than two days.'

'Right away, ma'am,' said Chow as they walked in. 'There are a handful of guards at the facility and only one prisoner. The place is not accessible by road, so choppers are the only way to get in or out. Hardly anyone knows this place actually exists. Tibetan monks had abandoned it centuries ago, leaving it to deteriorate over time. We rebuilt it five years ago and created a high-tech facility inside to keep an eye on the Indian border, as it's invisible to the eye.'

At around 20,000 ft above sea level, it was indeed a marvel.

They went to her room, which opened into a spacious balcony enclosed by a massive fibre shield. The view was breathtaking.

'Eighty kilometres from here, we hit the India border,' Chow said.

'That's very close.'

'Yes, but the path is impossible to cross. We have an army post near the border and a few kilometres of no-man zone with rough terrain. Beyond those mountains, it's just a cold desert. Would you care for a drink?' he added, while Nushen was lost admiring the rugged landscape.

'Sure.'

'Single malt?'

'Pour a big one.'

She entered the office after a quick shower.

'Tell me about Kalki,' she said, her team beside her.

'He is a nasty one—hasn't spoken a word yet. He enjoys pain, has no fear of anything and plays mind games with us. He has pushed me to such a level that I wish I could kill him right now,' he said in frustration. 'He killed a guard in Amsterdam using only two fingers. He had been bound in magnetic handcuffs since then, so he can't move his hands or legs.'

'Two fingers, you said?'

'Yes, some advance martial arts technique. He is lethal and would not hesitate to kill.'

'Intriguing,' Nushen mumbled.

'We don't have an ID match, but that's not a surprise. He looks too young to be who he is.'

'Well, looks can be deceptive. We both know that,' she said, picking up his photograph. His face intrigued her; there was no trace of panic or fear on him and he seemed no more than thirty years old.

'He's charismatic,' she said.

Chow made a face. 'Err ... Let's wait for a few days and see if you feel the same way.'

She chuckled.

'Are you his captor or is he yours?' she commented.

'You will soon know what I mean. We tried everything; we broke his bones, hammered nails onto his body, scrapped his skin, but nothing came out of it. He didn't even break under the electric chair and the pain beam, which burns water molecules below the skin. I've never seen anyone tolerate more than three seconds but he went on till the seventh second. We stopped then or he would have melted,' he added.

'That's incredible. Did you test his DNA? Anything there?'

'Yes. He is a normal human physically but he has mind powers.'

'Mind powers?'

'Yes, perhaps even mystic. He takes deep, insanely slow breaths. His body heals faster than anyone I have seen, even without wonder drugs. He messes with your brain; it's almost impossible to play tricks with him. We tried the nice card and gave him options of freedom, money and security but he didn't fall for that. We gave him the truth serum and he just stopped talking. His brain activity showed patterns similar to dreaming. Here, let me show you a few videos.'

Nushen watched a few important clips and realized this was not going to be easy. The man didn't respond to threats or torture, had extraordinary powers and they didn't have any information on his family or background to use to their advantage. She couldn't help but admire his courage and intellect. Whatever little the Chinese knew about Kalki, he was beyond what she had expected.

'Fascinating … do you think it's due to training administered by the Rudras?' she mused.

'Perhaps. It's rumoured that they have access to ancient methods of mind and body control. But you should watch this.'

Chow showed her a video where Neel woke up screaming from a nightmare. He was breathless and looked as if he had been strangled.

'He is in trauma. What must be bothering him?'

'God knows. Sorry—the Devil knows; this son of a bitch is from hell.'

They laughed.

'Has he made any requests at all?' she asked.

'None, except daring us to kill him.'

'I'm curious. How did we capture the most wanted man on Earth?'

'Frankly, I don't know. General Jian was closely monitoring this operation. No one knows but him.'

Nushen felt uneasy. Jian never did anything random; there was always a plan. What was Jian up to?

'What are you hiding, Chow?' she asked, sensing a slight hesitation in his voice.

Chow started to sweat. 'Err … nothing ma'am.'

'Chow!' she warned.

'I have heard from my sources that the Invisible Hand helped in securing him. General Jian wanted to personally meet Kalki; in fact, we were expecting him instead of you.'

Nushen hated the Invisible Hand. The group was headed by the most-wanted terrorist Master Zar, and not-so-secretly funded by General Jian, and its objective was to create a reign of terror across the globe by exploiting people in the name of religion, race, colour and money. They were against democracy and worked to instate dictatorship in countries. They were also known for discovering and unearthing extraordinary and supernatural weapons of mass destruction by tracing the history of various dynasties.

There were theories that the Invisible Hand was the offshoot of an ancient cult of assassins formed during the era of Genghis Khan, the Mongolian Emperor, to carry out heinous crimes and tasks that his army couldn't.

Intuition told Nushen that she was staring at a much bigger ploy. *I have to get Kalki talking … he could be the key to uncovering Jian's plan.*

'What is his current condition?'

Chow switched on a screen that showed Kalki's cell.

'He's weak. We haven't given him a bath and he is currently on half rations. We give him wonder drugs after every torture session to put him back together. And the routine continues every day.'

Neel was sitting upright on the floor with his eyes closed. He had a long beard and, although he looked weak, it appeared as though he was in ecstasy. The chains didn't seem to bother him.

'What is he doing with his fingers?' Nushen's bodyguard asked.

'The position of his fingers is called Jnana Mudra. It helps in uplifting one's body and spirit,' Nushen replied in a soft voice.

'What are you going to do?' asked Chow.

Nushen observed the screen for a long moment before answering, 'Clean him up and bring him to the interrogation room … naked.'

'Right away.'

'And get me a mask.'

'Get up,' the guard said roughly, walking into the cell with an agent. They kicked Neel with their leather boots and he silently took the beating.

'Seems like today is your lucky day. We're giving you a bath, you stinking rotter.'

They dragged him to the washroom, stripped him, tied him up in chains and turned on a hosepipe with tremendous water pressure. The freezing water hit him like a continuous array of needles.

They sprayed a cream to clean him up and dried him with a hot air blower that was a bit too hot to enjoy. Nonetheless, Neel was relieved that he finally got a bath.

Once he was clean, they strapped him to a chair and applied shaving cream on his cheeks and chin, scraping his face with a razor-sharp knife. The guard cut his skin at several places and his skin came off with his hair a lot of times.

'Don't move; you might kill yourself.'

'That's not a bad idea.'

'Don't worry; your death is very close. Enjoy this; it might be your last shave,' he said, applying anti-septic cream that burned his skin.

Finally, they dragged him naked to the interrogation room and strapped him to another chair, a powerful flashlight beaming on him from above and infront of him. He couldn't open his eyes easily. There was hardly any furniture in the room but he sensed someone sitting at a distance.

Nushen looked at him in flesh and blood for the first time; although weak, his body was muscular and athletic. She knew it was a body that was seasoned and prepared for worse days. His sharp nose and powerful jaw were masculine and tough, yet she saw warmth in his eyes. She had to admit that the man had a charismatic aura.

It was a long time since someone had seized her attention. She looked at him from face to toe, keenly studying his naked body. He had a lot of new scars and wounds inflicted during the interrogations but there were plenty of old ones too.

'Don't be shy. You can talk to me,' he said with a chuckle, breaking her train of thought.

His voice was deep and reassuring.

'I have to admit that I was admiring your body, Mr Kalki,' she said, getting up from her chair. Neel chuckled again.

'Bring up the lights,' she ordered, speaking into the comm placed in her ear.

Is that an American accent? Neel wondered. But intelligence officers spoke fluently in many accents, so that information was useless.

Chow turned on the lights in the room and he saw a tall, masked woman, getting closer.

She pulled out a chair and sat next to him. She smelled like heaven, bringing some life into the hell he was living in. He could only see her eyes under the mask she was wearing. *Dear God ...*

In those eyes, he saw something he had never seen before. They looked celestial in the true sense, as though a thousand stars were suspended and floating in each iris. He took a deep breath.

'I'm sorry my colleagues were tough on you,' she said.

Her voice is powerful yet insanely sensual, thought Neel.

'Tough—are you kidding me? Your agents are pathetic; they couldn't get a word out of me and went crying back to their bosses. Now, you're the new hotshot who has come to interrogate me by sweet-talking and manipulating me? Is that it? Well, game over, so let's cut the crap and get straight to the point.'

Bloody hell, thought Nushen. *He is a rogue, no gentleman material in this one.* But she knew she had to be patient and win his confidence. He could not be forced.

'Kalki, I'm here to give you a chance to make things right. You are an important man. Your people consider you their guardian angel, even though they have never seen you. You are a vigilante who brought justice to those in distress ... I respect you; I personally do.'

Neel didn't respond.

'We shouldn't have dealt with you this way. I'm not from the intelligence wing; I'm from the top brass of the country. I know you wanted to meet General Jian but he couldn't make it. I'm here, however, and I have power. I can set things right but I need you to cooperate.'

Neel laughed. 'Set things right? What does that even mean?'

'I can give you a chance to lead a normal life again. You can walk out of this prison and get your life back.'

'You think I'm an idiot? I know you will kill me one way or another. So really, Miss … Important Person, let's save everyone's time. I'm not giving you any information whatsoever. You can go ahead and kill me.'

'You are being foolish, Kalki. You're a businessman; you know how things work. The information you possess is worth billions of dollars. We know your company works closely with the Indian defence forces and you can now work for the Chinese defence forces. We can give you contracts worth ten times of what you get in India. Business is not country specific—it's global. China could become your number one client. Let's work out a deal. You name it and we will make it happen. Give me your terms.'

'Defence contracts with China?' he mocked. 'You don't understand me; you never will.'

'I want to understand you, Kalki. That's why I'm here.'

'How are you even sure I am Kalki?'

'Putting aside all the evidence that we have, my instincts say you are no ordinary man. You are too important to be dying in a prison. So, tell me, why did you want to meet General Jian?'

There was no response.

'What are your terms to cooperate with us? You can have anything you want.'

Neel thought for a while.

'Take your time,' she said. 'Would you like something to drink?'

'Anything, you said?' he asked, ignoring her last question.

'Yes. Ask for anything realistic and we will make it happen.'

Neel smiled. 'I want to see the face that is carrying those beautiful eyes … I'll start talking when I see your face.'

Nushen thought about it for a while and smiled, which he couldn't see. She had a feeling he would ask for it.

'Mr Kalki, I'm wearing the mask for a reason.'

'Because you're important.'

'Yes. If you see me, your chances of walking out of this facility diminish drastically unless you make yourself useful to us. Do you understand what you're asking for?'

'I understand. I will take my chances.'

'And you will start talking?'

'Yes.'

'Okay, I believe you. It's important that we keep our promises and build trust with each other, wouldn't you agree?'

'Agreed.'

She removed her mask and, right at that moment, time stood still for him. He took a deep breath. While she tried to correct the long golden locks covering her face, his mind went numb looking at her. He had never seen such unusual beauty before. He was in awe.

There was a glow in her skin, her face, her hair and her body—the same glow that existed in her voice. Such a glowing porcelain-like exterior was not human; such beauty was not human.

She was tall, well above six-feet, athletic and had a slender body, with the visage of a goddess.

Her eyes were still the most remarkable, of a colour that was a mix of turquoise and grey—like stardust. *Truly celestial ...*

She didn't look Chinese, Mongolian or even Caucasian. She was different, was all he could say. She was godlike. What was she?

'Mr Kalki?' She waited patiently, knowing it would take some time.

He didn't respond for a while, stuck looking into her eyes. And then it suddenly hit him. *Holy Mother of God!*

'So, it is really true ...'

'What do you mean?' she asked, perplexed.

'You can't be real ... you're different.'

'I get that a lot. Now, if we may start the discussions?'

'No, you are not just human, are you?'

'Excuse me?'

'You are what they call Nushen.'

She kept a straight face in spite of her shock. 'I have no idea what you are talking about. You make no sense.'

'Oh, come on. The Indian intelligence agency definitely knows about the super-soldier programme and Nushen and Shen were the code names for the first two that were produced. I had no idea these rumours were true until now.'

Produced? She didn't like the way he referred to her as a thing that was produced but she chose to ignore it.

'Mr Kalki, I think you are completely insane. I'm no super-soldier and I have no clue who or what is a Nushen.'

Neel laughed.

'Let's get to the point. Tell me about the projects your company is working on for the Indian army.'

Neel laughed again.

'What's so funny?'

'It's so easy to fool Nushen, the superhuman.'

She got up. 'What do you mean?'

'You heard it right. I lied. I'm not going to tell you anything,' he chuckled. Before he even realized, she struck his face so hard that he sputtered blood. There was a ringing sound in his head and he opened his mouth to spit out more blood.

'Now that's what I call a real slap. Teach that to your agents,' he struggled to say.

'A real man keeps his word,' she said, regaining her composure.

'You are not even Chinese, why are you working for them?' he asked, ignoring her remark.

'Don't you get that I'm your last hope of freedom?'

'You never lose your cool, do you? Is that because they made you in a laboratory?'

She punched his neck in response. He couldn't speak a word after that, coughing and wheezing like a rabid dog.

'Agent, take him and beat him until he collapses,' she ordered Chow in Mandarin. 'Let it be the reward for dishonouring his words.'

'You're a coward! You can't be a super-soldier,' he breathed out in Mandarin.

She ignored him.

'Open these dumb cuffs and we will see who beats whom,' Neel challenged in a choked voice.

Nushen turned and looked at him. She seemed totally relaxed.

'All right, then ... Open his cuffs!' ordered Nushen.

'Ma'am, no! He's playing you. Don't fall for it,' Chow warned over the comm.

'It's fine. Let's see what he is made of,' Nushen said with confidence.

Two guards came in and removed his chains. For the first time in weeks, he could move his hands freely. He stood up and felt his legs shaking; he had no strength.

'You want to fight me? Go ahead, show me what you got,' she challenged, without any hint of anger or fear on her face.

'Come on, now! Don't try to be all suave. Hit me if you ca—,' Before he could even complete his challenge, Nushen sprang into the air and kicked his chest so hard that he was flung back and hit the wall with a thud. While he fell face down on the floor, she landed on her feet effortlessly.

'Come on, get up,' she said, as her bodyguards and Chow rushed inside and stood near the door, pointing their guns at Neel.

When she saw that he was about to get up, she banged his head on the wall. Blood sputtered from his forehead and he dropped like a corpse to the floor.

'Get up! Is that all you can do? I thought you would at least give me a fight.'

He opened his eyes and mustered all his energy to stand up against the wall. 'I'm just getting started,' he said with a choked laugh. But he was bleeding profusely and could barely see anything; he collapsed.

'Is that so?' she chuckled. 'Take him and throw him back into his rat hole,' she told the guard.

She turned around to see him trying to get up again. She sighed.

'You are a stubborn fool, Mr Kalki. Do you want to die today? Because I'm in a mood to oblige,' she cautioned.

'Stop holding back. Or are you really just a coward?' Neel growled.

'As you wish … you're not going to recover from this one,' Nushen warned and sprang up again, turning mid-air to kick his head, but Neel was finally able to block her. In a fraction of a second, he used two of his fingers to touch her left leg, abdomen, neck and forehead in a sequence. It was as if he was pressing some secret buttons on the human body and she collapsed to the ground, immobile and struggling to breathe.

While her bodyguards rushed to her aid, Kalki collapsed beside her and passed out.

SIX

'Madam Nushen, you're awake—thank God!' Chow said when Nushen opened her eyes.

'Am I still alive?' she asked.

'Yes. You were unconscious for fourteen hours,' he confirmed, checking his wristwatch.

'How did he manage to do this?'

'Some ancient fighting technique, I would guess. The Chinese aren't the only ones good at martial arts … He paralysed the left part of your body because of which you went into a mild cardiac arrest and slipped into a coma.'

'Coma?'

'Yes, we didn't know if you would even wake up.'

She thought for a while.

'Well, we both know he wanted me in a momentary coma. If he wanted me dead, you would be burying my body right now,' she muttered and got up.

'Be careful. You need to rest,' her bodyguard rushed to her side.

'No, I feel fine,' she told him, stretching her limbs. 'Where is he?'

'In his cell. He was unconscious too but woke up an hour later. He has recovered; we gave him wonder drugs and put him in the synthesizer,' Chow replied.

The Chinese army had invested heavily in creating drugs and machines that could heal soldiers rapidly. As an offshoot of the *Homo Supernus* programme, they had breakthroughs in rapidly rebuilding broken bones, infusing new tissue to heal wounds, replenishing blood through drugs and so on.

For the entire day, Nushen watched Neel through the camera. He was in his usual meditation position, occasionally changing the mudras, and hardly opened his eyes.

What are you? What's your story? What is this fire that keeps you going? she thought. *So many questions …*

Nobody knew who he was or where he came from. How did he manage to conceal his past? This was the reason he was feared. He was a man with no face or identity.

'You know what they say, you could fall in love if you watch a person for too long,' her bodyguard said, and they laughed. They were akin to her family and ensured there was no dearth of humour.

'Seriously?' she asked and they fell silent as she switched on the news.

Much of the protests at Beijing were controlled and life was back to normal. President Wang had promised a better economy and millions of high-paying jobs with the influx of additional revenue to the country through security agreements with allies. Another channel showed an intense discussion in the scientific community on how this technology worked but no one had a clue.

Chow barged in and said, 'Take a look at this footage. It was taken when Neel was unconscious after your fight.'

Neel was uttering something in a feeble voice. 'Arya … Arya …' he called, twisting and turning as though he was in a nightmare. He started sweating and breathing heavily—and then he woke up.

Arya … Finally, we have a clue, Nushen thought.

She looked back at his cell. He had an unusual smile on his face.

Neel had closed his eyes and let his mind drift. He thought about his mother and the days of his childhood flashed before his eyes.

KALKI'S STORY ~ ORIGINS

Neel recalled his mother, Nikita, telling him about the day he was born. She had described it as the happiest day of their lives. 'Neel is a healthy baby, a very healthy one indeed,' the doctors had declared.

They were in a military hospital in the midst of the sprawling army campus in Belgaum, Karnataka. His father, Lieutenant-Colonel Digvijay was deployed in the Advance 'Strike' Corps training centre upon his personal request. He wanted to be at Nikita's side when his first child came in to the world.

The pleasant climate in Belgaum and the peaceful campus had given Nikita and Digvijay their best times during her nine months of pregnancy. Moreover, Digvijay enjoyed training soldiers who had been selected to be in the Indian Army's strike corps battalion, the razor-sharp tip of the Army's sphere, if one may call it.

When the nurse gave the baby to Digvijay, he looked at him with wonder in his eyes. 'He will make a good soldier one day,' he said with glee.

'He looks just like his mother,' said the nurse. It was true. He had her eyes, nose and chin.

❖

Nikita was born to a family of Kashmiri pandits who had been forced to flee the Kashmir valley when militancy and extremists had nearly wiped out the Brahmin community. Nikita's family had lost several members during that gruesome time and her grandfather had finally decided to move them to Delhi. They came from a modest background; her father worked in a government bank in Delhi, where Nikita and her sister, Kritika, studied and grew up.

Nikita met Digvijay in her college days, when Digvijay had moved to Delhi for studies. When Nikita had first asked Digvijay what he wanted to do in life, he had proudly said, 'I was born to be a soldier. I can't do anything else. I'm in love with the army.'

'Good,' Nikita had cheerfully responded. 'I dig soldiers.'

But deep-down, Nikita was fighting the demon of her ancestry. She wanted to fight the system. She hadn't come to terms with the fact that many of her family members had died in Kashmir and, although she grew up in Delhi, her heart was back in Kashmir. It was the place of her roots, her people. She failed to understand why people couldn't live peacefully in the valley like they did in the rest of India.

She admired that Digvijay wanted to defend her home that was Kashmir, where one day she wanted to go back with her father, who also pined for the place.

Digvijay, on the other hand, hailed from Bangalore and was brought up in a cosmopolitan army environment. His father was an influential leader in the Indian army. Digvijay and his father never really got along well and they hardly spoke or met. His father was elusive, quirky and known to have a bad temper. So, he grew up mostly under the care of his mother, with the army culture ingrained in him. He was a no-fuss guy with no lofty ambitions in life; he just wanted to be a warrior—to hold a gun and guard the country.

Digvijay eventually joined the army, while Nikita became a journalist in a major news channel. It was her desire to become a war, terrorism and external affairs reporter.

A few years after they got married, Digvijay joined the elite strike force of the Indian army. With a great physique, reflexes and mountaineering capabilities, he was a natural fit.

Nikita's hectic globetrotting as a journalist came to a halt when she unexpectedly became pregnant. They looked at each other and jumped in joy. 'The most wonderful things in the world happen unplanned!' Digvijay had said, lifting her up and kissing her belly. 'Can't wait for you, Junior.'

The nine months of pregnancy were a time they would cherish forever. The day he was born, they held the baby in their arms and kissed his tiny cheeks, deciding to name him Neel, derived from one of the many names of the Lord of the Lords, Shiva.

Neel Digvijay Kalki had arrived.

Two years had gone by in Belgaum and everything seemed to be going perfectly well until Digvijay was called by the Corps HQ for a critical mission. Unfortunately, he was killed in the operation.

When Nikita heard the news, her world came to an end. She had hoped that the news was just a bad dream but that was not to be.

When his body was wrapped in the tricolour and flown to New Delhi for cremation, Neel was too young to understand why his father wasn't getting up. 'Daddy, need Daddy ...' he kept saying, but his father wouldn't move.

Nikita did her best to stay strong for her son and resolved to bring him up alone. She took up a job in Delhi to stay close to her sister and her ailing parents.

Neel had proven that he was a genius at a tender age. He could solve complex problems, play sports skilfully, paint beautifully, write touching stories and communicate with people with exceptional clarity of thought and without any guidance or supervision. It was clear that he was different, born with abilities far exceeding his classmates and friends.

Nikita couldn't let her son's genius be wasted, so she worked twice as hard to earn as much as she could for Neel's schooling and future. She had at some level realized that life was uncertain and anything could happen anytime.

She was proven right. Neel was nine years old when Nikita was diagnosed with the final stage of leukaemia. She fought the disease for a year before realizing it was futile. Instead of getting into a state of depression, she picked herself up and decided to make the most of her time.

She had saved a decent amount of money for Neel from her job and, of course, she had her husband's army pension and ancestral property in Karnataka. This ensured that Neel did not have to bother about money for a long time to come. She then requested her sister, Kritika, to take care of him when she was gone.

She started writing her autobiography, since that was the only way she would leave behind something for Neel. He wouldn't have her physical presence but at least her words would become his guiding light and strength.

Neel knew there was something dreadful going on with his mother. He saw her go through various kinds of treatments, losing her hair because of chemotherapy and getting weaker by the day. It was a horrendous experience for him.

'I don't have much time,' Nikita said one night after dinner. They were staying alone after Nikita's parents had passed away a few years ago.

'Why do you say that?' Neel asked.

'I'm dying, Neel. Doctors can't cure me. I have cancer.'

'No, they will cure you. Don't lose hope, Mom. For my sake, you can't,' he said, as tears ran down his tender face.

'Krikita maasi will take care of you when I am gone. She loves you so much, Neel.'

'I don't want anyone else. Please, Mom, don't leave me. What did I do? Why are you punishing me? Why is God punishing me? First Dad left me and now you will. You can't leave me alone, Mom, you can't.'

Nikita couldn't control her tears as she hugged him close. 'I don't want to leave you, Neel, but I'm forced to.'

They cried a lot that night. It was a night Neel would never forget.

'I want you to promise me something.'

'No, no … Don't leave me. I'm not going to promise anything.' He shook his head.

His world, or whatever he knew about it, had come to an end. He had had an awful time understanding why his father had died and now this terrible news from his mother shook him completely.

'Neel, you have to promise me that you will never give up.'

'Give up what?'

'You will never give up believing in yourself. Never stop believing that you are born to do great things. It's my belief that you were born to change the world.'

'Mother, I am so unlucky … I don't care about the world. Just don't leave me alone.'

'You have to believe me. You will do great things, Neel. You are an exceptionally bright boy. Remember what your headmaster told you? He said you have a gift; you are a born genius. Let my words always linger in your mind. When in doubt, remember that your mother believes you were born to do great things.'

He was silent.

'I'm exhausted, Mom, none of the things you said mean anything to me. I just need you with me.'

'I will always be with you. In your soul; in your heart. You will never miss me. I'm leaving this diary behind as well.'

Neel hugged her tightly.

She died a few months later and everything changed for him after that. Life became hell; he shut himself into a cocoon and didn't want to come out of it, ever.

Neel moved to his aunt's place in Pune after his mother's death. Kritika had married Commander Dheeraj, one of his father's juniors from the army. Both Kritika and Dheeraj loved Neel very much and tried their best to bring him out of his misery.

He was upset with the world, with God and with life. In spite of being loved by his aunt and uncle, he mourned for his parents and missed them every single day. He tried to express his anger but didn't know how to. Soon, he found a vent through martial arts; he worked tirelessly on the skill and became pretty damn good at it.

He read his mother's diary again and again, finding solace in reading. Books became his best friends, through which he could escape to a different world.

A year after moving to Pune, his uncle was deployed in the north-east region to guard the Indo–Bangladesh border. The family shifted to Guwahati and Neel shifted to a new school.

Dheeraj was responsible for sending Bangladeshi refugees back across the border and had succeeded in sealing the loopholes along the border. This didn't go down well with the smugglers; they wanted him out of the picture.

Fate played a game yet again in Neel's life. In a planned ambush, a rain of bullets hit their vehicle on the way to Durga Puja. In the back seat, Dheeraj and

Kritika instantly flanked Neel on both sides. They were shot multiple times and were killed instantly.

'Maasi! Maasi!' he kept screaming in their arms.

Two more guards were shot dead in the front seat. The driver managed to ram the van ahead and fled the scene. Miraculously, there was not a single scratch on Neel.

His uncle and aunt had saved him by giving up their lives. He could still feel the vibrations of bullets hitting them as they protected him. He had felt them die against him.

Death had him in its grip yet hadn't taken him away. *Why? Why did you spare me?*

SEVEN

Neel woke up when he heard the door open.

Nushen walked in with a tray of food and kept it on the table.

'Look who's here to pay a visit,' taunted Neel.

'Do you have to be an ass all the time?' she asked, sitting down.

'Well, pretty much,' he said, looking hungrily at the food.

'Take a seat,' she said. 'Tell me, did you enjoy our fight?'

Neel laughed. 'It was kick-ass!'

He wanted to eat but couldn't move his hands. She tapped a few buttons on her phone and the magnetic handcuffs loosened; they looked at each other for a while, waiting to see what the other would do.

He then started tearing his bread and eating it in a hurry.

She waited until he was done. He drank the orange juice and kept the glass down.

'Thank you. This was the first time in weeks that I ate something decent.'

'You are welcome,' she acknowledged patiently.

'Are you always like this?' he asked.

'Sorry?'

'I mean—you never lose your cool.'

She didn't reply.

'Listen, I know we have our differences,' she ventured after a while.

'Differences? We're enemies,' he interrupted.

'We are enemies only if we choose to be. If we cooperate with each other, there is much we can accomplish,' she said. She had decided to try a different approach with Kalki.

'Accomplish?'

She kept her phone on the table, projecting a video footage in the air.

'Let me show you something. While you were locked up in here, China demonstrated its nuclear shield technology, which blocks and diffuses nuclear missiles mid-air,' she said, as the hologram proved her words.

'This technology, it's too advanced … How?' Neel asked in disbelief. *Such knowledge can only come from the Scripture of Gods,* he thought.

'Well, you're not the only one who can invent things, are you, Kalki?'

'This is not the normal Chinese style,' said a worried Neel. She didn't respond. Neel wondered how tense things might be in New Delhi. *Prime Minister Acharya must be looking for me … Damned timing!*

'This is classic General Jian, isn't it?' Neel added, standing up.

The statement surprised Nushen but she was happy that he had started talking.

He continued, 'Don't look surprised. I know that President Wang and General Jian don't get along very well. This event is too bizarre to be coming from the Chinese president. And to push the nuclear button without the president's approval, who else could it be?'

She was about to say something when he added, 'Your president has failed to contain him. Shame on you guys.'

'Careful,' she cautioned.

There was silence for a while, during which Neel tried to gauge which faction of the Chinese camp she belonged to—President Wang or General Jian's.

'Kalki, why did Jian want to meet you?'

He didn't respond.

'Look, it's important that you tell me whatever you know. I'm not from the intelligence; I used to be but I'm not anymore. I report directly to President Wang. There is a reason he sent me to talk to you and cut the intelligence wing out of it.'

Neel thought about it for a while. 'What's in it for me?'

'Now we're talking! If you cooperate with us, I will see to it that you are treated well and find a way to get you out of here. I can't promise you will be set free but you will lead a good life under our protection,' she said.

'You mean to say your dogs will never stop chasing me.'

'Kalki, you will be executed if you don't cooperate. This is your best chance and I will look after you personally. That's a promise.'

Neel tried to figure out whether she was telling the truth. *It doesn't matter. She's my best bet to get out of here,* he realized.

'Okay, I trust you.'

'Good decision, Mr Kalki. So, tell me, why did Jian want to meet you?'

'My best guess is that he wanted the pleasure of killing me personally. That's the only reason they kept me alive. After all, I have sabotaged several of his missions over the years,' he said.

'How did they catch you?'

'I walked into an ambush. It was a set-up.'

'That's it? Anything else you want to tell me?' she pressed.

'All I know is that General Jian and the Invisible Hand are planning something major. I don't know exactly what they're plotting but it has global impact, China included.'

'There's nothing in the chatter and our intelligence is too strong to miss this kind of a plot. So, what am I missing?'

'Not if your intelligence wing is run by General Jian.' She nodded.

'What do you think they are planning?' she asked.

'I don't know. But whatever it is, it can't bode well.'

'Thank you for this information, Kalki.' Nushen stood up, tapping a few buttons on her phone. The magnetic handcuffs pulled both his hands back together with a thud.

'Hey!' he yelled, trying to move his hands. 'That's rude!'

'Well, we have to be careful. You're that dangerous man who is snapping necks with two fingers!' With that, she walked out.

Unbelievable, he thought.

That was a start, she thought.

What had started as a mission to interrogate one of the most dangerous men alive was fast turning into something else. *Maybe President Wang's intuition was right about this,* she thought. It was not the first time the old man had sent her on a mission that looked trivial but turned out to be significant.

Just then, her phone rang.

She smiled. *Speak of the devil …*

'How is your health, sir?' Nushen asked in Mandarin. Wang's health had deteriorated since the nuclear strike, leaving her worried and alarmed.

'I'm still feeling sick, my child. It's old age; I need to retire but I fear there is no respite.'

'Sir, I strongly suggest you to take some time off and rest.'

'You know very well that I cannot do that. But I will try to get some rest.'

'I will check with the doctors. Is your family taking care of you?'

'Oh, yes, very well. Don't you worry.'

'Sir, I should come back immediately. Right away.'

'*Bu shi* (no),' he cut her off. 'Stay there and finish your mission. That's an order.'

She sighed. 'But, sir …'

'I will be fine. Trust me. How are things with Kalki?'

'He's no ordinary prisoner. He is exactly what they say he is—shrewd, intelligent and fearless—but I think I might be on to something. Kalki spoke about a plot Jian might have hatched.'

'What plot?'

'I don't know yet but I'll find out.'

'It's important to uncover what Jian was up to. I don't think we have much time and Kalki could be the key to getting our answers. Never forget what I told you that day: do whatever is necessary for the greater good of the nation. Spend more time, if required, and see what comes out of it.'

'Yes, sir. You take care.'

'God bless you, my child.'

He cut the call. She felt sad for not being by his side at his time of need. He had become a father figure; she looked up to him for everything and for him, she was the daughter he never had.

Shaking off her worry, she called all the key people at Beijing and alerted them to the possibility of a dangerous mission set in motion by Jian.

Next, she called her trusted agent, Han. 'What's the latest on Jian?'

'He's under tight security. No contact with anyone outside his cell.'

'Did anyone come to meet him? Any suspicious activity?'

'None. I would have called if anything like that had happened. He gets frustrated at times and smashes things. You know his sex addiction; he's having a tough time alone in prison.'

'That's good. I hope he rots there with his dick in his hand.'

Neel's head felt heavy when he opened his eyes the next morning. He hadn't slept a wink. How could he when his country needed him and he was stuck in a hellhole, about to be executed? His only card for getting out of there was Nushen and he knew she was a killer intelligence officer.

But I will take my chances, he told himself. *Nushen is my ticket.*

The door suddenly opened and Nushen barged into Neel's cell, looking visibly worried. She removed her comm from her ear and signalled the agent to take the camera offline.

'You were right. The Chinese intelligence wing has pledged its allegiance to General Jian; there is an unusual silence in the chatter. I can't trust anyone,' said Nushen.

'And why are you telling me this? Why should I care?' asked Neel.

She was pacing like a restless tigress.

'Kalki, I didn't tell you this yesterday but Jian is in prison right now for illegally pushing the nuclear button.'

She allowed some time for the news to sink in.

'That's good news, I think,' he replied after a while. 'Or else I might have been dead by now.'

'I have three of my trusted agents keeping an eye on him. They all say he hasn't communicated with anyone outside the prison. But I've had a bad feeling since yesterday.'

He chuckled. 'Again, I really don't care!'

'Perhaps you should. An unreliable source informed the intelligence agency that an attack on New Delhi is planned.'

Neel instantly got worried. 'Did you inform the Indian Intelligence Bureau?'

'Yes, I sent them whatever I had this morning but it's not very actionable and comes from a bad source. I don't think it's something to worry about.'

He sighed.

'Now, tell me whatever else you've been keeping from me'

Before he could answer, Agent Chow called on her phone.

'Yes, Agent?'

'The Indian prime minster will address the Parliament in New Delhi in ten minutes. Hurry!'

EIGHT

It was a scorching hot summer day in New Delhi. A lone ice cream vendor stood two kilometres away from the Parliament, which was cordoned off for the big day. He saw hundreds of cherry-topped government vehicles escorted by police vans going inside the Parliament in the early hours. Politicians from various parts of the country assembled in the building while traffic was stopped in and around the Parliament.

It was the annual three-day convention of the MPs and MLAs of the country, where they came together to showcase the progress the union and state governments had made during the year. Prime Minister Acharya had ensured the government ran akin to any publicly listed company, showcasing its quarterly and annual performance review. It had won him widespread popularity around the globe and several other countries had started following his model.

Today, it was going to be a more serious affair in the joint session of the Parliament, where leaders from both the houses would meet to discuss the new security policy in the wake of China's demonstration of the nuclear shield and the increase of threats from the terrorist group, the Invisible Hand.

'The situation is complex,' Acharya had spoken at the closed door all-party leadership summit the previous evening. 'Firstly, there is a threat from China because of their nuclear shield. We have negotiated a deal with President Wang and agreed to a peaceful and progressive relationship. However, General Jian's ambitions and control over the defence forces of China is a great concern for India.'

'Secondly, Pakistan's support to the Invisible Hand's Master Zar is also of grave concern,' he had said. 'Thirdly, the western nations have all panicked because of the Chinese supremacy. The US has increased its defence and R&D spend to develop technology to counter China's nuclear shield. Japan, UK, France, Germany, Israel and South Korea have joined the US in the effort.

'European countries have come together and created a United European Defence Agreement, under which they would act as one mega-nation to contribute to the overall security of the region.

'Russia has made a radical move by recreating a mega-country called Greater Russia, akin to the erstwhile USSR. They are directly working with China as a key ally. Likewise, several other countries have become allies of China. The question is: what is India going to do?'

Today, India would decide whether it would join a particular group or it would continue the Non Alignment Movement and not take sides—an ideology that was developed during the cold war by former Prime Minister Jawaharlal Nehru.

Reaching the parliament, Acharya stepped out of his car and was promptly joined by his secretary. 'Sir, we just received intelligence from the Chinese that the Invisible Hand is going to target the Parliament today. It might be a risk,' Ritesh said in Hindi, matching his strides with Acharya.

'Come on, Ritesh, you said it was a false report a month ago and now it's true again? We have ten minutes to begin the address.'

'Yes, sir, but this is a different source. I have tripled the forces around the Parliament and called for more air defence, as well as more security guards everywhere. We are moving people away from a three-kilometre radius. We also have the anti-missile shields up, so we are safe but—'

'There is no but. I can't let Zar, or whatever that clown is called, dictate when we hold Parliament session. The global media is covering today's event, you know that, right? We can't be afraid of some vague threats, Ritesh,' he said in frustration and came to a standstill.

'But, sir … we have the entire leadership of the country here today. It's what the Invisible Hand does; it identifies the right targets to inflict maximum damage. Can't we have your speech from another location? Just to be saf—' But he was cut off by Acharya.

'Son … look at me. That's not an option. How will they strike? Is that even possible?'

'It's almost impossible to strike here unless it's a hit from a satellite. But we checked the military satellites and none of them are in a position to strike within the next few hours.'

'Then let's keep this event going. I want to speak in front of all the representatives of the people of this country. This message is important to them and it's necessary that the world hears it from this very Parliament, the temple of our democracy. I can't change it.'

Ritesh nodded and hurried to make more security arrangements.

'Is Jagan attending the session?' Acharya asked his advisor.

'No, sir. The defence minister's office called to say he is still in the hospital. Some complications again.'

'I see. Have the home minister do his part, in that case.'

'Sure, sir. He is aware.'

'Good. I'm heading to the stage.' The house was full with MPs and MLAs from all over the country and they had made arrangements for the MLAs to be seated too. It was estimated that about 90 per cent of India's total government leadership was present in the building.

Cameras flashed and he was live on televisions around the globe.

'Namaste!' he said.

A lone man in his mid-twenties, clean-shaven and wearing a white t-shirt, waited some twenty odd kilometres from the Parliament in New Delhi. He held what looked like detonator. He stood on a deserted factory that spread over seven square kilometres and was barricaded all around so no one could peep inside the complex. The facility was a defunct cement-manufacturing unit of a business conglomerate that had been sold off to a local merchant four years ago.

The peculiar aspect of the facility was the excavation that went deep inside the ground to bring out soil that could be mixed in the cement and construction material. Two years ago, a machine had been secretly assembled and dropped into the earth. It was unlike any machine ever seen before; it was cylindrical in shape with a variety of mechanical hands that could protrude from anywhere and had a nuclear-powered engine that made absolutely no noise or vibration. It could go on without any external power for thirty years doing what it was built to do—excavation at two kilometres below the surface of earth. It created a circular tunnel inside the earth and built a structure around it by measuring the pressure from above and below, leaving absolutely no trace of any change in the earth above it.

It's unique technology made use of the chemical degradation of earth to dig without causing vibrations; it could dissolve rocks, soil, water, fossils, roots, and any substance that came in its way. All it did was degrade the soil as it moved and use that soil to build a hard structure around it, thus making a tunnel. It had taken the machine nearly eighteen months to travel twenty kilometres to get exactly below the Parliament.

The machine had then slowly moved its way up towards the centre of the Parliament, stopping only hundred meters below the ground. Master Zar's masterplan had taken over half a decade to materialize. His men had then transported bomb-making material to the site to assemble the bomb, which was capable of blowing up the entire building with a blast radius of 500 meters. They had zeroed down on a day and what was better than striking down the entire leadership in one go. But they were still waiting on a signal from Zar, who was watching PM Acharya live on television.

'We are at a distinctive juncture at this moment. The planet is on the brink of a catastrophic war if it's not contained right now,' said Acharya. 'Nations of the world have aligned themselves with various groups. The terrorists have mastered the art of guerrilla warfare and are striking at will. Cyber attack rates are at an all-time high and have brought a few nations to their knees. And, of course, we have the arms race and new breakthroughs that, on one hand, seem to protect us but can lead to the extinction of the human race, on the other.

'Just before I walked on to the stage to address you all, I was briefed by my secretary that there is an intelligence alert for a possible attack on the Parliament today.'

There was a commotion in the house but he waived his hand for silence.

'I'm not saying this to create panic. Be calm. Such threats have become routine and, in fact, they are in fashion these days. Any person sitting anywhere on earth can issue a warning and think he can disrupt the world.' People laughed as camera lights flashed.

'Should we back down and hide ourselves from these threats? No. Should we then step up our aggression

and eliminate our enemies? The answer again is no …
because we don't know who the enemy is. It's a complex
world out there. Should we align ourselves with NATO,
Greater Russia or China to protect ourselves? No,
because that won't solve any problems. It would only
cause more wars. Millions will die and we cannot let that
happen. India won't let that happen.'

There was a round of applause.

'India has a key role to play in keeping peace on this
planet. It's because of that we make it clear that we won't
align with anyone. Our Non Alignment Movement will
continue and more strongly so. We will continue to push
for peace, along with the UN, and bring back an era of
peace and prosperity.'

Sitting in a remote location somewhere in tribal
Pakistan, Master Zar dialled a number. *I see a dead man
talking,* Zar thought and laughed. 'Do it now. Finish the
job,' Zar said in Arabic to the young man in New Delhi
and the line went cold.

Meanwhile, Acharya continued his speech. 'The
enemies of peace will not succeed. Not today, not
tomorrow. This is not an issue of one nation anymore.
The world is more connected than ever before and we
have to stand together to root out this disease from the
face of earth. India will lead that grand initiative for
the world.'

There was a standing ovation.

Acharya gestured for everyone to sit and drank a
glass of water. He was about to continue when he felt

powerful tremors beneath him and he looked around in disbelief as his bodyguards ran up to him in panic. The walls started shaking and the roof collapsed, crushing the panicked people in the hall below.

NINE

※

The tremors were followed by a massive blast from beneath the ground that blew up the entire Parliament. Politicians tried to run but the impact threw everyone up in the air and burnt them alive.

PM Acharya and his entire cabinet were burnt to ashes in a matter of seconds. There were no survivors.

The cars and vehicles around the parliament had been thrown up into the air when the bomb had gone off. Such was the magnitude of the blast that every glass within the radius of a kilometre had shattered and the thunderous sound was heard for tens of miles away. Many buildings developed cracks while several collapsed. Electricity lines snapped at numerous places, causing fires. There was chaos on the ground as people ran for cover.

Spectators around the world could only watch in shock.

The fire fighters came rushing in to douse the fire but the blast covered a huge area. The earth was shattered for nearly half a kilometre around each side of the building, making it impossible to drive to the site. The choppers came in swiftly and started pouring water to clear the ground. Fire and thick black smoke rose high up in the air, making it hard for the police and security forces to move.

In ten minutes, the earth caved in and the entire structure fell through the ground, leaving only rubble above. Choppers captured the horrific scene on camera and aired it live. It was as though the earth had opened its mouth and gobbled the Parliament.

The temple of democracy had been destroyed in broad daylight and no one could have done anything. The monument that stood as a symbol of the biggest democracy on Earth was no more.

Nushen couldn't believe the turn of events.

The headlines on the screen read, 'Breaking News: Indian Parliament razed to ground. PM Killed. Leadership wiped out.'

She sank into her chair. *This was the plot … The attack must have happened from underground.* She immediately knew the underground excavation technology was of Chinese design. It was clear the world had never seen such sophisticated technology before. *Jian, what have you done?*

Her team was next to her.

'We have to be on high alert. There are going to be repercussions,' she said. Something told her the worst was yet to come.

'Yes, Nushen. I'll send a signal to all units.'

Nushen called President Wang's private number but it wasn't reachable. She tried his secretary and learned that he was in a meeting with the heads of the defence forces.

Damn! I should have been there with him, she thought.

'I have been trying to reach him since last night. Why is he not calling me back?' she asked.

'He is ill, and now busy handling the crisis. Give him some time.'

Something was wrong. 'How is his health?'

'The president is recovering. He has made progress but is still weak,' the secretary informed.

'Tell him I called and ask him to call me back without delay. It's urgent,' she said and hung up. She looked at her team. 'Be on stand by and assess the situation here. Come up with an evacuation plan just in case,' she ordered softly. They nodded and exited the room.

She then hurried to Neel to unravel what could happen next. *He needs to hear this,* she thought. *I hope Beijing isn't next.*

'Nushen, what is it?' he asked.

'I have some bad news.'

'What's the matter?'

'The Indian Parliament was bombed. No one was spared. Your PM, his entire cabinet, all the MPs and MLAs—they're gone.'

'What?'

She put her thumb on the wall, turning it into a screen, and turned on the news channel with a few taps. His stomach roiled as he watched the news. 'No!' he shouted. 'No! No!' He was struggling and trying to break free from his chains with all his might.

'Kalki, calm down! Calm down!' But he kept screaming and was inconsolable. She didn't know how to stop him; she waited for a few minutes for him to calm down.

'Prime Minister Acharya is dead … Do you know he was like a father to me? He was my biggest supporter!' he cried after a while.

'I'm sorry. I really am.'

'This was Chinese technology, wasn't it? You geniuses couldn't keep it from falling into the wrong hands!' he accused, eyes burning with anger.

'Hey, take it easy!' she retorted, without admitting that he was right. 'Jian is behind it. It's the plot you were talking about.'

'Nushen, what have you guys done? You couldn't protect your nuclear assets. This is the beginning of a domino effect. It will lead to a world war.'

'We screwed up, yes, but someone screwed up from your side as well. Someone important betrayed your country and you got played,' she pointed out.

She was right; Kalki had failed too. The entire world had failed that day. *I couldn't save you, Acharya … How will I ever live with myself?*

'This is all my fault. If I was out there, no one would have dared to do this. I ruined my country … I failed Acharya …' he kept mumbling.

Nushen was silent.

'Look, I don't pretend to know what pain you're going through but I'm with you in this fight. We are not enemies. It's very clear to me,' she said.

'My country needs me. You have to let me go,' he urged. He was a fallen man.

'You know that's not possible. Even if I wanted to, I couldn't; it's not in my control. This facility doesn't report to me and you are a threat to our national security. I have direct orders from President Wang to kill you before I go back to Beijing. I haven't been able to talk to him to change that order.'

Neel closed his eyes, helpless and surrendering to his situation. *How did I get stuck here?*

'Kalki, tell me anything that can help me! You mentioned a domino effect. What do you think they're planning to do next?' she asked.

'It's obvious, isn't it?'

'What is?'

'Jian will go for the throne. The time is ripe for a coup.'

'You're right! President Wang is in danger.' She ran outside, slamming the door behind her.

Neel was devastated, as he continued to watch the news channel. The television was a boon on this day. *Thank you, Nushen, for this little mercy.* He sighed.

The news showed that the Indian army had declared an emergency in the country, amidst the chaos and panic that had erupted. The heads of the three armed forces in India had immediately formed the Indian High Command (IHC) as the ruling power of the country. Defence Minister Jagan Singh had escaped the blast because of a hospital visit. The news report said he had been arrested as a suspect for interrogation. *Jagan, a traitor? That's impossible!*

A news conference was being aired live from New Delhi.

'Today will be marked as the darkest day of our history,' said General Vikram Singh, chief of the Indian army. 'We have lost our prime minister and all the MPs and MLAs of the country in a brutal attack by the terrorist outfit the Invisible Hand. Never before in the history of independent India have we faced such adversity. I know how difficult this situation is but you must have faith in the Indian defence forces and our resolve to give a befitting response to these terrorists.

'The country has been put under emergency and will remain so till we achieve some normalcy. We have no elected leaders left in India anymore and will have to fall back on the structure that holds the government together, the civil service that is the backbone of our government. The IAS and IPS officers and the secretaries will manage the government as long as it takes. The army will work with the police department to maintain law and order. Our top priority is the safety of our citizens and protecting our borders.

'I know a lot of riots have erupted across the country already, some of which are even communal in nature. The army will be deployed in strategic locations and the police force will maintain the situation. We have mobilized the reserve army personnel to a certain degree to avoid any threat to the country. There will be curfew in all the sensitive areas. It's my request to each and every citizen of our great nation to remain calm and

have faith in us. These are testing times but ones that
define our character as a nation. Let us stand united and
not let the terrorists win.'

A journalist asked, 'What will be your response to the
Invisible Hand?'

'Let me make something very clear: we will strike
back at the terror group and we will decimate them, no
matter where they are based or where they are hiding.
But it will be a time and day of our choice. I have no
other comments on this subject right now.'

'What about public life?'

'Everything will run normally. The state will go in
mourning this week but will resume soon after. The
sacrifices of Prime Minister Acharya and our leaders will
not go in vain. They were martyrs who died protecting
the peace in this world. They died as heroes and history
will remember them as such. Lastly, I want to make it
clear that India is not afraid. We will not back down. You
might hurt us but you won't succeed in breaking our
spirit. Jai Hind!'

The news channel then showed several other heads
of states, including US President Cooper, condemning
the catastrophic attack and saying they would stand with
India to punish the culprits and bring back democracy
in the country.

Neel couldn't take the pain and anger any longer. He
was about to turn it off when he read: 'Absence of Kalki
led to terrorist attack?'

The controversial yet popular news anchor, Heena
Khan, was saying, 'Today, as we stand at the edge of hope,
we are forced to ask the big question. Did the absence

of Kalki lead to the dreadful attack on our Parliament? We know for certain that the mysterious Astras Group, a shadow organisation that was supplying futuristic weapons and intel to the Indian defence forces, has been missing in action ever since Kalki disappeared. Where is Kalki? Is he still alive? That is the question everybody in the country is now asking.

'Some say that he is presumably dead. If that is true, we might be facing some dire consequences ..."

Footage of people holding pictures of Kalki in his mask were shown on the screen.

'Kalki, if you are listening to me right now, you need to hear this. You failed this country. You failed your prime minister. You failed in the most miserable way.'

Neel closed his eyes and took a deep breath. He didn't know what to do.

Within minutes of the press conference, news channels were reporting chaos all over India in reaction to Master Zar's response to General Vikram Singh's words. People were trying to flee the cities fearing attack.

'Today, the world has seen what we are capable of,' Zar said in the video. 'We can come to your home and kill all your leaders in broad daylight. No one can do anything about it. Let me tell you what will come upon you next: absolute annihilation. The majority of your population will die and the rest of you will become slaves to your new masters. Your country shall never be free again.

'Your military leader has given you false hope today. There is no one to counter our attacks. The two people who could have thought of standing up to us are now dead. One was your prime minister, Subhash Acharya. The other, your so-called guardian angel, the yoddha Kalki and his Astras group. Yes, he had been captured a few weeks back and was beheaded.

'Your country will soon become a living hell. Enjoy your last few days of freedom,' he proclaimed and laughed.

'I'm going to kill you!' Neel growled, seething with anger.

He wondered what his Astras team and General Ramsey were up to. He felt guilty for not being there for them. His mind then drifted to the day he had first met Ramsey—the day his life changed forever.

KALKI'S STORY – ENTER GENERAL RAMSEY

After the death of his uncle and aunt, Neel was in complete shock. He had lost everything in his life at the tender age of eleven and didn't know what was happening anymore; it was too much for him to understand why unfortunate things kept happening to him. *Why me?* he asked countless times, but he never got an answer. He was afraid of death; it followed him everywhere he went.

It had been two days since he had spoken a word or eaten anything. The army doctors were worried about his health but he had been flown down with the bodies to Pune for the cremations.

Recognizing Commander Dheeraj's sacrifice, the army honoured him with a 21-gun salute in the wreath-laying ceremony. Both the bodies were brought wrapped in tricolours and flowers, carried on the shoulders of soldiers. His relatives gathered around for the last rites; some of them he knew but most he had never seen before.

Although they all seemed to sympathise with him, he hadn't spoken a word with anyone, nor had he cried. His tear glands had given up; he had no more tears left to shed. Moreover, he was downright angry with life, fate, destiny or whatever they called it.

Looking at the pujari chanting mantras and arranging wood to burn the bodies, something had set ablaze inside him that day, something that frightened him—a feeling deep within that he knew wouldn't die down.

'The boy is cursed,' he overheard a relative tell someone. 'Anyone he goes with gets killed.'

Another woman said, 'He is the sole recipient of all the property now. I know he's bad luck but if you adopt him, you will enjoy the money.'

'No, thank you. I love my life more than money. Why don't you try?' the first one replied instantly.

The pujari called him forward to give fire to the bodies of his aunt and uncle. Reluctantly, he torched the wood and watched their bodies burn till the fire turned them into ashes. He didn't blink; he wanted to see every bit of it.

'I'm sorry for your loss, son. I want to take care of you. Come with me, let's go home,' said a relative after a while, putting a hand on his shoulder.

Neel looked at her with such anger in his eyes that she took a step back. 'Leave me alone. Why don't you go save yourself? I'm cursed; you will die if you come close to me,' he said, pushing her aside gently.

'You're evil,' she said, furious. 'No wonder everyone you know is dead.'

Neel felt abysmal, more so because it was true.

'No one will come for you. Mark my words.' She walked away.

He didn't reply.

As everyone stood wondering what would happen to the boy, murmurs came from the back of the crowd.

He looked back and saw a tall man with a grey beard, black suit and sunglasses approaching. Standing behind him were armed guards. One look at him and everyone broke into chaos, moving out of his way.

'The party is over. Get out of this place,' shouted the man, walking like he owned the ghat and the whole goddamn world.

'What a madman,' someone in the crowd said.

'Who said that? Who?'

No one replied.

'Get the hell out of here. Is this a freaking circus?'

They left hurriedly. The old man looked at the priest. 'Leave now,' he growled in a menacing voice, handing him a few thick notes. The pujari left in a hurry after telling Neel he would receive the ashes by the next morning.

The old man removed his shades and looked at Neel, standing silently next to him for a while. 'I hear you haven't eaten anything in the last two days. If you want my sympathy, you're not going to get it.'

'I don't need sympathy from anyone, let alone a stranger,' Neel said, annoyed.

The man guffawed. 'So, are you fasting for a particular reason?'

'I'm in no mood for an interrogation right now. Leave me alone, please,' he said and finally looked up at him.

The old man had an aura that commanded instant awe and respect, yet Neel thought he was somewhat snobby and obnoxious.

'You are quite sharp for an eleven-year-old.'

He didn't reply.

'There's a plane waiting. We have to hurry. Let's go,' he said and started walking.

'I'm sorry, why should I come with you again?'

'Because I happen to be your grandpa.'

They were in an army plane that took off from the air force base in Pune. He sat silently looking out of the window. When an attendant brought him food, Neel said he wasn't hungry.

'What's the matter, boy? You want to die of hunger?' his grandpa asked.

'I'm upset and when I'm upset, I don't eat.'

'I promise you will get the ashes tomorrow. Someone will bring them to you.'

'It's not about that.'

'I see. Very well, then. Continue to starve.'

'Where are we going?' Neel asked after a brief silence.

'To Bangalore. You will be admitted to an army school with a residential unit. It's one of the finest schools in the world, named after Netaji Subhash Chandra Bose.'

'So, I'm not staying with you?'

'No, I cannot be stuck with you. I have important work to do in my life.' He chortled.

A tear escaped his eye. He was devastated inside. He didn't have anyone to hold or cry with. He realized how having a loved one meant everything in life and he had lost all his loved ones. *And now someone calling himself my grandpa comes along ... acting like a cold, heartless man.*

'Don't feel bad. We will spend your vacations together and my doors will always be open for you, any time you want. I travel across the world for my work, so we can travel together whenever opportunity presents itself.'

There was silence for a long time.

'I imagined you to be older than what you seem to be,' Neel ventured.

'I am sixty-four but my strict exercise routine has worked for me; I am an army man, after all. Not to mention my excellent genes,' he said proudly.

'You look younger than fifty,' Neel said with a puzzled look.

His grandfather chuckled.

'Why didn't you visit me all these years?' Neel asked further.

'I don't like socialising. I like to be alone.'

'Do you hate me?'

'Of course not. What kind of a question is that?' his grandpa asked, shocked.

'Eleven years and you only appear after everyone is dead?' Neel said with disgust.

'Stop whining, will you? I'm your dad's father. You wouldn't be here if not for me.'

'No wonder grandma hated you,' said Neel.

'Did your mother tell you that?'

'Yes.'

'What else did she tell you?'

'That you're a madman. You never took care of your family; you never paid attention to my father when he was young. You didn't even come to my parent's wedding or when I was born.'

'Women talk too much, jibber-jabbering all the time.'

'You talk too much as well! Are you a woman?'

His grandfather didn't know how to react.

'What's the matter with you, grandpa? You didn't come when my mom died either.'

'Let me make something very clear. First, don't call me grandpa. I am Ramsey, General Ramsey; you will call me General. Second, I didn't know your mother that well. She died—people die every day. I can't attend everyone's funeral.'

'So, my mother is just people to you? You're sick!'

'Yes, I am.'

'Then why did you come today?'

'Dear heavens, how much do you talk? Can I have some silence now, please?'

'No, I need an answer or I'm going my own way. I don't need you to take care of me or get me admitted to any school. I'll go wherever I want to.'

'Do you know who you remind me of?'

'I don't care to know, General.'

'You remind me of myself and that's scary.'

'Does that mean I'm going to end up like you? I was hoping the worst was over.'

'What have I gotten myself into? You're the devil.'

'I'm like you, remember?'

General got up and left.

❖

His bungalow was inside a heavily guarded army campus. Neel thought it looked more like a laboratory and a war room than a home. There were equipment and files everywhere. Numerous blackboards filled with extensive writing occupied every corner. The bookshelves had what seemed like thousands of books stacked up and there was a huge world map on the wall with hundreds of lines drawn all across it. He tried to analyse its pattern but came up blank. *Must be battlefield plans,* he thought.

'What do you do, General?' Neel asked the next morning at the breakfast table.

'I'm a security adviser to the Prime Minister of India,' General Ramsey replied. 'I also work for the army in a division that makes weapons for the future. Something that you will not understand.'

'What kind of weapons do you make?'

'That's classified. Let's just say even the prime minister doesn't know what I'm working on.'

What a show-off, Neel thought and bit into a tasty slice of bread and jam. He was famished after having hardly eaten in the last seventy-two hours. He hadn't slept well, either, due to his nightmares. He had started having nightmares the day he learnt his mother had been diagnosed with cancer and they had never really stopped; with the recent turn of events, they had only increased.

'Listen, you asked me why I came for you yesterday. Well, here's the truth: I came for you because you are my blood. I couldn't let you be orphaned while I'm still alive and breathing,' Ramsey said.

'Anyone I love dies. Maybe it was a bad idea,' Neel uttered softly.

'Don't worry, boy,' he laughed. 'It's impossible for anyone to love me, including myself. I'm not here to babysit you. You're going to be on your own, like an adult, but I will be around and you will have a home.'

Neel wanted to hug him. *Thank you, Grandpa*, he wanted to say. *That's all I wanted to hear—that at least I have a home.* He wanted to cry his lungs out.

'Everything is taken care of. We will leave for your school in some time. Army school will make you tough and disciplined. Only the finest students go to that school and they didn't hesitate to accommodate you when they had a look at your grades. They said you seem to be some sort of a prodigy. You must have taken it from me.'

'How modest,' Neel said sarcastically.

'I know nothing about modesty; I'm a genius. Anyway, I don't really care how you fare in school, but make the most of it. I've asked them not to be soft on you, so you can be sure you won't get any sympathy for what happened. It will be a clean start.'

'Thank you, General. I really need that.'

'We need to leave. I have to drop you off at school and hurry to the airport to pick up my girlfriend.'

'You have a girlfriend?' He gaped.

'Yeah, she's pretty hot.'

'You're sixty-four!'

'So? I live my life. You want me to be some stooping, limping old man? Get out of here and get your bags.'

❖

A new chapter began in his life that day. He was about to meet Arya and Tiger, the two individuals who would turn his life around.

TEN

Nushen had tried her best to reach out to President Wang. She had asked all her trusted agents to ensure the president's safely but none of them were able to trace his whereabouts. She knew something terrible was going on in Beijing and decided to rush back to be at Wang's side.

'Madam Nushen,' called Agent Chow.

'Yes, Chow?' she said, putting on experimental next-generation combat vest she had borrowed from the research lab to test out. The body armour had a hard but lightweight exoskeleton that took the shape of the body, making it look like a body suit. It came with a control system that had nearly 500 tiny sensors and gadgets that could monitor vitals, control temperature, and inject medicine to heal instantly, as well as a solar-powered battery to self-sustain for months, a variety of weapons and ammunition, and a camouflaged exterior that could change colour.

She had to be prepared for the worst.

'You better hurry.'

'Now what?' Nushen loaded her gun.

'Some developments in Islamabad. There is a military coup in Pakistan; General Riaz is taking control.'

'Good Lord! This is getting out of control.'

The news showed Pakistani prime minister under house arrest and military leader General Riaz giving a statement: 'War is imminent and we must prepare our country for the worst possible situation. The Pakistani armed forces have jointly decided that it's best to handle the crisis ourselves rather than leaving it to the politicians.'

Several reports showed reactions from various countries around the world. The US president had asked the American forces in the region to be on high alert as China had been recognized as the provider of the technology for the terrorist attack in New Delhi.

'Pakistani nuclear missiles are presumed to be safe for the time being, but if the Invisible Hand succeeds in getting to them, they have already declared to use them against the US, UK, Israel and India,' said a report. The US had also beefed up its security around the Pakistani nuclear facility and some reports claimed that they had already secured them in some locations. This brought up the question of whether Pakistan would succumb to the military prowess of India, which was now under army rule and could act with aggression, having no political pullback.

'I assure you that we have the nuclear warheads with us,' lied General Riaz, although he fully knew that the US had taken control of all his nuclear assets. 'If any country threatens our existence, we will be forced to use our nuclear missiles.'

'The domino effect. It has started,' said Nushen.

'What?'

'World War Three.'

'What's happening in Beijing?' asked Chow, just as Nushen's phone rang. It was an unknown number.

'Yes?'

'Nushen, you have to get out of there.'

'Shirou?' He was one of her trusted agents from Beijing.

'Yes, this is Shirou. Jian has killed President Wang.'

'What? How?'

'An internal coup is under way. Jian has taken over the communist party council and everyone is supporting him. It was long-term planning. He was the mastermind behind everything. The Indian attack, the Pakistani coup—they were all his doing and now he's back for revenge.'

'What do you mean?'

'He executed his father and Defence Minister Yang Shu. The rest of the leaders opposing him have been captured and you are the only one free at the moment. They will declare in a week that President Wang died of natural causes.'

'That bastard! I will not spare him.'

She cursed herself for trusting Han and the agents to restrict Jian's access to the outside world. *Never trust anyone. Never,* she admonished herself.

'Where is Jian right now? What's the line of command in the army?'

'Nushen, you don't have time. Jian knows you are there and he wants you captured. Get out of there, now!'

But it was too late. The door opened and two guards shot Nushen's bodyguards. They fell to the ground, dead. She ducked for cover behind the tables as Chow fired from the other side and killed them both.

'Nushen, we have to hurry. Move to the chopper,' Chow said when the alarm went off.

'I need to get Kalki. He's leverage.'

'Are you sure?'

'Yes, he will be my hostage! I need him.'

'Attention, attention. Listen carefully. Change in command at the military headquarters. General Jian is the new commander-in-chief. Orders are to capture Agent Nushen and kill anyone who gets in the way. Do not shoot at Agent Nushen. I repeat, do not shoot at Agent Nushen,' came an announcement from the speaker.

Nushen picked up additional body armour, loaded her guns and stowed her knives and ammunition. They ran towards Kalki's cell.

'How many soldiers remain?'

'Some ten odd. We can take them down. I will hold them here; you get him out,' Chow said, taking guard.

While Chow fired bullets at the soldiers who had followed them, she ran as fast as she could. She opened the door and said, 'Let's go.'

'That was fast,' Neel replied.

'President Wang is dead. Jian has attempted a coup. We need to get out of here,' she gave the command to drop his chains on her phone.

'So, my words proved true … Jian actually went for the kill.'

'We don't have time for chit-chat,' she cut in.

'Nice suit, by the way,' he said, looking at her combat vest.

'You need one too. Here, take this.' She handed him the spare vest.

'Are you actually saving me?'

'Don't kid yourself. I will put a bullet in your head if you try to get away.'

Yeah, right! I'm gone the first chance I get, he thought.

They could hear gunshots nearby. They didn't have time to think; he hurriedly put on the bodysuit. 'Press this sensor and it will cover your head.' She touched a sensor near his neck and a hood appeared from behind the armour. It had a vision assistance system to enhance eyesight and gave statistics and alerts in real time.

'This tech is neat,' he commented as they ran towards the exit corridor. They looked like space-age ninjas, covered from head-to-toe while the exterior changed to a greyish tinge to camouflage with the stone walls.

Chow had shot down five men when they reached him. 'We have to use the tunnel that opens up on the other side,' he said.

'What if they are guarding it?'

'We'll have to take that chance. Right now, they're waiting for us outside this exit and we are dead the moment we go out.'

'All right,' she said and stuck two bombs on the wall. 'This will keep them distracted.'

They ran down the tunnels leading to the other side of the building. She remotely detonated the bombs when they were mid-way and the structure collapsed behind them, closing the tunnel. When they reached the end, Chow went outside to see if the coast was clear.

'Get back,' he shouted.

Two guards fired at Chow, shooting him on his legs and shoulder.

'Run! I will cover you,' Chow cried.

The soldiers were still shooting, so they hid behind the wall. Nushen went to the other side of the window and shot down a soldier.

'Give me a gun! I can take down a few of them,' Neel urged, looking alert.

'I'm not a fool! I'm not giving you a gun,' she yelled.

Chow started spraying bullets all around and two soldiers died immediately.

'All clear. Go now. Go!'

Their body armour changed to white to camouflage with the snow. They ran towards the chopper while Chow continued to fire. He figured that everyone was dead by now. They were about to enter the chopper when Neel saw a solider standing at a distance with a gun that looked dangerous.

'Is that a laser gun?'

'Shit! Yes! A couple of hits and this suit will give up. We have to hurry,' said Nushen.

It was too late. Neel saw him shooting straight at her.

'Nushen, move!' He pushed her aside. The laser beams missed her but at least ten hit Neel. Most of them hit him on the vest but a few cut through the suit and struck his hands and torso. 'Bloody hell!' he screamed. Blood ran down his chest and flowed out of his hands, even as he entered the copter and picked up a machine gun. Nushen had been hit on her hand too.

She fired up the engine while Neel kept shooting heavily at the soldier. 'Die, die, die!' he yelled but couldn't tell if the soldier was dead. He looked to the other side and saw Chow lying motionless on the ground. His sight was getting blurrier the more blood he lost. 'Your agent is dead.'

'Come on! Come on!' Nushen screamed. The engine started roaring just as the soldier returned with a rocket launcher. 'Damn! Incoming, Nushen. It's a launcher. Take off now!' Neel shouted, firing at the soldier.

The missile came in hot, and though it missed the chopper by a whisker as they took off, the fire engulfed the tail of the chopper, sending it into a tailspin.

'We have to jump, Kalki ... Kalki!' she called at the top of her lungs. His eyes were closing; he had lost too much blood. She looked down. They were more than 20,000 feet up. She tried to control the helicopter to get as far as she could but, soon enough, they were spiralling down.

The chopper alarm went off, warning of another incoming missile.

'Dammit!' she picked him up and ran towards the edge of the chopper, jumping out just as it burst into flames.

ELEVEN

The first time Neel woke up, it was to a hazy and icy world and he could barely open his eyes. He saw snow everywhere and felt as if he was floating. The next time he opened his eyes, he was leaning against the trunk of a tree. He remembered closing his eyes and slipping into another world.

'Arya … Arya …' he heard himself mumble when he couldn't feel his feet on the ground.

Nushen kept him down. She was tired beyond her superhuman abilities after carrying Neel for miles and tending to his wounds. The laser beam had burned his skin but luckily the bodysuit had contained the medicinal supplies to heal his skin. He was now in a drugged state because of the wonder drugs she had administered from the emergency kit. If it weren't for the suit, he would have been killed.

Nushen had to then stitch herself up, and her left hand was bruised. Although she had missed adventures of this nature, what was unfolding in front of her was a question of life and death—not just for them but for billions of people on Earth. All she wanted was to get to a safe haven as far away as possible from the crash site, while ensuring they didn't leave a trail for the army dogs and drones to follow.

She looked at the distant mountain peaks far ahead of her. To save them, she had to conquer those peaks. She stood up, breathing heavily. *I won't let you down, President Wang. I will avenge your death. I will kill Jian ...*

Agent Han called General Jian in Beijing. '*Xiānshēng* (sir), we have lost Nushen.'

'How?' he shouted.

'Sorry, sir. She escaped with the prisoner, Kalki.'

'This is ridiculous!'

Han was silent.

He yelled in frustration and banged his fist on the table. 'I need her at any cost, do you understand? If you don't bring her to me alive, I will cut your head into a thousand pieces.'

Neel strained to open his eyes and noticed a fire next to him. Although it didn't help much, it was a welcome sight. He looked around what seemed like a small cave, closed off by a stack of wood.

He tried to get up but his abdomen hurt like hell and his vision was still blurry. He noticed his left arm was hit as well and had been bandaged but blood still dripped out slowly. Luckily, the bodysuit had helped protect him and the laser beam had missed critical organs. There was a flesh wound on his right hamstring. He lifted his neck to see what had happened to his stomach, pulling at the bandages slowly, and saw stitches on the raw wounds. It was a gruesome scene. *Goddammit! I'm a mess,* he thought.

Someone removed the stack of wood and walked in. He carefully looked up and saw Nushen with a gun in her hand.

'You're finally awake. How do you feel?'

'I feel like shit.'

'Don't try to pull any stunts. I won't hesitate to shoot you,' she warned. 'And don't assume for a split second that you are free. You're my prisoner now.'

'Why did you save me?' he asked.

'Didn't you hear me? You're a high-value asset. I can trade you with the Chinese or the Indians or anyone for a price or a favour.'

'Fabulous! Perhaps it was a mistake saving you,' he said. 'I should have let the laser gun take you down.'

She looked at him but didn't reply.

'How can I forget? You are a superhuman, not human. Everything is a calculated move for you,' he muttered. 'I'm a mere pawn on your chessboard.'

'Who are you kidding? You're not a saint either. In fact, we are essentially the same. Given a chance, you wouldn't hesitate to kill me and cross the border.'

This time it was Neel who didn't reply.

'How did we get here?' he asked sometime later, while she was removing her bodysuit. He could see the bandages on her left arm.

'You don't remember?'

Neel tried to recollect but his mind was in a jumbled haze. He remembered jumping from the helicopter while Nushen held him tightly. He remembered seeing the chopper in flames before drifting in the air with the propeller parachute. He remembered that he had lost too much blood and had fallen unconscious. He also remembered that, upon touchdown, Nushen had carried him and had tried everything to keep him alive. It all felt like a distant dream.

'I remember faintly … Where are we now?'

'Somewhere near the border, on the Chinese side. We're probably in the no-man zone; it looks safe. We are far from civilization and the forest has been blanketed by snow. The land is not habitable but we have to survive here for a few days.'

He nodded.

'I had to carry you for nearly forty kilometres to find this cave. There were planes and drones flying all around, trying to find us. The camouflage helped, along with the fact that they probably don't expect us to negotiate this impossible terrain. But we are not safe here either; we have to keep moving.'

She stopped him as he tried to get up. 'You shouldn't strain yourself. We can stay here for a few days. It wasn't easy to fix you, so don't cause more problems. You've lost of a lot of blood but the drugs I gave you will heal you fast.'

'You really are an expert surgeon?'

'Yes. Among other things, I am a doctor and a surgeon.'

He chuckled. 'I can't believe the way you have done all this, as though I was in the ICU.'

'I have skills,' she mumbled. 'I have to hunt. We need food and animal hide to stay warm; the bodysuits took a hit and so we can't rely on them too long. I will be back before dark. Just stay still and don't get up. Here's your water and some chocolate and energy bars if you get hungry. Your meds will ensure you get a sound sleep.'

'Okay.'

'Don't try to escape. You will die out there. I'm the only one who can keep you alive right now.'

'Of course.'

'You can throw these pieces of wood into the fire. It will go for a day, so you can keep yourself warm. See you soon.'

He saw her go out with his blurry vision, before he closed his eyes and slipped into sleep.

By the time the sun had set, Nushen was back with two dead rabbits and some nuts. She had also carved hard wood to make two containers for holding water. When she entered the cave, she saw that the fire was out and it was freezing. She touched his cold forehead and cursed, *Damn! He's been sleeping for too long.*

She hurriedly lit the fire with wood, struggling to get it going at first but succeeding nonetheless. She rubbed his face with her hands and hugged him to share warmth. For some strange reason, this gave her a sense of comfort. She stretched her legs and closed her eyes, still holding him as she realized her body needed rest. *Human bodies are the best heaters …*

'You're back,' he said a few hours later. She got up hastily.

'Yes, yes. Err … How are you feeling now?' she asked, slightly embarrassed for holding him as he slept.

He was struggling to talk. 'I need to take a leak.'

'Oh! Okay, you can go in this wooden container I made.'

'No, take me out. I want to see what's out there.'

'That's a bad idea. It's cold and you can't walk. Your stitches might come off.'

'Please, Nushen.'

'All right, but be careful. Hold my arms.' She slowly lifted him. He cried out when he set his foot on the ground. 'Easy, easy,' she said.

Breathing heavily, he marshalled all his energy into standing up. His abdomen hurt and his stitches felt as if they might come off.

When they stepped outside, he was stunned. There was a near full moon in the sky, which helped him get a good view of the terrain. 'This is the abode of the gods!' he exclaimed in spite of all the pain. They were at a tremendous height, on a cliff, with a treacherous slope right outside and winds blowing strong. One step more and he would fall ten thousand feet down to death. 'How did you manage to get me here?'

'I must admit that it wasn't exactly a walk in the park.'

He chuckled. He felt as though he was standing on the clouds.

'You think it's easy to stay clear of the drones you have built? Or the Chinese drones, for that matter? We are invisible to them right now.'

'And the stack of wood?'

'I had to make a few trips. There is a forest up on the other side of this mountain.'

'No one can find us here,' he said and spread his arm to feel the wind. It was chilly to the point of leaving frostbites, but refreshing at the same time.

'We have to get back in there soon or we could get frostbite. Do your business quickly and let's get going.'

'Okay,' he said and moved his zipper down with one hand. She looked the other way. He did his business and zipped back up.

'All cool?' she asked with a hint of smile.

'Oh, yes. It's been a while since I peed into a void like this,' he said. She couldn't help but laugh. 'Let's go back.'

Once inside, she peeled the rabbits and roasted them over the fire. 'Those look yum,' he said.

'They weren't easy to catch. I had to dig deep to get them out. Enjoy them because your next meal might just be rats.'

Neel laughed. 'So, is this military training?'

'You can say that. We had to camp at various forests around the world and survive for weeks, if not months, without proper food or water. I've been through some pretty tough camps.'

'What next? What's your plan?' he asked.

'We have to wait until you get better. You will heal fast.'

'Honestly, why are you risking your life for me? I will only slow you down. What do you want me as a leverage for?'

She looked at him in silence. After a while, she said, 'You don't have patience, do you? Always the curious type?'

'You can say that.'

She cut a few pieces of the rabbit and gave them to him. 'You're right. I need you for something.'

'What?'

'We have plenty of time to talk about that, I assure you. You will get your answers. But tell me this ... who is Arya?'

He looked at her angelic face. She was an enigma. He didn't know whether to trust her or not. There was something about her aura that kept him on the edge; a tension in the air that was only growing as time passed.

He couldn't risk telling her anything, not yet. But his mind flashed back to his school days when Tiger and Arya were about to enter his life.

KALKI'S STORY - TIGER ROARS

The Netaji Subhash Chandra Bose School, where his grandfather General Ramsey had admitted him, was part of a massive university run by the army. With state-of-the-art infrastructure, beautiful trees, lawns and fountains, and the unending stadiums for various sports, it looked simply marvellous to Neel.

From day one, he kept to himself in the school and never tried making any friends. He effortlessly aced most of the subjects in his class, especially maths, science and history, but his social skills were a problem; he almost always failed in any task that required working in a team. Soon, he was labelled a freak.

Kids did everything to trouble him at the hostel. Several boys would beat him up when they didn't get any reaction from him and wet his bed before he went to sleep. They tore his books and assignments regularly.

A bully called Tiger become his nemesis. When Neel refused to salute him in the dorm one day, he punched him hard in the stomach.

'You assmonkey, the day you salute me is the day I will spare you. Get that, butt breath?' he warned and punched him again twice. He was known for using swear words generously.

Neel fell to the ground but didn't react; he never did. At some level, he wanted to get beaten up and experience physical pain. He liked the pain; he didn't know why, but he did.

He usually went to the library after and cried silently behind the books. Whenever a bad incident happened, he missed his mother more than ever. *Why? Why did you leave me?*

One day in the eighth grade, he was reading a book on the power of the mind by Swami Vivekananda. He read that if you take up one idea and live, breathe, think and dream that idea and that idea alone, it would lead you to success. He also read that if you truly wanted something, the universe would conspire to take you towards realizing that idea.

For some reason, he was suddenly clear on what he had to do with his life—*I have to end terrorism in India!* The death of his family members had ruined his life and he blamed terrorism for it. *I will stop terrorism and ensure no other child becomes an orphan like me.*

He went to the auditorium lawns to sit under the trees and work on a strategy to rescue India. He was so excited. *But how?* He had no idea.

Before he could get started, though, he heard someone crying in pain. He ran towards the rear of the building and was shocked to see a bunch of bigger kids beating his classmate, Tiger. *Tiger, the bully, is getting beaten black and blue? Ha! He deserves it,* was his first reaction. But the bigger kids didn't seem to be from his school and two of them were beating him with hockey sticks. He got concerned.

'Hey, let him go! Who are you guys?' Neel shouted. 'How did you get in here?'

'Who is this wimp? Bring him here,' the leader commanded, and two boys came to grab Neel. Tiger fell to the ground, groaning in pain.

They came running towards Neel but he took them by surprise and knocked them down in two back-to-back kicks to their groin. They fell to the ground, gasping for breath and clutching their crotches.

The rest of the boys left Tiger and came to attack him. 'You're dead meat,' the leader shouted but before he could attack, Neel moved sideways and aimed a punch at his neck. The leader fell down instantly. The other two boys looked at each other and decided to run. Neel kicked the three boys who had fallen to the ground over and over again. There was rage on his face, so much so that he couldn't control himself. He picked them up and beat them down again.

'Neel, you have to stop. Neel!' Tiger screamed, limping towards him. 'Stop. You'll kill them.' He pushed Neel back with whatever strength he had left.

'Are you okay, Tiger?' Neel asked, breathing heavily.

'Do I look okay? Get me a bloody doctor,' he cried, blood oozing from his wounds.

Neel ran to the auditorium and dialled the security, who came in and took the three boys. He then escorted Tiger to the dispensary.

'If you expect me to thank you, I'm not going to,' Tiger said, lying down on the dispensary bed with bandages all over. He was terribly embarrassed that Neel of all the people had helped him.

'I'm not expecting anything,' mumbled Neel, reading a book.

'I owe you one though. You had my back, now I will have your back. That's it, nothing more!'

Neel smiled. 'Sure. But you don't have to.'

'Why can't I? I will do whatever I wish!' Tiger hit back.

Neel nodded.

After a while, Tiger cleared his throat and asked 'Why did you save your enemy, Neel?'

'Because it was the right thing to do. I couldn't stand there and watch. Moreover, you are not my enemy; you're just a bully.'

Tiger didn't understand this philosophy and it wasn't important for him to understand it either. He was grateful that Neel had saved him but was too proud to admit it. 'How do you fight so well?'

'I started learning martial arts when I was very young. I got my black belt in Guwahati.'

'I thought you were a wimp, a weakling. But you surprised me.'

Neel laughed.

'And what was that rage on your face? Were you about to kill them?' Tiger asked further.

'Well, when you hit your enemy, you hit them so hard that they never dare think about coming back again. That's what I was doing.'

'That's it? I feel the real reason was your pent up feelings and frustration busted out. You just had to get it out of your system. I have heard about your past.'

'To tell you the truth, you are right. I felt good after that. I guess punishing bad guys could be my stress buster,' Neel confided.

'Cool, that sounds fun. We can do it together,' Tiger added.

'Beat up bad guys together?'

'Yeah, totally!'

Neel smiled and went back to reading his book.

After a few minutes, Tiger cleared his throat again. 'So, are we partners now or what?' he asked, holding his hand up for a high-five.

Neel thought for a while but something told him to let himself go.

'Do I have a choice?' Neel asked.

'No!'

They both burst into laughter and high-fived.

Thus began a friendship that changed their lives.

When he was fourteen, Neel was selected for a top-secret military programme called Prodigy 25, in which students with the best minds and diverse abilities were selected to for training in next-generation warfare. Children with extraordinary capabilities were chosen and brought together to create a formidable group that would defend the future of the country for decades to come. They would be trained in every aspect of warfare, including combat, science, technology, politics and espionage.

It was here that he started a team called the Astras to retaliate against Russian and Chinese cyberattacks on online military infrastructure.

'Astra means weapon,' said Neel, looking at the ten-odd members of the team who were keen on being part of this mission. He had even managed to pull in Tiger into his team. 'We will create technology that is unprecedented.'

Soon, the premise escaped cyber defence and they started innovating in a number of areas, including space travel, robotics, bioengineering, battlefield strategies, combat and weapons.

While Neel built on their cyber hacking capability with AI and software engines called ultrabots, Tiger focused on bioengineering and chemicals. He was fond of genetics, evolution and anthropology and his acumen in those areas became an asset to Astras. Moreover, they both excelled in martial arts and combat strategies and proved to be phenomenal in mock drills, where they hit enemy camps with exceptional accuracy. Along with the team, Neel and Tiger spent hours learning karate, judo, ju-jitsu and Indian martial arts techniques.

Tiger proved to be Neel's biggest asset. His full name was Tiger Singh and he was from a family in remote Punjab where it was a tradition for every male (and female, for the past decade) in the lineage to serve in the Indian armed forces. They took pride in the medals they had won over the generations and the blood they had shed to protect their country. All Tiger knew from birth was that he would one day become a soldier in the Indian army and die in battle. Being with Neel and becoming a part of his vision was everything he had asked for in his life.

For some reason, General Ramsey was worried about Neel's unusual life.

'What are you reading?' he asked, walking into his room. Neel had just turned sixteen.

He didn't respond.

'Your obsession with AI and weapons is not healthy. There is more to life than this.'

'Why are you not happy with me doing exactly the same thing you do?' Neel hit back.

Ramsey was silent.

'Why didn't you want me to be part of the Prodigy 25 programme?' he asked.

'You went ahead anyway! Why are you complaining?' his grandfather countered. 'Son, why are you screwing up your life? You don't have any friends apart from that bull of a boy, Tiger, and you're called anti-social in school. If you just … try to be normal, everything will be all right. You have to forget your past and move on.'

'I cannot forget what has happened; I cannot forget how I lost everyone. I can't be normal like others, so I have stopped wasting my time. I don't even know what normal means.'

'For God's sake, boy. At times, I worry about what you're going to end up as.'

'I'm very clear about what I want to be.'

'And that is?'

'I won't let anyone go through what I went through. No child should lose his or her parents.'

Ramsey laughed. 'That's right. Such a practical goal. Wake up! You can't protect everyone. People die in wars. Our soldiers die so our countrymen don't shed blood. It's an honour that our family has sacrificed so many people to protect our country. Their deaths were not in vain.'

'I can at least try to stop it.'

'So you want to become a soldier?'

Neel chuckled.

'Oh, I get it. You are inspired by those superhero movies? You want to become a mercenary, a vigilante? A masked man saving people's lives?'

'You're hilarious.' He laughed. 'Tell me one thing. Who controls the defence forces?'

'The Prime Minister of India.'

'And who controls the prime minister?'

'The people.'

'Come on, General. Don't be so naïve. Who truly controls the prime minister?'

Ramsey thought for a while. 'The businessmen.'

'Bingo! I want to be a businessman,' Neel affirmed and showed him the book he was reading, *Economics of War*. 'I want to be *the* businessman who rules the defence sector.'

Ramsey stared at him, stunned.

By the time he was eighteen and in college, the Astras Group, through the Prodigy 25 programme, had won contracts from the IT Department of the Indian Defence Ministry to protect nearly 10 per cent of its cyber assets. With their proprietary artificial intelligence engine called ultrabots, they had stunned the world with what India could achieve. In parallel, they had started creating promising weapons and machines. Neel came up with the concept of ultra-drones, which were futuristic drones that could be used to guard the borders in rough terrains, but competing against giants to win contracts for drones seemed impossible.

'Professor Vati, we need funding. I can't build these machines without grants. Why can't the army fund me?' a frustrated Neel asked his physics professor who was incharge of the Prodigy 25 programme. She had been one of his biggest supporters and often called him the 'chosen one', though he never understood why.

'My boy, you cannot say they didn't support you. Your company is already one of the biggest in the cyber defence sector. Why not use its profits to fund your R&D for a couple of years?' she asked.

'It's not remotely enough to build what I have in mind,' he complained.

'I wish I had a magic wand to get you the funding out of thin air! However, as always, I will see what I can do. Okay? But no promises,' she advised. 'That reminds me, you had issues with creating high-quality alloys for your robots, isn't it?'

'Yes,' said Neel. 'I'm struggling with it.'

'Here, take this journal that details an advanced method of making alloys. It's top secret, classified. And don't ask me who wrote it.'

Neel glanced through it. 'Sanskrit? That too encrypted?'

'Yes, it's encrypted for a reason. See if it's useful and keep it to yourself. Now, I'm getting late for my class,' she said.

'Where is the key? How do I decrypt it?'

'Well, you have to figure out the key yourself,' she concluded, walking away.

Intrigued by the journal, Neel and Tiger came out of the faculty office and stopped dead in their tracks. In the corridor, amongst the hundred-odd students, they saw a face that had become the talk of the entire college since she had joined a few months ago.

'Can you hear my heart slamming in my chest?' Tiger asked breathlessly.

'Yes. Can you hear mine?' Neel breathed. The first time he had laid eyes on Arya Sharma, he had instantly fallen for her.

'Yeah. Why don't you ask her out?'

'Why don't you ask her out?' Neel retorted.

'Dude, because she is totally into you—and you're totally into her. Just cut the crap and do something already,' Tiger stressed as she walked closer.

'Hey, guys! What did the professor say?' Arya was part of the same Robotics class as them.

'The usual. Nothing new. We're not getting the funding,' Tiger replied.

She made a sad face.

'Think about the Fight Club! It's not a bad idea,' she said, looking at Neel. 'Let's go check it out, at least.'

She handed over the tickets.

❖

'Kalki! Kalki! What happened?'

Neel's eyes were moist. He looked at Nushen but didn't respond.

'Kalki, who is Arya?'

'She was the love of my life …' he whispered, lost in thought.

'Why do I see tears in your eyes?'

He didn't reply, in spite of her asking him repeatedly.

'Did something happen to her? Is she not alive?'

'Anyone who gets close to me is taken away,' he said quietly, looking into the fire.

She moved closer to him, holding his shoulders and looking deep into his eyes. 'I'm sorry,' she uttered softly. She kissed his forehead, then brought her lips next to his. 'You should rest now.'

He leaned forward and touched her lips with his. A bolt of electricity passed through his body; his heart slammed in his chest.

'Nushen,' he started, but she cut him off.

'Shh, not now. We will discuss everything when the time comes. You need to rest up.'

Neel nodded and closed his eyes, while she held him in her arms. She stared into the fire for a long time.

Everything is fair in love and war … Everything is fucked up in love and war …

She smiled.

TWELVE

—✲—

'Wake up, it's morning.'

He opened his blurry eyes.

'You've been sleeping for over fourteen hours. How are you feeling?' Nushen asked.

'Much better!'

'Your abdomen seems to be healing fast,' she exclaimed, surprised to see rapid improvement. 'Your body heals almost as fast as mine.'

'As fast as a superhuman? That's definitely a compliment.'

'How is this possible?'

'Ancient techniques that I have learnt over the years.'

'Ancient techniques?'

'Maybe I'll tell you someday.'

She nodded.

'The good news is that, at this rate, you will only take a few days to heal, not weeks.'

'I'm feeling pretty good already. I guess I'm ready to go.' He tried to get up.

'Kalki, no! Not right now.'

He took a deep breath. She was right; he needed a few more days.

'Stay still,' she said, taking a bowl of warm water and dipping a cloth in it. She removed his shirt, and wiped his chest and arms with the cloth.

'This is bliss,' he breathed out. She smiled slightly and continued to rub his torso, skirting around the wounds.

'Oh!' he blurted, when she slid his pants down. *Dear God.*

She poured warm water on him and rubbed him further, holding back a smile. 'Don't get too excited.'

'That's not humanly possibly when a goddess is doing things to you,' he muttered, taking a deep breath. She stopped and took a look at his face. His mind was in a tizzy.

'Err ... I think I need to go ... to fetch some water and food,' she cleared her throat and slid his pants back on. 'Clearly your body is not able to control its excitement.'

She got up and walked away in a hurry.

Damn, thought Neel.

Meanwhile, in Beijing, a top newspaper reported:

President Wang reportedly died of a cardiac arrest. He took his final breath peacefully in sleep while his family was attending to him. The Father of Modern China, as he was widely known, had taken the country from being a rising power to a superpower second to none, ending the supremacy of western countries. His family is devastated and so are the citizens of China.

During his final days, the president had entrusted General Jian to take over his position as the commander of the defence forces and the supreme leader of the Chinese Communist Party. The cabinet and the top brass have unanimously supported this decision and voted General Jian to the top position.

Jian had read the article and given his consent for the tone of the message that was being sent out to the media. His PR department was on an overdrive, hailing him as the best thing that could have happened to China and that he had the absolute blessings of his father.

He walked towards his father's body, kept for everyone to pay final tributes in the Hall of People.

I didn't have to do this Father, he thought. *You may not believe me, but I feel bad for what I did to you. It was inevitable. You wouldn't let me do anything. You had me thrown in a prison and left me no choice. This dragon cannot be caged; this dragon cannot be a puppet … I have my vision for this world and it can only be realized with blood. And it has started with your blood, Father …*

His agents had meticulously executed the plan to assassinate President Wang. They had administered genetically engineered bacteria in his food and the infection in his vital organs had slowly grown as no medicine worked, ultimately killing him. The death was made to look natural.

I am now the supreme leader of the most powerful nation on Earth! I feel power running through my veins, Father! I will be called Jian the Conqueror for ages to come. I will be called a god!

'Let's proceed with the death ceremony,' he told his chief advisor, Shanyuan.

'Millions are waiting outside to pay homage, General,' Shanyuan replied. 'It's one of the biggest gatherings of humans in the history of the world.'

'Give them a chance to say goodbye, then,' Jian instructed.

While heading back, he saw his younger brother, Renshu, standing in a corner with an expressionless face. He was the last remaining member of the family. Jian and Renshu didn't get along and he had figured out what Jian had done to his father. They looked at each other but neither of them spoke.

Jian walked into his new office, which had once belonged to President Wang. His larger than life painting hung on the wall behind the desk. Jian stood on the chair, took it in his hands and flung it to the floor.

'I'm the new emperor!' he roared in Mandarin. Everyone stood stunned. 'Han, how do we celebrate the coronation of a new emperor?' he asked, getting down from the chair.

'With the blood of traitors, sir!' Agent Han replied.

'Very well said. Bring in the traitors,' he ordered, and Han hurried out.

He looked at his secretary. 'Move out all this trash and bring in Master Genghis Khan's throne.'

'Yes, sir.' She bowed and moved out.

Han came in and behind him walked the eleven trusted lieutenants of President Wang and Nushen's core team. Although they were in chains, they stood with their heads held high with dignity and pride.

'You're a traitor!' said a senior advisor, while another spat on him.

'You are making me very angry,' Jian barked, holding a sword in his hand. 'I'm offering you a peaceful death; don't force me to keep you alive and cut you piece by piece every day.'

As they continued to protest and snarl at him, the guards held them down one by one. In a frenzy, Jian took up his sword and swung to cut their heads off, colouring the walls of the office red. Their blood flowed on the floor, seeping through the doors and touching the steps of the highest office in China.

'Tyranny and cruelty are the only virtues of a great conqueror. I want blood spilt every day. I want people slaughtered across the world,' he said, looking at his bloody hands. 'No more peace.'

'What are the orders for India and Pakistan, sir?' Han asked, who had been promoted as the head of the intelligence wing. Han had betrayed Nushen and won Jian's trust.

Jian laughed.

'Well, the plan is already in action. We just have to sit back and enjoy the show!'

'Are the defence forces along the Chinese border prepared?' asked General Vikram Singh, the head of the newly formed Indian High Command (IHC). He was in a meeting with his chief reporting officers to draw up battle plans in case China or Pakistan were to attack India.

He had worked with the navy chief and the air chief marshal to salvage the situation in the country. There were rampant riots, arson, strikes, bandhs and morchas, to name a few law and order issues, everywhere. Nearly 3400 people were dead in terrorist attacks and bomb blasts, as the Invisible Hand had activated its sleeper cells. People were scared to step out, business was badly hit, the stock exchange had crashed and the prices for food and consumer goods had skyrocketed.

Ajay Pradhan, the influential principal secretary and head of the Prime Minister's Office, played a major role in controlling all the government related aspects.

Ajay Pradhan was a shrewd, cunning and powerful bureaucrat who had been the nerve centre of the PMO for almost a decade. He was an IAS officer and had risen through the ranks swiftly because of his acute sense of politics and business acumen. He controlled every file that moved in the PMO and Parliament; he influenced every policy or plan that the government came up with. He was also notorious for creating rifts between factions to ensure his agenda was pushed. 'You are *the* Narad Muni,' PM Acharya had joked once, but the truth was that he knew how to get things moving in the capital and Acharya had been fond of him.

He had miraculously escaped the Parliament bombing as he had been on an official trip to Britain during the time. When he came back, he had worked with General Vikram Singh to set up the IHC. Although General Singh was the head of the high command, along with chiefs of the navy and air force, it was Pradhan who controlled the government for them.

He had that ensured nothing changed in the running of the country or the states. IAS officers had replaced the politicians and ran the government smoothly. 'The days of the babus are finally here!' Pradhan had told officers from across the country after the IHC was formed.

That day, when everyone left the room after the IHC review meeting, General Talwar stayed back. He was Vikram Singh's trusted man and supported him throughout. General Singh had promoted him when emergency had been declared and had entrusted him with several functions of the army and IHC.

General Singh looked angry. 'How could General Riaz imprison his own PM? I had sincerely hoped the days of enmity with Pakistan were behind us. He has ruined everything that Acharya had worked for in the last few years.'

'Sir, we cannot trust the Pakistanis. We should attack before they do,' said Talwar.

'No, Talwar. We cannot start a war. With the current unrest in the country, millions of lives are at stake. Peaceful dialogue has to be our first option,' Singh opined in a pained voice. 'Moreover, this is all about Riaz and the ISI, not the people of Pakistan.'

'Sorry, sir, but isn't ISI always in power? Aren't ISI and the corrupt Pakistani army always the true enemy of both the countries? I'm unable to control my anger in the face of the unprovoked firing going on in Kashmir right now. Should we just sit here and do nothing?' Talwar asked as tea was served.

'Ask them to give a befitting reply but nothing more than that. Understood?' General Singh ordered.

'Yes, sir,' said Talwar, jumping up from his seat. 'I will send ex-Defence Minister Jagan in. He wants to speak with you.'

'Jagan is here?' asked General Singh, surprised.

'Yes, sir, we have brought him from house arrest as he had been insisting.'

'Okay, send him in.'

After Talwar left the room, Jagan came inside.

'General Singh, you have to give me a clean chit. Absolve me right now and I will stand next to you to resolve this crisis. You know I'm stuck in this situation through no fault of mine. We have worked together for nearly a decade,' Jagan pleaded.

'I understand, Jagan. Our investigations have proven you innocent. It was a mistake arresting you but we had to do what was right for the country. We had to investigate. Talwar strongly believed that you were involved in the Parliament attack and we didn't want to take any chances,' Singh replied, sipping his tea.

'General! How could you let this happen to me!? After what we have gone through together to modernise our army ... There is something off about General Talwar, I'm telling you. Our investigations have revealed that he has connections with the Invisible Hand. You need to believe—'

'I'm going to order them to release you. You will be back to working with Pradhan,' Singh interrupted. He had started sweating profusely.

'General, what happened?'

He was unable to breath. His eyes turned red, as though they were about to pop out, and he clutched his chest, falling to the floor. His body wriggled for a few seconds, then stopped moving.

Jagan hurriedly called in the guards but by the time they came in, General Singh was lying dead on the ground.

At the same time, Talwar and Pradhan walked into the room and saw him dead.

'Jagan, what have you done? What's in that water?' Talwar asked, horrified, when they saw that Jagan was sprinkling water on him.

'I didn't do anything! I was just sitting here when he started coughing and struggling to breathe.'

Singh's body had turned blue.

'He has poisoned the General,' said Talwar, while Pradhan stared at Jagan in shock. Pradhan knew very well that it was impossible for Jagan to have done something like this. In fact, he had put his best experts into proving Jagan wasn't guilty but here he was again with Jagan in the middle of another conspiracy.

'Pradhan, you know I haven't done it. Please save me. I'm being made a pawn in this conspiracy. This was all done by Talwar,' he cried.

'Arrest that traitor before I shoot him in his head,' ordered Talwar. The guards handcuffed Jagan, even as he kept shouting that he was innocent.

'Search him. He must have the weapon with him,' Talwar instructed. The guards did as ordered, finding a tiny tube in his pocket. Upon examination, they realised it was some kind of poison.

'Sir, this is the potential weapon he used to kill the General,' said the guard.

Jagan was speechless. 'I have no idea what that is. This is all a set up. Talwar, you bastard, you're a traitor! You have sold your soul to the Invisible Hand,' Jagan yelled, while the guards dragged him out of the room.

When everyone had left the room, Talwar turned to Pradhan. There was a brief silence.

'What do you think, Pradhan? Am I right in thinking that Jagan did this?' He knew Pradhan had lobbied to get Jagan released.

Pradhan thought for a while. *Talwar, you traitor … you have backstabbed your own country. But this is not the time to oppose you. You will have me killed too. I have to take care of this country and its citizens. I have to stay alive, no matter what.*

'I think you're right,' said Pradhan, clearing his throat. 'I made a mistake in judging Jagan. He would have killed you too. Luckily, you came out of the room before he worked his magic in here. We will investigate it. Justice will be served.'

General Talwar nodded.

'Pradhan, I know this is too early and that General Vikram Singh's body is still not cold enough to talk about this but a country cannot run without its head. There is a void at the top, now that he is dead,' said Talwar.

'You're right. The country will fall into further chaos once this news gets out. We need a successor to take over immediately in order to pacify the country and, according to seniority, you are next in the chain of command. By the rules of the military, you are the new chief of army. It will automatically make you the head of IHC.'

Talwar nodded in appreciation. 'You are my right-hand man in running this country, Pradhan!'

Pradhan faked a smile and said, 'Congratulations, General. You are the new supreme leader of India.'

The next day, there was a press conference to announce General Talwar's appointment as the chief of the Indian army and the head of IHC.

The public went into chaos at the news of General Singh's murder and former Defence Minister Jagan's second arrest. The tension in India was palpable.

'What the hell is going on between you and General Jian anyway? Why is he after you?' Neel asked, when Nushen returned at noon.

Nushen was silent.

'Why did the announcement say "capture Nushen but don't harm her"? Why does he want you alive? I need answers!' he stressed.

'All right …' she said after a while. 'I will tell you about my life and why Jian is haunting me like a ghost—not as a bargain to get to know more about you, but because I want you to know who I really am. I want you to know who our common enemy is and the kind a maniac we are dealing with.'

Neel stared at her in surprise.

'They say the beginning of a new species is always tumultuous and mine was no exception …'

NUSHEN'S STORY ~ DAWN OF HOMO SUPERNUS

※

A few decades ago, a Chinese scientist named Dr Mike Chang and a German bioengineering pioneer, Dr Robert Muller, started working on a secret project that was code-named *Homo Supernus*. The idea was to create superior humans, primarily for defence purposes but the benefits of which could be taken to the general public later on. These new humans would be better in every aspect—strength, tolerance to diseases, immunity, physical appearance, aging, healing, intelligence, reflexes, control over emotions and so on.

Although this project would give an incredible advantage to the Chinese military, with the introduction of super-soldiers, it also had the potential to further mankind by curing diseases, increasing human life span and whatnot. It could also pave the way for designer babies—the possibilities were endless.

Instead of genetically modifying the genes, Chang and Muller initially took a different approach. They termed the method as 'perfect selection'. Everything in nature follows a theory called natural selection. Better genes, organs and species get selected by nature to go forward and nature kills the ones that are weak. This was termed as 'survival of the fittest' by Darwin.

Instead of depending on nature to select the genes, Chang and Muller decided to choose the perfect combination and create humans using a gene pool with superior attributes. To achieve this, scientists toiled for five years to narrow down a set of genes from various bloodlines that could be the perfect combination to create *Homo supernus*, the name they chose for the next evolution of *Homo sapiens*.

Chang's research led them to narrowing down and isolating ancient bloodlines with incredible and even supernatural capabilities. Over the centuries, and across various civilizations, there had existed races with unique attributes, which people back then spoke about as magical, godly, evil or mythical. The key was to combine those attributes to create a single fabric of DNA. In the quest to acquire this DNA, they unearthed ancient tombs, went after the secret societies and mutant clans, kidnapped people of royal bloodlines and did everything to isolate genes of value. The best set of genes were methodically chosen to create superhumans.

Another six years went by in trying to convert theory into practical results. Hundreds of babies were produced in labs by implanting embryos in gestational surrogate mothers. The results were bizarre, to say the least. The babies were born with deformities—sometimes with a leg missing, sometimes with no head and so on. The genetic mashup they had created wasn't stable and had become unpredictable, sometimes making the foetus grow too much and rupture the womb.

'Dr Chang, we have funded billions of dollars in the last two decades but the results are gruesome. You are producing one-legged monsters when we asked you to produce super-soldiers. I cannot convince the leadership to continue this programme anymore,' said a furious Mr Yin, who was funding the project on behalf of the Chinese army. He had paid a surprise visit to inspect their progress and had been shocked nearly to death when he saw a surrogate with her belly ruptured.

'Please, Mr Yin, we need two more years. These are necessary steps to get to our goal. We are very close. We will get you your super soldiers. You have to trust me,' Chang urged.

'My patience is running thin. People are laughing at me, Chang. I'm giving you one last year and then you are cut off.'

'*Xièxiè*. Thank you. We will make it happen, I promise.'

But Chang and Muller had hit a dead end and nothing seemed to be working in their favour. They had even tried to bring in animal chromosomes but it had ended badly.

They frantically started various experiments by altering the DNA to create perfect superhumans. In one such project, they implanted two babies in each surrogate with some variations in each twin. Like their other experiments, this failed too—but for one exception.

There was one pair of twins—a male and a female— that showed exceptional promise. The heartbeats were perfect, the growth rate was increasing frantically and they looked completely healthy in every aspect. They ran a number of experiments and the results were unbelievably good. Within two months, they were bigger than normal five-month old babies. After several tests on the surrogate and the foetuses, they concluded that these would be the first set of *Homo Supernus*.

The mood in the facility was ecstatic. However, the surrogate suffered unbearable pain as the foetuses grew rapidly. Her body couldn't handle the parasitic behaviour of the babies in the womb. By the fifth month, she had succumbed and they had to extract the babies by cutting her open.

Chang and Muller heaved a sigh of relief when they saw the newborns. The babies were beyond what they had expected; they looked extraordinary, with god-like features and a glow to their skin. They looked unlike anything the world had ever seen before. They were the *Homo Supernus*.

'My white knights have arrived!' Chang proclaimed.

It was celebration time at the research centre while the babies were artificially incubated till their seventh month. They named the boy 'Shen', Mandarin for god, and the female 'Nu Shen', Mandarin for goddess.

Several key people in the Chinese army learned about the success in the weeks to follow and everyone was ecstatic about the fact that China had produced super-soldiers—a feat that no other country in the world had accomplished. Everyone was eager to see the two children.

Unfortunately, the Americans got wind of their success through a double agent. The leadership at the US intelligence wing, the CIA, decided to end the mission at any cost as it would be a definite threat to US domination and national security. Before the Chinese could even plan for tests and future development, the CIA had taken out both Chang and Muller in separate accidents. They were killed along with their assistants and the labs were burnt in a coordinated mission on a single day, so that no one with core knowledge on the project remained alive.

This was dreadful news for the Chinese army, which didn't know how to proceed. They couldn't raise an issue over what the US had done as it was a top-secret project.

New scientists were assigned to take the project forward but they struggled to replicate the success. Instead, they traumatized the two babies with numerous tests, so much so that at one point they almost lost the children. They were exposed to heavy lab tests and experiments of various kinds—health, intelligence, social and so on.

They conducted experiments where they deliberately hurt the babies and learnt that they healed three times faster than humans and aged three times slower, giving them a life expectancy of over 200 years. There were experiments to check their reflexes in adverse conditions, like escaping arrows that were shot at them. Nushen's reflexes were better than Shen's, as she was lean and agile, but Shen was twice as strong as her in terms of physical strength.

Despite the trauma of these harsh experiments, they both grew up to be strong individuals with superhuman abilities by the age of ten. Surprisingly, they continued to discover their abilities. No one knew what they were capable of or what they could evolve into, except Muller and Chang themselves.

They certainly looked different; their faces, their features, their hair and their body types were too good to be real. They had a radiance in every part of their body that was visibly different than humans. Their eyesight, hearing, olfactory abilities and reflexes were also better. Their eyes were different, as though diamonds sparkled inside them. All this came with the additional burden of having to wear lenses and make-up to look normal. Moreover, they were devoid of love, as everybody looked at them as the results of an experiment. They were nicknamed 'lab rats' by the intelligence agents who guarded them all the time.

As they grew up, they picked up skills in combat, military strategies, warfare and martial arts. Their intellectual capabilities were superior to humans and they had abilities to specialize in a number of fields, including medicine, surgery, metallurgy, carpentry, arts, science and technology—making them multiskilled soldiers. By the age of fourteen, they knew all the major concepts of arts, science, technology, medical, finance and economics. They could even perform complex surgeries on humans and animals.

By the age of fifteen, it was time for them to get separated as they were deployed in different missions of the Chinese intelligence agencies, where they performed increasingly complex covert missions. Thus began their journey, which would change the world for years to come.

Nushen met President Wang, the most powerful man in China, when she was nineteen.

She was being bestowed the highest award won by an intelligence officer for her remarkable 100 per cent success rate in nearly a dozen covert operations, the most recent being the extraction of Chinese traders held hostage in Somalia by extremists. For this, she was taken into the President's office in Beijing, where the most powerful men in China were present, including the secretary of defence.

President Wang was introduced to Nushen. She saluted him and looked right ahead without any eye contact.

'Nushen, you are indeed a marvel that China has created. Your dedication to this country is unparalleled,' he said in a hoarse but gentle voice. She could see that age had taken its toll on him.

'Thank you, sir,' she replied in Mandarin and saluted him again.

He pinned the medal on her regalia and shook her hand.

'It's an honour to be the one giving you this medal.' He smiled.

'The honour is mine, sir.'

He asked the rest of the people to leave the room. 'Care to serve some tea for the old man?'

'It will be my pleasure, sir.'

While she poured him tea and mixed honey, he said, 'I must admit that your beauty is beyond what I had heard of.'

She couldn't help but smile. Dressed in the meticulous Chinese army uniform, she stood six feet tall with a perfectly toned body, radiant skin and glowing hair. Her hair was originally blonde but she changed it often to suit her assignments; she had coloured it black in her most recent cover-up.

'What a pity that we have to hide you from the world. Your eyes—no one on earth has that colour.' He touched her face to examine her skin. She felt uncomfortable, being treated like an alien. *What is the old man doing?*

'Nushen.'

'Sir.'

'Take a seat,' he said, sitting next to her.

'I have three sons but I don't have any daughters, though I have always wanted one … Sons never have the attachment that daughters have. It's sad but it's true.'

She didn't know what point he was trying to make. She was trying to judge him but she didn't sense any ill will in his demeanour.

'I want you deputed to our central defence advisory committee. You will report directly to me and handle projects that I play closer to my chest.'

'Thank you. It will be an honour to serve you, sir.' Nushen couldn't believe what he was saying; it meant everything to her to report directly to him.

'You will not serve me; you will serve China. You will always act for the good of the Chinese people and you will never make choices against the bigger interests of the country, even if you are under any sort of pressure— internal or external. Understood?'

'Yes, sir. If I have the honour of giving my life to China, I would happily do so.'

'No, Nushen. You have to survive for China and its people. Things can go bad any time and it's up to us to get things in order. You shall remain in Beijing from now on.'

She was ecstatic but tried to control her smile.

'Two pieces of advice for you. One—don't trust anyone. This is Beijing; The world's eyes and ears are in this city, so be watchful.'

'And the second, sir?'

'Avoid meeting my second son, General Jian Wang. If ever you cross paths with him, I need to know about it.'

'Yes, sir,' she said and took his leave after saluting him. She wondered what made him mention his son.

She was soon about to find out.

NUSHEN'S STORY – PROPHECY OF THE LAST KING

━━━━✦━━━━

'Sir, we have some news,' Agent Chang, an intelligence officer, had said when he had learnt that Nushen was posted in Beijing.

'It better be good if you're calling on this line,' Jian growled, whipping a young woman whose hands were tied to the headboard. She wore nothing but a slave collar around her neck, with a leash attached to it. He put Chang on speaker phone.

The officer could hear the girl moaning in pain.

'Sorry to disturb you, sir. Looks like a bad time to call.'

'Well, not that bad perhaps. Let's play a guessing game.' He gave a sinister laugh. 'Guess who's my latest slave?'

'Sir, it is not my place to answer that question,' Chang said hesitantly.

'Agent, it's an order.'

The officer didn't know what to say, so he kept quiet. Jian was known for his bad temper and erratic behaviour. No one ever understood his mood swings. 'I have no idea, sir,' he said, his voice hardly audible.

'It's Meifen Lin.'

'The movie star?'

'Oh, did you hear that slave girl? My agent is surprised to hear your name.'

Chang could hear the girl crying out loud.

'Stop crying,' he yelled and whipped her with the leash. She squeaked and stopped making any sound immediately. At eighteen years old, she was the latest star in the Chinese movie industry and had changed the pecking order with her debut movie.

'You always get the woman you want, sir,' said Chang.

'Wrong. I always get *whatever* I want ... Now, tell me, what's the matter?'

'Sir, we have news that Nushen is in town.'

'What?' Jian froze.

'Yes. She is in Beijing and now reporting directly to President Wang.'

Jian pulled himself out, much to Meifen's relief.

'The Goddess is here?' he exclaimed, lost in thought. People in the defence and political circles spoke about the tales of her beauty; she had become their ultimate fantasy. No one had seen her but everybody called her the Goddess.

Jian was indeed one of the most powerful people in China; he occupied a seat in the People's Communist Party of China and was an influential man in the armed forces. All this meant that when he wanted something, he usually got it. This time, he wanted Nushen.

Jian looked up at the wall of his majestic bedroom, where a life-sized painting of Genghis Khan, the Mongolian emperor who had ruled from west to east in the twelfth century, hung. Jian was a follower of Genghis Khan, heavily influenced by his philosophy, and patronized a cult of mercenaries called the Invisible Hand, which was believed to be started by the great conqueror himself in the year 1211 AD. In time, Jian had become Invisible Hand's biggest benefactor and strategic leader. He had vowed to make them the powerhouse required to rule the world.

Below the painting, Genghis Khan's words were engraved — *"I'm the punishment of God … If you had not committed great sins, God would not have sent a punishment like me upon you …"*

Genghis Khan was known as the most feared conqueror of all times; having conquered and ruled a land bigger than anyone had in history and killed forty million people in his conquests, reducing 11 per cent of the world's population at that time.

It was also known that a vast percentage of the world's population could be traced back to Genghis Khan. He was the direct ancestor of 8 per cent of the Central Asian population, amounting to seventeen million males, making him the biggest hero of copulation in the history of mankind. He had raped and mated with women in every kingdom he had conquered, in the process getting thousands of women pregnant.

Being a sex addict, Jian took inspiration from every aspect of Genghis Khan's life. He was a congenial sex maniac and womanizer. When any new actress or celebrity in China came on the horizon, she would always become his sex slave if he liked her. He subjected them to bondage and kinky sex in his private hideouts.

It was another matter that those who pleased him reached heights of success in their respective fields through Jian's influence. In short, if Jian picked a girl, it meant both—a path to great success and a path to horrific slavery. No one could do anything to him in China; he was that powerful. The media never wrote anything bad about him, he controlled the police and he had a vice-like grip over the political and army circles. His name was a synonym for absolute power.

Nushen was Jian's ultimate fantasy and he had strong reasons behind it. According to an ancient Chinese prophecy called the Prophecy of the Last King, an angel not from the human race would marry a king and make him the most powerful ruler to have ever ruled the surface of Earth. He had taken the prophecy literally.

When he had first heard about Nushen, his mind had set ablaze with fantasies of what he could do to the body of a goddess. But the *Homo Supernus* was one project he could never get close to. The day he had seen a sixteen-year-old Nushen's image, he had lost his mind. His relentless search for her had not succeeded, mostly because President Wang ensured no one even in the army knew her whereabouts.

Now that she was in Beijing, he didn't want to waste a single minute.

'Chang, find out how to get a meeting with her. My father would do anything to keep her away from me but I need to get her. At any cost.'

'Yes, sir. I am on it.'

It took Jian a few months to get a meeting with the elusive Nushen. Because of his frantic hunt for her, news had leaked in the intelligence circles that someone important called Nushen needed to be tracked. When the American intelligence got wind of Jian's hunt, they sensed a rift within the Chinese faction and also connected the dots to link Nushen with the super-soldier programme started by Dr Chang. The CIA began its own hunt for the superwoman and the news reached the Indian intelligence wing, RAW. That was how Neel had gotten the news from his sources in the RAW.

Both President Wang and Nushen knew about Jian's unending pursuit for her. 'Sir, he will not stop. Please allow me to meet him once. Let's put an end to this,' Nushen had urged Wang and, because she was right, the old man had reluctantly agreed.

When she walked into his office, Jian thought she was beyond his imagination. Everything about her was different and yet so human. Her beauty was beyond human.

'Dr Chang has indeed created the greatest masterpiece in human history,' Jian praised.

She didn't reply.

'Welcome, Nushen, the daughter of China, the Goddess … come inside. Can you please ask your team to stay outside? I have matters of great importance to discuss.'

Nushen nodded to her team and they left the room.

'Impressive,' she said, looking at the majestic room full of ancient war artefacts, dominated by Genghis Khan's era and legacy.

'Not as impressive as you are,' said Jian. *You will be the best of my collector's items,* he thought.

She chose to ignore him again.

'I'm a connoisseur of art, weapons and women,' he added.

'I'm well aware. Your reputation precedes you,' she said, guarded in her approach. She noticed he was not at ease; he was trying to figure out a way to approach her. She cut in before he could respond. 'General Jian. Can we leave aside the pleasantries and get to the point now? Why did you want to meet me?'

'Take a seat, Nushen.'

Nushen sat down across from him.

'I'm not going to beat around the bush,' he started, but he was interrupted by a knock on the door.

'Who is it? I don't want to be disturbed!' Jian yelled, losing his patience.

'Master, it's Meifen. I have brought some tea as requested,' said a female voice.

'Oh, yes. Come in,' Jian said with glee. He wanted to show his prized possession to Nushen. A beautiful young woman came in with a tray. She was naked, barring the diamond studded slave collar she was wearing.

Nushen looked at her in shock. 'Are you Meifen Lin?'

'Yes, she is. She is also my slave. Does it surprise you that she has landed all the leading roles in the industry lately?'

'How would you like your tea, ma'am?' she asked without looking at Nushen's face. Jian's slaves could never look at anyone's face directly.

'I'm a huge fan of yours, Meifen. Your acting is simply brilliant. I'm stunned to see you in this condition,' Nushen said. She saw no reaction on Meifen's face and figured Meifen was beyond the point of feeling ashamed.

Nushen looked at her beautiful face and body till she left the room. Jian cleared his throat to snap Nushen out of her thoughts.

'General, I'm impressed by your collections and really, you are living a life of a king. Now, can we get to business? I'm running out of time.'

'I'm a true king, Nushen. A true king.'

'Not yet.'

'Yes, not until I have found my queen,' he got up from his majestic throne. 'I want to propose a union of our interests that is critical to the future of China and this world. I'll also be direct in telling you that it has been my fantasy to make love to the only superwoman on earth.'

She looked at him with a blank face, unsurprised.

He continued, 'There is an ancient prophecy, the Prophecy of the Last King, that says the King of China will wed an angel not of the human race and together they will rule the world.'

'Correction: the prophecy says she marries a king—not specifically a king from China ... and I'm not big on prophecies.'

'I am.'

'I'm sure, and very conveniently so.'

He banged his fists on the table but saw no reaction on her face.

'The days of peace are going to end soon. You are well aware that we are sitting on the brink of a world war that is bound to happen, no matter how much we try to push it further, and we, as a nation, are well prepared this time, unlike the last one. I will not let anyone dominate us anymore, especially the Japanese, Americans or Europeans. Democracy around the world will end, colonization will return and mega-countries will be formed. And I will fulfil what Genghis Khan couldn't: I will rule the entire world. When that happens, it will be your fortune to be my woman. To be my queen. It's an honour I'm giving you.'

Nushen had only heard of his dangerous ideals and beliefs but today she witnessed it in person. *President Wang was right*, she thought. *This guy is a maniac; one who cannot be given more power.*

'It will be a strategic alliance between you and me. And, of course, our progeny will ascend the throne of China to bring on the era of *Homo Supernus*.'

Nushen's mouth dropped open involuntarily.

'Are you even listening to yourself, General? Do you take drugs?' she asked.

He was upset but controlled himself. 'No, I'm a teetotaller.'

'President Wang had warned me about your extremist views and beliefs. Unfortunately, I don't subscribe to the same school of thought. My vision is more of preventing the disaster, rather than planning it. My job and my purpose in life is the very reason you and I can't get wedded.'

'What do you mean?'

'My job is to kill people who are a threat to China, like you. It's only the system and President Wang who stand between us; or you would have been a dead man. And you're talking about marriage?'

Jian angrily picked two knifes from the table and flung them to the wall. They struck the forehead of a beautiful woman on a twelfth-century painting.

'President Wang will not protect China. It will be me,' he roared. 'The day my brother, his favourite son Feng Wang, died, he changed. He is a pussy now; he doesn't enjoy the trust of the armed forces or the political class. Everything he does right now makes good sense for a soft China but the world doesn't need a soft China. I'm the stronghold of this country. You are too naïve a super-soldier to ignore this fact. His days are numbered, Nushen.'

Nushen knew about President Wang's tragedies; the loss of his eldest son had changed him completely, and for the good.

'General, I heard your proposal, and the importance it holds to the grand scheme of things according to you, but I have to respectfully turn it down.'

'Why?'

'Honestly, I loathe the very fact that China has people like you in power. I know your designs for creating mayhem in the world by backing the Invisible Hand. You want to break things just to fulfil your fantasies of being a tyrannical king but guess what, we won't let that happen. Your dreams won't be fulfilled,' she avowed and got up.

'You're making a mistake, Nushen. You have insulted me today and I will neither forget nor forgive. So, unless you want me to make your life a living hell, sit down right now!' he yelled.

'No one gives me orders except President Wang.' She started walking.

'You walk out of that door today and there is no looking back. The blessings of my father will end the day he will die and that's not too far. Then there will be no one to save you from me. I will have you as a slave in my dungeon, marry you and have you bear my children. Or at the least, I *will* kill you.'

'Consider yourself fortunate that, because of your father, you are still breathing right now. Take it from me: the day the old man dies, no one can save you from me. Till then, goodbye.'

'Sir, why don't you curb Jian? He is vehemently talking about taking the reins,' Nushen asked President Wang.

'We will give him one more chance. I spoke to him in great detail last evening and I hope he takes my suggestions seriously. Don't forget that I am a father; I have neglected him throughout my life. I favoured my firstborn, and raised him to become a hero, but everything changed after his death.' Wang sighed. 'Jian tried very hard to get my attention and love but I wasn't there for him. Unfortunately, he was drawn to the philosophies and beliefs of Invisible Hand. Influenced by them, he chose a wrong path and things started getting out of control. Whenever he did get my attention, it was for some brilliant thing that he had achieved through extremely dangerous ways. I blame myself for what he is today and I hope I can guide him now.'

Nushen doubted it would have any effect on Jian; it was, perhaps, too late. The only way out, according to her, was to cut him out of the system and get rid of the Invisible Hand from its roots.

'It's the same case with Shen, your brother. His ways are a bit too radical. He is violent and can be corrupted,' Wang added.

Nushen was silent.

'But you, Nushen, your judgement is impeccable. It's my belief that you cannot be corrupted. I have been watching you and your brother for a very long time. You are different from him; you have always kept your nation ahead of yourself. I know the sacrifices you have made for your country, even after being treated like a lab experiment and subjected to extremities without the comfort of a parent. I know for a fact that you believe China is your parent, and it truly is. The nation itself has given birth to you and protected you. You are the daughter of China.'

'Clearly, you have read my personal diaries,' she said. Nushen had struggled to fit in the world as a normal human, something she could never completely achieve.

He chuckled. 'Ah … yes. I have. Your vision is a gift to this world but unfortunately the world is not ready for it. I hope that you are able to live long enough to bring the change required to create the world you think we all deserve.'

'Your words mean the world to me, sir. You have been very supportive of me. I hope I can do justice to your trust.'

'You will. It's natural for you. I believe it's your destiny.'

At times, she couldn't understand why Wang trusted her so much and took such personal interest in her matters. 'Sir, can I tell you something personal?'

'Yes, of course. What is it?'

'Sir, I'm sure this great nation is my mother and father but you have been more than a parent to me. You are the closest to a parent figure in my life. I thought I should tell you that.'

A smile appeared on his wrinkled face. 'You are the daughter I never had, Nushen.' For the first time in her entire life, someone had called her a daughter and truly meant it. A tear escaped her eyes but she quickly wiped it off and got her emotions in control. She was never one to let her emotions clog her mind.

She saluted him; he saluted back. There were no hugs or embraces and she went back to the world with a strange yet comforting feeling. *So this is how it feels to have a parent,* she wondered.

That week, she had made a sworn enemy who wanted to make her a slave and, at the same time, had found a caring parent who wouldn't let anyone come close to her.

THIRTEEN

While Nushen narrated her story to Kalki, she couldn't help but feel guilty for not being there for President Wang when he needed her the most.

'So, he wants to marry you and fulfil the prophecy?' Neel chuckled.

'We can laugh about it but he strongly believes in it,' Nushen replied.

They were silent for a while.

'Once you are able to trek, I will accompany you to the Indian border, then return to Beijing,' said Nushen.

'What? Why?' Neel asked, shocked. 'I thought you wanted me as leverage.'

'Oh, yeah. Don't think for a second that I'm letting you go just like that. I will call you for favours from time-to-time and you will hold your end of the bargain. You owe your life to me.'

'And why would I do that exactly? You think I'm that honourable a man?'

'You really don't get it, do you?'

'Kindly explain.'

'Sure. Think of it this way: I mean business, just like you do. I have sworn allegiance to my country to protect it from enemies, just like you have. I lost President Wang, just like you lost Prime Minister Acharya. General Jian is my enemy, just like he is yours. I want to kill him at any cost, just like you do. Enemy of an enemy is a friend … Now, do you get it?'

Neel was quiet.

'You are one of the few people who can disrupt what General Jian has planned outside of China. I assume he and his allies have already bought everyone else in India. There is little hope but you possess the resources to upset him and help me win back my country,' she concluded.

Neel looked into her eyes; he could see rage whenever she spoke about Jian. *One thing is for sure, she hates him and wants to destroy him. Hate is a powerful emotion.*

'Look, I want you as my ally; that's why I saved you. Not because of some petty leverage. Your path and mine are the same. I will go back to Beijing, save Shen and destabilise Jian.'

'That's it? That's your plan?'

'Pretty much,' she retorted instead. 'I'm saving you because you will be my weapon against him.'

He tried to decipher whether she really meant what she said. *There is something about you, Nushen, that you are not telling me … but my gut tells me to become your ally.*

'I understand. Everything is fair in love and war,' Neel said finally.

'Everything is fucked up in love and war,' she countered.

There was a long silence after that.

'So, are we allies?'

'Yes, we're allies,' he confirmed. They looked into each other's eyes and shook hands, knowing this pact was not meant to be broken no matter what.

'Jian won't rest until he finds you, will he?' he probed.

'No. He's obsessed with me.'

'What do you think his next move will be?'

'Something big and disruptive.'

'Cheers!' They toasted at the victory dinner held to celebrate General Jian's ascension to power. As everyone downed a peg, Jian, being a teetotaller, gulped water. He laughed as he looked at everyone celebrating his victory. He had been waiting for this day since he was a child. He was now the emperor and rightly so, in his mind. *Father, I wish you were here to see this.*

To materialise the masterplan, it had taken decades of effort by none other than the Invisible Hand. They had waited ages for a leader like Jian, someone with the madness and rage to do whatever it took to wage wars against the world and enslave millions.

Now that they had Jian, the masters at the mercenary cult had done everything to make it a success. The cult had a complex structure of leadership, with six masters governing their council. Master Zar was appointed as the head of their military and terrorism division; he had made them proud indeed.

Two decades ago, they had begun by instating their key men to take over as dictators in every country that mattered and now controlled dictators in several countries, including Pakistan, Middle East, northern Africa, North Korea and South East Asia.

India was a key country and they had made inroads there as well by instating General Talwar. They had carefully groomed him and ensured that he climbed the ladder to one day take over the Indian army. They didn't believe in luck; they believed in planning and executing the plan to perfection—and they had executed it beautifully. No one knew who Talwar really was.

'My army will march the Earth and conquer every country. We will wipe out anyone who stands up to us,' roared Jian. Today, he had the defence forces under his command, and the Invisible Hand at his disposal to do everything the army couldn't, just like Genghis Khan once had. He felt omnipotent.

'Hail Jian! Hail Jian!' chanted everyone.

Shanyuan slipped him a paper with something written on it. *Urgent call*, it read.

He excused himself and went to his room to take the call.

'Good evening, my friend,' said Zar.

'Evening, Master Zar. I'm a very happy man today. Our plans are finally yielding results.'

'Indeed. I have better news. We will soon have the location of Shambala locked in. Our mole in the Rudras has succeeded in decrypting the map to a great degree.'

'Excellent! I cannot wait.'

'There is another matter. The masters are suggesting we move to the next phase. Should we begin our onslaught?' Zar asked.

'Yes, the time is right. Give them hell. The world should crumble at our feet.'

In New Delhi, General Talwar summoned Pradhan and the RAW chief, Rathore.

'Cancel all the contracts awarded to Astras Group, be it for network security, ultra-drones or any other weapons programme. Take control of their operations, seize their bank accounts and arrest anyone who works for their group. I want to ban Kalki's every operation. Make it impossible for them to operate.'

'Sir, we don't have any documents related to Astras Group—their whereabouts, how they operate, bank details, it's all a secret,' said Rathore.

'Is this true, Pradhan? How is that even feasible?'

'Yes, this was the condition put forth by Kalki. They needed unconditional anonymity to work with us. PM Acharya had approved it. We don't know how their payments were made, how they delivered the weapons or how they supported us. We cannot even trace where they operate from.'

'How could we act in this fashion? We are the government! They can't tell us how to operate.'

'General, without Astras Group, there would be no security for our online assets, no drones guarding our borders, no weapons capable of defeating the enemy. You, of all people, know what they have accomplished for the country,' pointed out Pradhan.

'Enough. People might think he is the hero but I know he is the villain. He is a vigilante—a loose cannon!

I don't want such rogue elements in our system; we can never control them. Their time is up and I need them eliminated. How do we catch them?'

'Kalki is already dead, sir. What's the point?' asked Rathore.

'He is dead just because that terrorist Zar said so? Has anyone seen his dead body?'

'No.'

'Then he is alive, I need a way to get rid of Astras from the roots.'

Pradhan thought for a while.

'There is one way we can get to them … It's through this device called the Rift, which holds all the information. Only PM Acharya had access to it and, now that he is gone, it's not possible to access it. The device is impossible to hack into. I have heard that it has information about their secret locations, all the weapons programmes, payment details, battle plans and whatnot,' said Pradhan.

A smile appeared on Talwar's face.

'Get the best hackers in the world working on this. I don't care how much we have to spend; I want that device cracked,' he ordered Rathore.

'Yes, sir. What about ex-Defence Minister Jagan?'

'Leave him to me. I will deal with him.'

Master Zar messaged his aide in Mumbai, who worked as a software engineer in a reputed MNC and was the head of the sleeper cell unit in Mumbai.

'You have the go ahead. Activate all sleeper cells. Detonate bombs simultaneously in all cities on D-day,' the encrypted message read, which he took fifteen minutes to decipher. He hastily started sending encrypted messages to all his counterparts around India.

Similar messages were sent to the Invisible Hand's sleeper cells in the US, UK, France, Germany, Israel and Japan. His aides had been waiting for this day for the last two years.

The next day, bombs went off simultaneously in Mumbai, Bangalore, New Delhi and Chennai, killing tens of thousands of people and sending the country into chaos. There was panic everywhere and the paramilitary was deployed to control the situation. Curfew was instated in all the metros and the nation was shut down.

Just when people thought the worst was over, there was a blast at the other end of the world in New York that brought down the One World Trade Centre, built after the twin towers had been destroyed decades ago. Blasts took place in Chicago, San Francisco and Washington, D.C., bringing the country to a halt.

Similar blasts were reported in London, derailing the entire Tube infrastructure and burning all the running trains, leading to the deaths of thousands of passengers. The city was on fire along the Tube lines.

The whole world had come to a halt that day, with blasts across major cities in all time zones. No one knew how the sleeper cells had escaped the heavy security and sniffer dogs everywhere. The truth was that the bombs had been placed at those locations about a year ago and the technology used was unprecedented because it didn't use conventional material for the bombs. So in spite of being in front of everyone's eyes, no one had detected the bombs.

The Invisible Hand had brought the mightiest countries to their knees. The group claimed responsibility for the blasts and warned that their agenda was to enslave the world.

FOURTEEN

❦

'He who neither drinks, nor smokes, nor dances, he who preaches and even occasionally practices piety, temperance and celibacy, is generally a saint, or a mahatma or more likely a humbug but he certainly won't make a leader or for that matter a good soldier,' Neel quoted as Nushen laughed her heart out. Cut off from the world, they were oblivious to everything happening beyond the mountains.

'True that. Who said it?' she asked with a smile that was no longer guarded.

They were sitting outside a small cabin they had put together on a mountain peak, camouflaged between the trees and snow. They had moved out of their cave and set up a new base closer to the border.

In their hands, they held cheap liquor that Nushen had bought, or rather stolen, from the nearest village along with other essentials they needed to survive the cold. With her exceptional speed, she had trekked for thirty hours non-stop, hiding from police and anyone who might be looking for her. Anyone else would have taken over two weeks to carry out a similar trek.

Upon return, she had been relieved to see that Kalki had recovered exceptionally well. It was merely five days after they had escaped from the prison and he could now walk.

'It's a saying in the Indian army, quoted by our Field Marshal Sam Manekshaw,' he replied.

'He was a great man. I salute him,' she said, saluting. She was high after a long time and so was he.

They sat next to the fire for a long time, talking about their adventures and trading stories of their childhoods. Although neither could reveal any sensitive information about their lives, they spoke about several other topics and got to know each other well.

'We always think peace is the natural order in the world, that peace is the state of the universe when balanced, but we are wrong. Chaos is the state of natural order,' mused Neel. 'The world always goes back to being chaotic … It's a cycle. We cannot have more than fifty years of global peace; it's unprecedented. This time we went nearly a century without a global war. The universe created this set up to bring upon us the reign of chaos. It couldn't take peace anymore; peace was too boring for it.'

Nushen nodded in agreement, throwing wood into the fire.

'It's also true that when the universe creates mayhem, it also creates anomalies who rise to become the defenders of the oppressed. What remains to be seen is whether you and I, the anomalies in question, can actually rise to the occasion. And if yes, how long will we take to protect the people before millions die?'

'I'm convinced that we cannot stop bloodshed,' Nushen asserted. 'But I'm equally convinced that we will avenge our countrymen who lost their lives. I have faith in the universe. I believe we met so that we could fight this war shoulder-to-shoulder.'

Neel held a stick and got to his feet. He walked ahead and looked at the valley that would lead to the Indian border. *I'm coming back soon, Mother. Give me the strength to get back on my feet.*

They didn't talk for a long time, both trying to comprehend what was unravelling around them and how they would fight back. They felt helpless because they couldn't do anything; they only hoped to get back to their world soon enough to start fixing things.

Nushen walked to Neel with a bottle in her hand.

'Want to hear another army slogan?' he asked.

'Yes,' she smiled, sipping the liquor.

'Catch them by their balls, their hearts and minds will follow,' said Neel and she spurted out the liquor, laughing.

'This is the first time I'm seeing you act like a human, Nushen. Normally, you are so calm, stoic and in control of your senses. Is it a gift or a curse given by the *Homo Supernus* team?' he asked as they sat back down.

'Well, it's a gift. I was made this way. I neither panic nor get hyper with happiness. It allows me to take sound decisions, especially in combat and stressful situations where it's a matter of life and death. For instance, even when the situation was dire, I decided to pull you out of that prison because my mind didn't panic.'

He smiled.

You are the most beautiful woman I have ever seen in my life, he wanted to tell her.

'Can I ask you something?' she said.

'Yeah, of course.'

'Why did you save me from that laser gun?' she asked, looking into his eyes. 'Why did you risk your life? You could have just escaped if I was dead.'

'Do I really need to answer that?'

'Yes, you do.'

He chuckled. 'I have tried to eliminate General Jian and Master Zar a dozen times but never succeeded. I had realised long back that you don't belong to Jian's faction. When the announcement to capture you alive came, I knew you weren't my enemy anymore. You were my natural ally and I had to keep you alive, no matter what. You are my ticket to ending the Invisible Hand's vicious crusade.'

Nushen nodded.

'And then, of course…' he cleared his throat. 'I couldn't escape the tension, the force, the power that kept drawing me towards you. I would be damned if I let you die without understanding what this rage in my soul is all about.'

She looked deep into his eyes and held his gaze, leaning forward and kissing him. They held on tightly to each other, realizing that they had both longed for this moment for a long time.

'I wanted you the first time I saw you,' she whispered, while he kissed her neck.

'I can't wait any longer,' he whispered back, breathing heavily.

While they made love under the clear skies and stars shining down at them, he wanted to capture that moment for a lifetime. *There is a connection. I cannot deny it and I cannot escape it.* It had been a long time since someone had stirred his mind and body like Nushen had.

Once they both reached their climax, she leaned forward and kissed him, still in the grip of carnal pleasure.

She slid down beside him and they lay on the ground, catching their breath. They looked at each other and started laughing heartily. 'I was supposed to kill you but here I am making love to you!'

As they lay by the fire, looking at the night sky and the stars, Neel couldn't help but think about Arya.

Arya ...

He thought back to when she had stormed into his life and turned everything upside down.

KALKI'S STORY –
GLADIATORS OF STEEL

'What is this fight club you keep talking about?' Neel asked Arya. *She's so beautiful,* he thought. With long straight hair, a beautiful smile, a hint of a dimple, nice set of teeth, brown eyes and lips to die for, she was a genuine beauty. She had stolen his heart the first time he had seen her in college a few months ago.

She is a tomboy, he guessed. It was her eyes; they gave away her secret, hiding some sort of adventure behind them.

Neel tried not to look into her eyes, for it would give away his secret—that he had a huge crush on her. On the other hand, she had given him enough hints that she was into him. The sexual tension between them was palpable.

'It's this underground event that's the new rage in the city. It happens once a month and the kick is that no one knows where it happens! They blindfold you and take you to the venue, where fights are conducted amidst a crazy crowd. Everyone there has to wear a mask, so it's totally clandestine,' she said with excitement.

'What kind of fights?' asked Tiger.

'It's unlike anything you would have seen. Machines fight each other.'

'Machines?' asked Neel, suddenly excited.

'Yes. Machines fight in a huge cage. They have different characters, get-ups, swords and whatnot.'

'Have you been there yourself?'

'Only once, a few months ago. It was kick-ass. I think you should take your ultra-drone to these fights and see how you stack up against other combat machines. I heard the money is good if you win, which can keep your R&D going a bit.'

Neel was intrigued but something was not adding up.

'How do you know so much about it? I have never heard of it,' Neel asked suspiciously.

'Well, my ex-boyfriend was this real grease monkey; he loved playing with cars, bikes and gadgets. He was the one who exposed me to this crazy underground world,' she explained. 'It can get addictive. I was hooked to robotics from there on.'

Neel looked at Tiger. 'What do you think?'

'I think we should totally check it out. It's sounds dope, man!' Tiger decided.

'Awesome! We have about four weeks to prep for the next fight. I'll let the organizers know that we're bringing the ultra-drone,' she cheered. 'See ya later. I'll swing by the lab sometime.'

'Bye!' they said. Neel couldn't take his eyes off her.

'Tiger, something isn't adding up. I cannot be wrong about this feeling. Can you do a quick background check on her? See where she is from, which school did she go to, her parents, et cetera?'

'Horse shit! Are you crazy? Don't be weird, man. Just go on a date with her before someone else takes her out. You just heard her, right? She spoke about her ex-boyfriend. She's dropping you hints!'

'Look at her, Tiger. She is sexy as hell, enigmatic … and she had to land in our robotics class! What are the odds? Such a beautiful package has to be complicated. Trust me. That's the law of nature.'

Tiger laughed.

'Okay, Neel baba,' he said, folding his hands to do Namaste. 'You prep the machines and I will do the recce on her.'

The ultra-drones, or ultras, that Neel's Astras Group had created were humanoid robots that could retract their legs and arms to become drones. They could hover in the air with four rotors and go up to Mach 1 speed. Due to an in-built AI software, they could process a ton of data thrown at them, helping them take decisions at runtime like humans. However, they were still in the nascent stages and their bodies didn't have robust shields to protect against onslaught or firing.

To be able to fight other robots, Neel had to use better alloys and programme them to get better at reflexes, martial arts and hand-to-hand combat techniques. They had to learn on the go and improvise in real time to beat the enemy. With only a few weeks remaining for the fight, he had a daunting task ahead of him but it was not impossible.

Let me read Professor Vati's journal, Neel thought. *Let's see if it's of any help.*

He opened the book and started reading the Sanskrit script. Despite his mastery over the language, he couldn't decode a word of it. *What is this technique? Why did she give me such an obscure classified document?*

He tried hard to focus on the words, trying to figure out the pattern and encryption. He drew a few snippets on the whiteboard, applying different methods to crack it. After nearly an hour, he gave up and went to his classes. But he couldn't get the script out of his mind, he wanted to crack it at any cost.

He went back to it that evening and kept staring at it until that one moment when the book started making sense. 'Yes!' he screamed with euphoria and started reading with vigour. It had all been in front of him this whole time. The book was double-encrypted and the key kept changing with every sentence. His mind needed to process everything at once to understand it. And for him, there was no need to write the decoded text anywhere, he could read it in a flow once he understood how to decode.

While he read through few pages, he realised it was a scientific text unlike any other. The approach of making alloys was unheard of. *What is this journal? Who has written it?*

He turned pages to the end of the journal to read the reference material.

There was only one source written.

'Source: Scripture of Gods,' it read. *Scripture of Gods?*

He quickly googled and found nothing on the internet about such a book. *What is going on?* Being an expert hacker, he searched through the dark web and after an hour, found a reference in a classified Indian Space Research Organisation's three-decade old document on a space programme. It was mentioned that certain aspects of the satellite launch vehicle propulsion technology were borrowed from the Scripture of Gods.

Again there was no information about the author.

'What happened?' asked Tiger, walking in and finding a troubled look on Neel's face.

'Nothing… I just broke the code of Professor Vati's journal.'

'Awesome! Listen, I have some news … Bud, you were right. She's a ghost,' Tiger declared.

'What do you mean?'

'None of her friends really know about her background and my contacts at the admin department said her file has nothing in it. Zilch!'

Neel hurriedly logged into his computer and hacked into the university database within a few minutes. He hadn't wanted to do it in the first place, as it sounded cheap, but it had to be done.

He looked at Tiger, shocked.

'There is nothing in her file except her name. Not even an address or date of birth,' he announced, throwing his hands up in the air.

'How is that even possible?'

'Do you think she's honeypotting me?' Neel asked.

'What on earth is honeypotting?'

'It's a term used in secret services where a girl lures a target by arousing him. Don't you see? She's perfectly my type. Beautiful, mysterious, loves robotics and even has a dimple. It can't all be a coincidence. She is trying to get me to do something,' he explained.

'You're overthinking it, Neel. Give her some time and things will be fine. Let's be cool with her, okay? Don't ruin it. She's the first girl you've had a crush on.'

Neel nodded but wasn't convinced.

'All set to roll?' Arya asked on the eve of the match. They were all dressed up in their favourite attire. Anyone could have thought it was Halloween night but only they knew that the stakes were much higher. Arya had designed costumes for each one of them in the previous weeks. They all wore highly stylised black leather bodysuits and masks of different types. Neel wore a black mask with the letter 'K', indicating Kalki, written on it to cover the top of his face.

For Tiger, the mask was styled with stripes like a tiger and Arya herself wore just a slim mask to cover her eyes. They looked like a team straight out of the movie *Matrix*, but with masks.

At the age of eighteen, Neel stood over six feet tall with a lean yet muscular body. Tiger, on the other hand, was a year older than Neel and had a massive build, bulky muscles, and towered over most of the population at six feet six inches.

'Wow,' Tiger exclaimed when he looked in the mirror.

'Let's go beat the shit out of those machines, baby!' Arya cheered.

Out of nowhere, Neel threw a soda can at her and she caught it within a split second, revealing exceptional reflexes.

'Thirsty?' Neel asked.

'Are you nuts? Do you hate my face or something? It could have hit me hard,' Arya snapped, getting annoyed with him.

'Nice reflexes!' he replied. *Those reflexes are not normal. You are something else, Arya ... What are you hiding from me?*

'Neel, why have you been acting like such a jerk to me? You've been trying to pull this shit on me for the last few weeks. You won't let me help you in building your machine and you didn't take any of my suggestions for modifications to the ultras. You avoid me in class and even in the canteen. Why do you hate me all of a sudden?' Arya asked, looking visibly upset.

Tiger looked at Neel with disgust. *Full-time ass-faced moron,* he thought.

'We're getting late. Can we leave now?' Neel said, ignoring her allegations.

She was furious but controlled her anger, walking out. They followed her to the parking lot, where the robot was loaded in a trailer.

'They should be here any minute now,' she said, checking her mobile.

Neel looked at his ultra-drone. Standing six feet tall, it looked strong and not to be messed with. But only he knew there was a lot needed to be upgraded.

He had worked relentlessly to use the knowledge in the journal to forge the alloy with the rudimentary equipment he had at his disposal in the lab. He was awestruck with the results, he had succeeded in creating a lightweight yet superstrong material. However, all that he had managed to forge were the shield and the body armour of his robot. The rest of the body was still old.

His machine had quick reflexes with strong arms and knuckles to punch back. Two swords hung on its back and it was loaded with powerful AI to fight till it either kills or gets killed. They had run thousands of simulations and live tests on combats and the results had been wonderful. Neel was confident but nervous about tonight's bout.

A monstrous truck approached and two masked men got down.

'Load up!' one yelled.

They hooked the trailer to their truck and it started chugging away. 'Come on in!' The men put a sack on each one of their heads and told them to sit inside the truck. Neel and Tiger hated the feeling; they couldn't see anything and felt suffocated.

'Relax. It won't take much time,' Arya assured.

It took nearly an hour to reach the venue. When the gunny bags were removed, they were awestruck by what they saw. It was nothing short of a rave party; there was a big crowd cheering and dancing around the stage, where skimpily clad girls were dancing. The beats were exotic and the bass shook the room.

The security personnel frisked them and took away their mobile phones. 'No guns or cameras allowed. What happens in the Fight Club, stays in the Fight Club,' read a board at the entrance.

While Tiger and Arya started jiving to the music, Neel's stomach churned. It would be the first time his machine would face a real adversary. It was not just a match; it was his life's work.

He looked around and saw that everyone was wearing a mask. It was a magical world where people were dancing, drinking, smoking, kissing and he was sure, in some corners, even having an orgy. It was a free world where nothing was prohibited, a world he had never seen before. *You put on a mask and you have the liberty to do just anything*, Neel mused.

While he was lost in the crowd, he heard an announcement.

'Are you ready for some steel?' yelled the anchor.

'Yes!' everyone hooted.

'Tonight will be one of the best you have seen in a long time. Let the games begin,' he announced. Earth-shaking music followed, as choppers flew towards the stage with the cage. They dropped the cage and the ground crew rushed to assemble it.

'Get ready for the fight of your life! Behold the Gladiators of Steel! The first bout tonight is Nebuchadnezzar versus the new kid of the block ... the Ultra!' he bellowed.

The crowd erupted in joy as they eagerly waited for the machines to get in the cage.

'For the new folks out here, let me tell you the rules. Well, there is only one rule in the cage. Kill or get killed.'

'Kill or Get Killed!' shouted the crowd.

'What? We are the first?' Neel yelled. They ran to the back of the arena and booted the ultra-drone.

'Come on, boy! We have to face this. You're smart and you can fly. You can do this,' Neel said, controlling his robot through the portable tablet in his hand, and the machine moved to the arena through the tunnel. The trio walked behind the Ultra until they saw the opponent standing in the middle of the cage.

'I think I just peed my pants a little,' said Tiger, looking at the Nebuchadnezzar. It was greyish black in colour, with a texture that made it look alien. Black horns came out of its head, back and shoulders and it was at least ten feet tall; it had a presence that could scare the opponent before the fight even began.

'He may be the incarnation of the devil himself but you can beat him. Go get him, boy!' Neel cheered as he hit engage on his tablet.

A bugle sound reverberated through the arena and the machines ran towards each other, colliding with force. They traded blows, metal parts flowing up in the air with each punch or kick. It was like the Roman amphitheatre where gladiators fought to death, only this one looked a notch higher. It was a hair-raising experience to see the machines clash in that brutal and raw fashion.

Less than ninety seconds into the fight, Nebuchadnezzar took out a giant sword from its back and struck Ultra's shield. The crowd was suddenly mute. Such was the strength of Ultra's alloy that the powerful sword broke into two pieces. No one had survived a blow of Nebuchadnezzar's sword before.

The trio jumped up and down with joy.

However, the euphoria was short lived as the opponent held Ultra's neck and twisted it.

'What was that?' cried Tiger, as he heard a cracking sound.

'The neck and joints are still old. They are weak,' said Neel. 'I didn't have time to create every single nut and bolt with the new alloy.'

Nebuchadnezzar tore Ultra's neck apart and flung it away. The head crashed into the cage and fell to the ground, while the body of the Ultra moved around like a headless chicken.

Neel fell to the ground when he saw what had happened and Tiger covered his face. 'Come on, guys, let's lose with dignity. Get up,' Arya urged.

'Kill! Kill! Kill!' chanted the crowd.

Nebuchadnezzar held the Ultra and rammed it into the cake. Neel's machine fell to the ground and collapsed.

Back in the lab, they all sat silently staring at the floor. It was the worst night of Neel and Tiger's lives.

'I'm not building machines again. I quit,' Neel declared, feeling awfully hurt.

'Don't be foolish. You need to learn from your mistakes and move on,' Arya advised. 'On the bright side, your new alloy proved to be phenomenal. Only if you had taken my suggestions for modifying your robot. But you didn't pay heed. You are too arrogant.'

'I only listen to my friends,' snapped Neel.

'So that's what this is about. I never belonged in this group; I'm not even a friend.'

'Arya, just ignore him,' Tiger said, but he was interrupted by Neel.

'Friend? We know you're hiding things from us. Friendship is about transparency and trust. We don't even know who the hell you are.'

'What did you say?' she asked, furious.

'Yes, we scanned your records in the admin database. You're a ghost. Tell me, who are you really?'

She stood up.

'You went behind my back to check my background? How dare you! You could have just asked me, Neel. Did you ever bother to ask?' she questioned.

It was true; he had never bothered to ask her directly until that night.

She turned to Tiger. 'Tiger, you have hurt me. I didn't expect this from you … To hell with you two.' She slammed the door behind her.

KALKI'S STORY – THE RUDRAS

※

They didn't see Arya at college for a week, during which they constantly looked for her everywhere but to no avail.

'You've got to see this,' Tiger yelled, walking into the lab. He showed Neel a video where Arya was fighting a male opponent in karate class. 'It's going viral on the college network. Someone posted it fifteen minutes ago.'

Neel couldn't believe the way she was fighting; She had incredible reflexes and he had never seen the techniques she was using before. In four flat kicks, she had knocked down her black belt opponent, the college champion, and made him look like a rookie.

A knock sounded on the door.

'Come in,' Tiger called.

Arya walked in all sweaty, her hair messed up.

'Hey! What up?' She waved.

They looked at her with their mouths hanging open.

'Are you for real?' asked Tiger.

'Well, I had to take out my frustration on someone!' She scowled at Neel.

'Where had you vanished?' Neel asked.

'Why are you so bothered?' she retorted, taking a seat in front of them.

'Fair enough. But tell me this, are you still not going to accept you are hiding something from us?' asked Neel.

'Again? Are you possessed by Sherlock's ghost?' Arya snapped.

'Tiger, show her the footage.'

The computer screen showed her entering the library in the Literature department.

'What exactly do you do in the Literature department?' Neel inquired.

'I can't visit the library now?' she hit back, furious.

'In the last few months, you have spent most of your days and even nights in that library. Tell me, is that normal? What business do you have in that department?'

Arya was about to respond, when Tiger interrupted. 'Arya, please. We are your friends. Don't hide things from us. Tell the truth.'

She took a deep breath, looking down and running her fingers through her hair.

'Are you in some sort of trouble?' asked Neel.

'No. I mean not personally, but I'm trying to fix a grave threat.'

'What?'

'I cannot tell you because the truth will to put your lives in danger,' she muttered, getting up. 'We have to go, aren't we getting late for the class?'

'Lives in danger?' asked Tiger.

'No, we are not going anywhere until we sort this out,' stressed Neel with an intense look.

She threw up her arms in frustration, and walked up and down the lab, thinking hard.

'Are you sure about this?' she asked after a while, as they both sat infront of her.

'Yes!' they said.

'Okay then. Come with me.'

She took them to the old library in the Literature department and through a door with a sign reading 'Access Restricted' after entering a passcode on the security system.

The door opened to a long tunnel lit by wall-mounted lamps.

At the end of the tunnel, they saw several chambers and corridors.

'Get into this chamber before anyone sees us,' she said.

The chamber led them to an underground cellar through narrow stairs. What looked like a creepy old stone basement soon gave way to a swanky lab straight out of a science-fiction movie. Machines and weapons of various shapes and sizes were stacked on the walls in glass enclosures.

They couldn't believe their eyes.

'What is this place?' mouthed Neel, astonished. Tiger was dumbstruck.

'This is the lab used to prototype weapons,' answered Arya.

'What a collection!' Tiger exclaimed, picking up a gun that looked ancient yet ultra-modern.

'Don't touch anything!' warned Arya. He hurriedly put it down.

While Neel was keenly observing the machines and weapons, they saw a lady working on a desk in the corner.

'Professor Vati?' Neel recognised her.

'Hello, Neel, Tiger. How are you two doing today?' she greeted. Their jaws dropped when she turned towards them.

'Professor, am I hallucinating or has your skin really turned blue?' asked Neel.

She laughed. 'Take a seat. This is my natural colour.'

'Natural colour? Are you an alien?' Tiger asked, bewildered.

'No, I'm not an alien. I will explain it a bit later, but tell me this—could you crack the encryption of that journal?' she asked Neel.

Neel couldn't speak.

'Err… I was searching for you to tell you this but yes, professor. I cracked it and went a step ahead by using the technique and formula to forge the alloy. It was the most fascinating scientific text I have ever read. Truly revolutionary,' Neel said with wonder in his eyes.

'Well done, my chosen one!' The professor looked excited. 'Very few people have been able to successfully read it. A handful.'

Neel looked puzzled. *What?*

'Was it encrypted for a reason? Is it military classified information,' he looked around. 'This lab, it is a secret military facility, isn't it?'

The professor ignored his question and walked to the shelf. She picked up a thick ancient book and kept it on the table.

'We have many such texts that are ages ahead of our time in science and technology. So much so that we cannot even implement most of it ... This book is a complete text on Alchemy, Chemistry and Metallurgy.'

'This is the same type of encryption,' Neel mumbled.

'I have tried decoding it countless times, but never succeeded,' Arya interrupted.

He looked at Arya and went back to decoding the script. It only took him a few minutes to complete the first chapter. He looked up at Vati and asked, 'This is the Scripture of Gods?'

'Yes, this is one of the original works. It's called the—'

'Scripture of Rasāyana!' Neel completed her sentence, reading its title.

She nodded and smiled.

'How many such works do you have?'

'Nine original scriptures with nine volumes each. So, eighty-one in total,' Vati said.

'Who are you people?' asked Tiger, getting up from his seat. 'My head is about to burst with the whole suspense thingy. Tell us what is going on?'

'We are the protectors of the knowledge the books contain,' she replied. 'We operate more like a secret society and are not associated with any government or military organisation.'

'Protectors? What kind of knowledge are you talking about?' Neel asked.

'For example, one of the books is about physiological warfare and the touch of death. The book explains how to kill a person with a simple touch—by reversing the pulse of the human body,' answered Arya.

'That cannot be true. No way,' Tiger countered.

'Do you want me to demonstrate?' asked the professor.

'Never mind,' they chorused.

'Relax, I'm not going to kill you.'

She touched three spots in a sequence on their temple. They instantly closed their eyes and started taking deep breaths.

'What do you see?'

'I can see a hues of colour … Purple, red, yellow, green. What did you do to me?' Tiger cried out.

Vati touched their temple again and they returned to normalcy. 'That was just to show you that you have certain hotspots on your body that can be triggered by a simple touch. We can trigger hundreds of such actions and emotions through the knowledge in the scripture. You can think about it as a super-advance Marma technique. It's dangerous and access is given only to those who are in the combat wing.'

Neel and Tiger looked at each other in shock.

Professor continued. 'For a long time, we have been the guardians of this knowledge. We have also worked over the centuries to enhance it. Today, we have about eight hundred scriptures and enemies want access to what we possess. Twice in our history, our enemies have succeeded in disrupting our organisation. They even took some of our scriptures a few centuries ago. We have recovered a few of these books over the decades but several are still missing. So, what we do here is dangerous.'

'Centuries? This technology is centuries old? But it's ultra-next-generation! How is it possible?' asked Neel.

'Not just centuries, it's thousands of years old,' said Arya. 'The society is ancient.'

'What's it called?' asked Tiger.

'We are called The Rudras,' revealed Vati.

Rudras? Neel connected the dots.

He had read about the myths of the Rudras on the internet and newspapers. While there were rumours that famous people throughout history had been part of the secret society, none were confirmed as facts. He had read reports that Aryabhata, Isaac Newton, Albert Einstein, Tesla and Homi Bhabha had been in the Rudras, along with kings and leaders from various eras. King Chhatrapati Shivaji, Pope Paul V, Charlie Chaplin, Swami Vivekananda and several other names had also done the rounds. Whatever the myths were, this revelation by Professor Vati was unsettling to say the least.

'I'm unable to digest any of this!' said Neel.

'I know it's not easy to digest, but you have experienced the scripts first-hand now. The secrecy is important because we carry a monumental burden,' began Vati. 'Rudras' mission is not only to protect ancient knowledge but also to guard the world against apocalyptic events.

The potential of the knowledge our ancestors possessed was unimaginable. They had attained what we refer to as Absolute Knowledge, a state where humans attain the knowledge equivalent to that of a god. This is akin to the singularity, when machines attain the knowledge and sentience humans possess. And when creations become as knowledgeable as their creators, disruption is bound to happen.'

'Our society was revived and brought under a consolidated body by Emperor Chandragupta Maurya in 316 bc. But it was indeed the brainchild of Chanakya himself,' added Arya.

'Chandragupta Maurya?' questioned Neel.

'Chanakya?' asked Tiger.

'Yes.'

Neel and Tiger both gulped a glass of water.

'Are you guys okay?' asked Arya.

They nodded, lost in thought. Reality was slowly sinking in.

'Why are you hiding this from the world? You could help humanity with this technology,' asked Neel.

'Good question,' Arya said. 'I hadn't been able to understand this myself for a long time. Let me explain. The secret society is just an observer; we don't alter the course of the world. Unless it is a matter of grave importance or the possibility of being apocalyptic. For instance, the time smallpox had threatened to wipe out humanity by killing millions, we had helped in creating the vaccine. But wars, natural calamities and diseases are necessary to keep the balance on Earth or else the population will go out of control.'

'That's not good. You need to protect everyone if you have the power to do so,' said Neel.

'What if that power is used for destruction? What would you do then?' Arya asked.

Neel was silent.

'That is why we have to keep it a secret. We intervene only when it is absolutely necessary. We have functioned this way for centuries and we will continue to do so until the end of time,' she continued.

'How did you get into it?' Tiger asked.

'That's a story for another time but I can tell you that before coming here, I was in the Trishul city.'

'Trishul city? Never heard of it,' said Neel.

'You'll probably never hear about it again. It's a secret underground city of the Rudras. Nobody knows its location. I have now been deployed to Bangalore,' she said.

They were silent for a while.

'That brings us to the key aspect—our enemies,' Professor Vati broke the silence.

'The Invisible Hand?' guessed Neel.

'They are the most formidable, but not the only one. The Invisible Hand intends to enslave the world by unearthing the Weapons of Gods.'

'Weapons of Gods?' interrupted Neel.

'They seek the ultimate weapons of destruction created by our founding fathers, which are called Weapons of Gods. They are rumoured to be hidden deep inside the city of Shambala, a lost city buried somewhere in the Himalayas. These weapons are believed to be more powerful than any other created by mankind, including nuclear weapons.'

'Shambala is real?' asked Tiger.

'What can these weapons do?' Neel asked at the same time.

'They are weapons of unimaginable power—ones that can destroy the universe. According to ancient scriptures, the war chest includes weapons that can control matter and change things at will; and weapons that can control the weather or rise the seas to annihilate everything in its path. These weapons are not just myths.'

'So, the Rudras know where Shambala actually is?' asked Neel.

'No, we don't,' she admitted. 'Few centuries ago, we lost the scriptures that had information about Shambala and the Invisible Hand killed all our gurus and council members with knowledge of its whereabouts. We are not sure whether the scriptures are currently in their possession or not but we know it's impossible to decipher them.'

'What if they succeed in breaking the code?' Neel asked.

'That is always a possibility but the only thing we can do is prepare for that day. Whoever controls those weapons will control the world.'

'Professor, can we get to the point?' interrupted Arya.

'Yes, yes, my dear… We have a grave problem at hand and time is of the essence,' spoke Professor Vati.

'Arya and few of our agents had gone to collect critical intelligence from a trusted source. We received a report last week that the Invisible Hand plans on transporting a tactical nuclear weapon to India through the Pakistani border. We are not sure where and how they plan to detonate it but millions could die and no one can stop them because the nuke is supposedly surrounded by this radioactive material called Calamitous. In sufficient quantity, Calamitous can kill anyone in a two-kilometre radius.'

'Is this a confirmed report?' asked Neel, looking concerned.

'Yes, my source confirmed it. Luckily, they don't have enough of it at this moment as it's a painfully slow process to create Calamitous. We have a few weeks until they have a significant quantity,' Arya chipped in.

'If that chemical can kill everyone around it, how will the Invisible Hand carry it?' asked Tiger.

'That's a valid point. I'm sure they must have developed shields to protect themselves.'

'Well, you will stop the Invisible Hand, right?' asked Neel.

'That's the sad part … The Rudras are led by a council of nine people and they haven't yet taken a decision on whether we should intervene or not. As a rule, we only intervene if an apocalyptic event is about to happen; they aren't sure if a nuclear attack on India qualifies,' said Vati.

'Is the council run by heartless people?' Neel asked incredulously. 'And what do you think?'

'I personally think that we have to stop the Invisible Hand at any cost. The Indian army is planning a few things but we need backup plans to mitigate risks.'

'Backup plans?'

'Yes! Neel, I want to giving you a chance. I know your burning desire to do something substantial for this country. So, this is your chance!'

'Me?' panicked Neel. 'How can I stop a nuclear weapon?'

'That is something for you to decide. I have shown you a path already.' She smiled, pointing towards the

Scripture of Rasāyana. 'You can have it, but it doesn't leave this lab.'

Professor got up and started walking.

Neel looked at Tiger and Arya, confused and scared.

'Professor,' shouted Tiger. 'Aren't you forgetting to clarify something?'

'What?' she turned back.

'Why are you blue in colour today?'

She chuckled.

'Oh, I'm just getting old. I turned 124 years old last month.' She smiled. 'One of our forefathers invented a technique to rejuvenate body cells by throwing out toxins. When these toxins are flushed out, they leave a blue tinge on your skin over the years.'

'I don't get it. You were fine the last time I saw you,' said Tiger, baffled.

'That's just a simple cream to remove the pigmentation,' she answered, applying a cream on her hand and turning it back to normal. 'It usually stays for a few days.'

'You cannot be 124 years old, you are more like forty,' said Neel.

Professor laughed and said 'This technique can help in staying alive for centuries if you wish. It's required for some of us in the Rudras to ensure continuity as well as transfer of knowledge and experience from generation to generation. It seems like a boon, but you soon realise it's a burden. Now, off I go, leaving you three to decide what to do next.'

Things were moving too fast for Neel and Tiger.

Arya and Tiger looked expectantly at Neel after Professor Vati left the cellar.

'Bro, what's the plan?' asked Tiger, his stomach churning. Although the mission was adventurous, it was a huge undertaking.

Neel looked at his trembling hands. 'I am scared and my mind is numb,' his voice barely audible.

'Guys, I know this is too much to digest so suddenly but war and terrorism don't come announced. I'm scared, too, but I believe in our team. We can accomplish anything together. And remember, you already have a body of work behind you. I went through the software you built for the Ultra; it's unprecedented. It's genius. You didn't have the necessary tools before, but you have them now.'

Neel and Tiger still looked doubtful.

'Do you know I was asked to read the Book of Rasāyana last year because of my IQ?' Arya went on.

'What's your IQ?' inquired Tiger.

'145, but I still couldn't crack that book.'

Neel was shocked.

'Do you think I can't crack decryptions and sequences? Think about it,' she added.

'Of course, you can. They are pretty straight forward … How am I able to read it?' Neel wondered.

'I don't know, Neel. But I know this—the book chose to reveal itself to you. Our ancestors and their collective wisdom is showing you a path. Be brave and honour them. Be the soldier they want you to be. We will give our one hundred per cent and then if we fail, that's fine. But if we don't, we don't deserve to protect this country.'

She is right... Destiny had shown him a path to fulfil his vision; he was not the one who would miss this great honour to stand up for his country.

'Thank you, Arya,' he said and picked up the book, but still feeling uneasy within.

'What is the Blade of the Snake?' asked Neel, when Professor Vati came to the lab the next day. Neel had spent the entire night decoding and studying the scripture.

Vati smiled.

'The book teaches you how to unlearn things that you have learned about matter,' she said, as Arya and Tiger walked in.

'Precisely,' said Neel. 'We need to programme matter at the fundamental level as a building block rather than creating parts to make a yantra. This is hardcore science; how can it be ancient?'

'Well, our ancestors attained "absolute knowledge" thousands of years ago. The script that you are reading is just the A of the alphabet in terms of complexity and what they teach about our universe, or should I say multiverse.

'The inherent strength of matter is that it can be programmed the way you want it. It can become anything. Matter is very much like your software; you only need to know how to instruct it. And that's what the blade will help you accomplish,' the professor enlightened, walking towards a secret door behind one of the massive artillery guns kept in the lab. She placed her hand on a scanner on the wall, and it gave way to a hidden chamber.

When they walked inside, the chamber looked ancient with carvings and paintings on the stone walls. In a corner, there was a giant metallic tower with an opening of a hearth at the bottom.

'This is ancient,' uttered Tiger.

'I have never been here before,' said Arya, mesmerised by the patterns and carvings.

'Think of this as the most advanced 3D printer ever created. It can bring anything you want to life but the instructions will be given through this device called the Blade of the Snake.' Vati handed him the blade, which was nothing but two fangs of a cobra with a little golden hue to them. It was heavy and had rings for wearing it in two fingers.

'How does it work?' asked Neel.

'Think of it as a communication device for rendering your schematics in the air. To give you a visual, we have integrated it with a hologram machine,' she said. She wore the blade in her hand and drew a circle in the air, the hologram machine drawing it out with a blue line. They could see it, turn it, zoom in or out and interact with it using hand gestures. She drew an infinity in the air and they moved back as the synthesizer roared to life. The machine huffed and puffed and, within a minute, created a giant metallic ball.

The trio was awestruck by its power.

'How old is this machine again?' asked Tiger.

'Well, no one really knows. It is believed that this yantra was retrieved from the Weapons of Gods warchest. We have added a few modern touches, that's all. Remember, the scripture is your teacher. It will tell you everything about matter, chemicals, metals, alchemy, this machine and a hundred other things. How you interpret and use that knowledge is totally up to you and your mental capability.

'The machine has a way to understand what you are thinking when you wear the blade, which acts like an interface. I drew a circle and a ball came out. It knows my mind; it understands my gestures. It's not easy to build a weapon that can work like magic; it requires complex construction at an atomic level. For instance, how will you build a material to withstand Calamitous?'

Neel didn't have an answer.

'Now, it's your choice whether you want to help your country or not. Whether you choose to believe in the ancient wisdom of the Rudras or not. That is a decision only you can make.

If you choose to proceed, your imagination will be your only limitation. You are God when you wear this device … We need to see what you would do with that advantage to stop the enemy at the gates.'

Later that day, the trio sat down to make a plan.

'Guys, we are taking up this challenge,' announced Neel with determination.

Arya smiled.

'Yes!' cheered Tiger.

'The plan is simple. Let's create a machine to stop our enemy dead in its tracks. Let's split the tasks; Arya, you focus on creating a robust engine. Get the schematics for the best engines that power the most heavy-duty machines. Can you do that?'

'Yes, I can access the Rudras servers. We have a repository of new-age fusion reactors.'

'Brilliant. Next, let's upgrade the AI software of the Ultra. We need a cool interface; a character we can speak to.'

'On it, boss.' She saluted.

They smiled.

'Tiger, focus on the core structure that can withstand radioactive material. Arya can get you access to the latest tech from Rudras. Another thing, I want the machine to feel alive. I want it to have skin. We need to create flesh and blood!'

'We're going to smash those terrorists like ripe papayas!' Tiger yelled.

They laughed and high-fived.

'I will work with this book and see how this giant fella works,' said Neel, pointing to the synthesizer and the blade.

FIFTEEN

❧

Back in the present, General Talwar got a call from General Jian on his private number.

'Good morning, General Jian.'

'Morning, General Talwar. You have made us proud. Everything is going as planned.'

'Thank you, General. Tell me, what is the urgent matter?'

'I have some important news. We were able to decrypt the map to Shambala and it points to three possible locations, all of them on your side of the border.'

'That's excellent news! Where exactly?' He stood up from his chair.

'Ladakh. We will need to carry out an excavation unparalleled to any other in human history. We don't know the exact location and the terrain is going to pose a problem.'

'What do you want me to do?'

'We cannot excavate with civilians or the army around. We'll have to clear the whole area.'

'All of Ladakh?'

'Fifty per cent, give or take. Can you come up with a strategy to make that happen? It would have been better if the land was China's but it's disputed. Maybe it's time we reclaim it … I know that increases your problems but it needs to be done.'

Talwar thought for a while.

'It's a tough one but I'll try to work something out. Perhaps a war will do the trick.'

'Cowardly attack by the Invisible Hand kills 1,20,000 civilians in India,' read a newspaper in New Delhi.

'One million people dead in one day. World on a war with Invisible Hand,' read a newspaper in New York.

India was rattled by the attacks of the terrorist group. Every town, city and state had started preparing for war, calling on the youth to rise against the onslaught of enemies, both internal and external; several national bodies of political parties, think tanks and religious groups had sworn to protect their people no matter what.

Prices for food grains and commodities had skyrocketed and people had started withdrawing their money from banks, forcing them to close down the ATMs to control liquidity. Meanwhile, unemployment had increased steadily. The stock market had crashed, wiping out trillions of dollars of wealth globally; the global financial market had collapsed into a bear market for a long time to come. People were predicting another world war.

General Talwar made an appearance on the news, alongside the UN Secretary General, and condemned General Riaz for harbouring the Invisible Hand on

Pakistani soil. The world's leading countries supported India's right to defend itself and imposed unparalleled economic curbs and sanctions on Pakistan.

'I'm here to say enough is enough; India was never one for bloodshed but war begets war. When the Invisible Hand destroyed our parliament and killed our leadership, we hoped that Pakistan would bring them to justice. But they did nothing ... And now, the Invisible Hand has killed a million innocent civilians. Do you expect us to act as spectators? No. We will attack our enemies and exact our justice. If the Pakistani government and army will not take action against the terrorist group, then we will,' concluded General Talwar.

'Sir, are you hinting at a war with Pakistan?' asked a journalist.

'Yes. From this minute on, we are at war with Pakistan until we decimate all the terror hubs. We won't hurt its civilians; we are only after the terrorists who have hurt ours,' he declared.

On the other side of the border, General Riaz responded, 'If India attacks us, we are fully capable of defending our soil and people. They cannot plunder our country in the name of destroying terror hubs. They just want a reason; there is no credible proof that the Invisible Hand operates from our soil. However, if they want war, we will give them war.'

Thus, the war began.

After the press conference in New Delhi, Talwar was on his way back to the prison where ex-Defence Minister

Jagan was held captive. On the way, he saw posters of Kalki on every wall and every flyover. 'Kalki. We want you back. Protect us,' one poster read. 'Protector of India. Save us. We need you, Kalki,' read another.

His blood boiled looking at them; he asked his secretary to get them cleared immediately but heard back that the posters came back every day and they were not able to stop them.

Now in a bad mood, he walked briskly to the cell where Jagan was housed, sifting through the messages on his phone. One message in particular irked him; Rathore's team had been unable to break into the Rift.

'Rathore, I don't like seeing mails of your incompetence,' he barked into the phone.

'We are trying everything we can, sir, but that device is impossible to hack into. Experts from all over the world are working around the clock to try to crack it,' Rathore pleaded.

'If you don't crack it by next week, you can put down your resignation letter. Am I clear?'

Rathore went silent.

'Am I clear?' Talwar yelled.

'Yes, sir,' he replied hesitantly before the line went dead.

The guards opened the cell. Talwar walked in to see Jagan in a miserable condition; he was in heavy chains and looked weak and beaten up. He had been tortured for days without food or water to get information on Kalki but the man had not spoken a word.

Talwar intentionally sobered down to sympathise with him.

'Jagan, why are you torturing yourself? You are rotting here, my friend. Just tell us about the Astras Group; give us their account details, their locations, their secret projects. Don't you want to get out of this prison?' he asked softly, as though he cared for him deeply.

Jagan gave him a faint smile. 'To hell with you.'

'Don't fight me ... I want to set you free. You can be our witness and bring that criminal Kalki to trial. Why would you protect him?'

'I have made myself clear again and again. I don't intend to tell you anything. I couldn't even if I wanted to; I don't know anything about Kalki and Astras. Only Acharya knew about him and his projects.'

'Can you, at least, tell me how to access the information on the device that had been in Acharya's possession?'

'No one except Acharya could have opened the Rift. That's the truth.'

'The information on the Astras group has to exist somewhere apart from the Rift. I learned from the CBI that you destroyed some papers after the terrorists killed Acharya. Tell me something, anything, and I will spare your life.'

Jagan laughed. 'You will never be able to find Astras; they are truly invisible. Acharya gave them that invisibility.'

'Do you want to die in this cell?' Talwar asked, trying hard to control his anger.

'Do I have a choice? I will be killed one way or another, won't I?'

'That's not true. Prove yourself to be useful and I will personally help you. Give up that traitor.'

'You are the traitor, Talwar, you are! Kalki is a true soldier of India; a faithful son who will return to destroy you. You are a stooge of the Invisible Hand; my investigations can prove it. You won't survive for too long. The truth will come out eventually,' Jagan shouted with whatever strength he had left in him.

'That's enough!' Talwar thundered, looking around to check if anyone was there. 'Let me tell you a secret: it was me who set you up. I killed General Vikram Singh and put all the blame on you. And yes, I'm very much a part of the Invisible Hand,' he said softly and laughed.

'You bastard!' Jagan screamed, trying with all his might to attack Talwar, who pushed him back and kicked him hard. Jagan fell down to the ground, gasping. 'You won't succeed. Take it from me; Kalki will hunt you down like a rabid dog!' He spat on Talwar's face.

Seething, Talwar wiped his face with his palm, removed his gun from the holster and shot Jagan in his head.

It was two days after Nushen had come back from the trek in the village. They had decided to start their journey towards the Indian border that morning.

Nushen heard a noise in the early morning hours but couldn't notice anything when she looked around. She planted a kiss on Kalki's chest and closed her eyes.

She opened her eyes again a minute later.

'Kalki, wake up. There's someone out there,' she whispered. He woke up instantly and slowly moved towards the backdoor of the tiny cabin.

'Damn!' Neel whispered when he spotted a Chinese drone. It looked like a UFO and had tentacles with cameras, weapons and tools to manoeuvre things. Because the cabin was heavily camouflaged with dry wood and branches, it kept scanning the area to confirm whether it had found anything suspicious.

'Is this a pilot-controlled drone?' asked Neel.

'No. It's on autopilot. It must have identified us by our heat signatures through its infrared sensors. It's definitely going to send back a signal. We need to get out of here,' Nushen said, alert like a tigress on a hunt. If it wasn't for her superhuman hearing abilities, they would be dead by now. The drone scanned the area again and, finding a thermal heat signature behind the cabin, turned towards them.

'Run!' Nushen pushed Neel forward. The drone opened fire, its bullets cutting through the trees and branches standing in the way as they slid down the slope. It sent a live visual back to the drone station.

'We have a visual from Drone 62,' the operator from the drone station informed the Beijing HQ. 'Should we alert General Jian?'

'If you can confirm it's Nushen, then yes,' said Agent Han.

'Sending two more drones to confirm,' said the operator.

Two nearby drones were alerted and dispatched, scheduled to reach their location in less than ten minutes.

'We don't have much time. We have to escape it,' screamed Nushen.

'Should we split up?' Neel yelled back, as they dodged not only the bullets but also the falling trees and branches. Nushen could have easily outrun the drone but she couldn't leave Neel behind.

'No, we can't risk it. Let's go towards the border!'

'The trees are sliding down. The drone might think we are going down with them,' Neel suggested.

'Yeah. Let's go backwards. Here, now!' She pulled him up by his hand and they stopped sliding, hiding behind one of the trees. The drone went ahead and they used the opportunity to run up the slope.

'Run! Run! Run!' she urged. They ran as fast as they could but with his wounds still not completely healed, Neel was struggling to catch up. The drone was searching everywhere but couldn't locate them. They hid behind two separate trees as it came back up the hill to scan the area again, hovering close to where Nushen was hiding.

Oh, boy! she thought. Neel could see it moving towards her; it must have sensed her heat signature.

He found a rock next to his tree and threw it down the slope with all his strength. It created a thumping sound as it spiralled down; the drone stopped abruptly and followed the noise.

'Nice work,' Nushen said, sprinting ahead. 'Let's move!'

Neel's abdomen was hurting but he managed to pull himself up with Nushen. When they reached the mountaintop, she went inside their cabin to collect the bags they had kept ready for the journey.

'Let's leave before more drones arrive,' she said as they hastily put on their bodysuits and enabled the camouflage.

'Wait!'

'What?'

'We have to split. There is no way we can make it to the border, especially with my condition. I will lead them away from you so at least you will have a chance of getting it out of here alive,' he advised.

'You fool! You will die if we do that. I can easily outrun them. Haven't you seen me run? You move towards the Indian border and do whatever it takes to cross it; I will take the drone with me. Don't worry, they will never catch me.'

It was true. Nushen could run faster than any human on Earth.

'So here we part ways,' said Neel, holding her close as he kissed her. 'Take care of yourself.'

'I will be fine. It's you I'm worried about,' she replied. 'Kalki … I would hate it if there comes a day when I have to choose between you and my country.'

'We both know what we will choose. That's the tragedy of our story. Sleeping with the enemy comes at a price, but that's what makes it exciting and larger than life.'

They kissed again, not wanting to let go.

'There's a drone waiting to kill us,' Nushen said, finally. He sighed.

'Do we have a name for what's going on between us?'

'Shh!' She put her finger on his lips. 'Don't. I can't make any promises, nor do I want any. I had the time of my life up in these mountains with you; I will treasure it forever in my mind. Let it stay like this … unspoken, unbound, uncomplicated.'

Neel nodded in agreement.

'Until next time,' she said, looking deep into his eyes, and broke away from him.

'When will that be?' he asked.

'Honestly, I don't know. But I'll be damned if we never meet again.'

'Until next time then. Godspeed,' he bid adieu and she started running. He could see her sprinting faster than a cheetah, easily avoiding colliding with the trees and using the branches to jump ahead. *Holy shit! That's insanely fast*, he wondered.

Neel pressed the sensor to put on the helmet of his bodysuit, the camouflage turning white to match the snow. He sat on the ledge they had prepared and zoomed downhill, towards the Indian border.

SIXTEEN

In the outskirts of Hong Kong, a busy film crew was wrapping up a shoot. One of the most popular Chinese actresses, Meifen Lin, was playing the lead in this movie. After the last shot of the day, she entered her plush makeup van, a state-of-the-art palace on wheels with everything an actor could possibly need.

She came into the van, closed the door and went into the bathroom, splashing water on her face. Meifen dropped her clothes to the floor and stood in front of the mirror, looking at the scars left by whipping and caning on delicate body. She turned around to see the marks on back. Her eyes filled with tears as she remembered Jian; she trembled with fear at his mere thought.

'Tears don't suit a pretty face like yours,' said a voice from the shadows.

Meifen shrieked and pulled her towel up. 'Who is it? How did you get in here?' she asked in shock, but it was not unusual for stalkers to cross any boundaries to get close to her.

She was about to press a panic button when the person emerged out of the shadows. It was Nushen.

'Goddess! You?' said Meifen, surprised and scared at the same time.

'Yes, it's me.'

'Everyone is searching for you. We thought you had escaped to India with that vigilante, Kalki.'

Nushen had misguided the drone that had been chasing her and sprinted non-stop for ten hours to reach a nearby town, where she had discreetly alerted one of her key contacts to send her a chopper to fly to Hong Kong. She hadn't wasted a single minute once she had landed.

'Well, my work is here, not in India. I won't run from my country. I have to fix what has been done.'

'Why are you here? I told you I can't help you anymore.'

Since the time Nushen had seen her at Jian's office, she had constantly followed her every move. She had secretly approached her and convinced her to spy on Jian and, although Meifen had been apprehensive, she had agreed, giving her valuable information for a few years until she couldn't take the stress anymore.

Nushen placed her hands on Meifen's shoulders and turned her towards the mirror. Meifen took a deep breath. She knew Nushen was a dangerous woman and could kill her in a split second if she wanted to.

'I'm here to offer you a favour,' Nushen said from behind her. 'I'm here to offer you freedom. Because Jian will never let you go … Ever.'

'I—I don't understand,' Meifen said softly. Nushen walked around to come face-to-face with her.

'You are his favourite slave, aren't you? It's been years and he has still not got enough of you.'

Nushen could see the frustration and anger on Meifen's face. 'I don't know why he doesn't get tired of fucking me. He's making me train his new slaves and I feel horrible putting these girls through the same hell I went through. The thought of taking my life crosses my mind every day but I stay alive for my family. But now that he has become the president, maybe it's just a matter of time before I end my life.' Tears filled her eyes.

'I won't let that happen, all right? Now, tell me, does he still share things with you?'

'He shares nothing with me but I can hear things whenever I'm around. He has become comfortable with me, so he openly talks on the phone and even meets people in front of me. That's how I knew about you and Kalki. He threatened to kill me and my family if I said anything to anyone.'

'I need to know everything you know,' said Nushen.

'No. He will kill me, Goddess.'

'No, he won't. He will never know. You have nothing to fear, I promise. He hurts you a lot, doesn't he?' she asked, touching the scars on her breasts.

'He's an animal. He treats me like a whore. I want to kill him; I hate him so much. He has ruined my life,' Meifen cried, unable to control her emotions any longer.

'I can put an end to this, but I need your help,' Nushen promised, wiping her tears and embracing her.

'What do you want me to do?'

'Take this device and keep it within a three-feet distance from his phones when he is not around. It's a wireless hacking device; it will work by itself and download all the data from his phones without leaving any trace behind. It just needs three minutes to do its job.'

Meifen looked at the tiny device in her hand. 'What if I get caught?'

'You won't. Remember, you've done this before. Just keep it in your bag and put it close enough to his phones. It will help us understand his plans and eliminate him. You are the only one who can do this, Meifen. Do you understand? This is important for your country, not just for you alone. Will you do it?'

'Yes, I'll do it.' She took a deep breath, making up her mind. 'But I want you to promise that my family will be safe if anything happens to me.'

'Nothing is going to happen to you, I promise. I have regrouped my supporters and they will make arrangements for your family right away. And remember: don't talk about our meeting to anyone. You speak to anyone about it and you're dead. Do you understand?'

She nodded.

'This is the number you need to call in case you want to reach me. Just memorise it.'

Meifen kept it in her handbag and hugged Nushen. 'Please save me.'

'I'll save you. It's a promise.'

Ten of the most trusted military and intelligence wing leaders sat in front of Jian in the headquarters at Beijing. When he had overthrown his father, he had rejigged the top brass of the country with his close aides. He didn't want any sort of mutiny or discord in the power circles; anyone who was remotely likely to question his authority was eliminated along with their families. 'Leave no trace of their lineage or existence. Kill them all,' he had ordered, and there had been bloodshed across the country as every possible threat was eliminated.

There were, of course, a few exceptions and one was Shen, whom they hadn't been able to capture.

'What was the last known location of Shen?' asked Jian.

'We lost him somewhere in Tibet. We had waited for quite some time to see if Nushen would approach him, but she didn't. We swooped in to pick him up but he had escaped by that time.'

'That's bad news. I want him dead, understood?'

'Understood, sir. It will be done.'

'Where is Nushen?'

'She was spotted in Hong Kong; she was using different get-ups but our camera scans were able to spot a woman with matching heat signature, body type and gait. We are sure it was her.'

Hong Kong? 'She must be regrouping her team, trying to pull a surprise attack or something.'

'You're right, sir,' Han chipped in.

Why, Goddess? Why must you trouble me so much? thought Jian.

'We've laid a trap for her. We haven't taken out a few of her trusted agents; they don't even suspect that we are on to them. She will contact them sooner or later, and when that happens, we will be waiting,' said Shanyuan.

'She is both our biggest threat and the biggest trophy. I want her alive; without a scratch on her body,' ordered Jian.

'Sir, that makes it really difficult for us. Our options will be limited,' said an intelligence officer.

'She is the future queen of China. One scratch on her body and I will have your head eaten by crocodiles. Is that clear?' Jian growled.

'Yes, sir.'

'Announce a reward of 70 Million Yuan for anyone who gives information on Nushen or Shen. Someone will talk. They will definitely make a mistake somewhere,' he said.

The time was 5.18 p.m. In the heart of the Kowloon island in Hong Kong stood a skyscraper 150 stories high. On the thirty-fourth floor, a lone woman had taken position with her long-range sniper rifle, aiming at a building 700 meters away at the other end of the street.

Masquerading as a middle-aged man, Nushen wore an attire that made her look like an electrician. A voice modulation device changed her voice to match a man's.

It had been over four hours since she had been waiting patiently, without moving an inch. A few empty energy drink cans and straws were littered around. Her eyes were strained and she had a strong urge to pee. *Come on, Han, where are you?*

She had hacked into the airport system to get alerts on her key targets and the CCTV cameras in Beijing airport had identified Agent Han, sending an alert to her phone at 6.25 a.m. She had learned from her sources that he had boarded a flight to Hong Kong and was pretty sure he had come to hunt her down. She had made some mistakes and it was obvious that the Chinese intelligence wing knew she was here.

The building she was aiming at housed a quiet bakery on the ground floor and a two-floor apartment above it. It used to be Nushen's safe house during the days when she worked in the intelligence wing. Not many knew about this location and she knew with certainty that Han would check this hideout himself to get clues about her, even if he wasn't expecting to arrest her by catching her off-guard.

Han had betrayed her in the worst possible way. He had been her right-hand man and had won her trust by undertaking many critical missions for her over the years. He had protected her even, saving her life once. *Then why?* It had been hard to believe that he had double-crossed her but, in hindsight, he had always been an ambitious man. It was obvious that Jian must have promised him position, power and money. *But how could you think I would leave you alive, Han? I don't forgive people who betray me, don't you know that?*

A black SUV pulled up in front of the bakery and she became attentive, getting ready to pull the trigger. It had to be him. Three men got out of the car. They were facing the bakery and she didn't have a clean shot. *Show your face, dammit!* she thought in irritation.

Before she could get a glimpse of who they were, the men went inside the bakery. She moved her aim to the first-floor windows. There was some movement; then the lights came on. The curtains were open, so she could see clearly that one of the agents was Han.

There you are, traitor! she breathed out slowly and took aim. They were moving around in the building and could be seen from different windows. For nearly five minutes, she tried to take him out but wasn't able to get a clean shot. After finding nothing at the house, they were about to leave. *No, no, no! Come on!*

Han suddenly stopped and moved to the open window. He was examining it when he finally gave her a clean shot.

Boom! She fired, the bullet hitting him right in between his eyes, and he fell to the ground instantly as his skull burst open. *Goodbye, Han. That's the price you pay for backstabbing me.*

Before the other two agents could call for backup, she killed them in two clean shots. In a matter of minutes, Nushen had packed up her rifle and was on her way out. One of her men pulled up in a taxi in front of the building and they casually drove into the traffic.

One down, several to go. I'm going to kill all your trusted dogs one by one, Jian, and then I'm coming for you …

They dragged Agent Shirou to General Jian's chamber, which now looked completely like the seventeenth century courtroom of Emperor Genghis Khan, with antiques and artefacts from that era decorating the room. Jian sat on the throne, which archaeologists had confirmed had once been the throne of Genghis Khan himself.

Shirou was thrown to the floor in front of Jian's throne.

'General, he hasn't spoken a word about Nushen,' said Agent Chang. They had picked Shirou up after a CCTV camera had captured him talking to an old woman, whom the computer had recognized as Nushen based on her expressions and physical attributes. Of course, the woman had looked nothing like Nushen but everyone in this room knew that she was a master of disguise. They couldn't trace where she had gone, so they had captured Shirou instead.

'Agent Shirou, Nushen's trusted dog. See what your plight is now,' said Jian, who was frustrated with Nushen killing three of his trusted cabinet ministers and agents.

'General, there has been a terrible mistake. I have always been loyal to you. I have no knowledge of Nushen's whereabouts,' he begged.

Jian laughed and walked behind his throne to where swords of different shapes and sizes hung on the wall. He picked up one of the longest and creepiest looking swords, which looked like it could cut an elephant's neck in one go. He examined the bleeding edge of the sword and walked up to Shirou.

'Shirou, I'm willing to forgive you if you tell the truth and help me get to Nushen. Do you know why you are still alive? It's not because we didn't know you were part of Nushen's stronghold, but because you were bait. We have always kept a watch on you. We knew she would come back to you one day because you helped her escape with that terrorist, Kalki.'

He swung the sword around as he walked, twisting and turning it, showing off his mastery in swordsmanship.

'You must know that I mean no harm to Nushen. I intend to marry her; she is the future queen of the world,' he added, coming back to stand in front of Shirou, who was kneeling face down on the floor.

'That's right, the queen of the world,' he continued. 'You know, Shirou, this world has never seen a supreme leader. Never. But that will soon change and I will rule every country and every person on Earth.' He let out a sinister laugh and placed the sword above Shirou's neck.

'Tell me, where is Nushen? What are her next plans?'

Shirou didn't reply and held his breath, his heart having almost given up inside his chest.

'Hold out his hands. They go first,' Jian told the guards.

'No. No. No, I swear I don't know anything. Please, you have to trust me,' begged Shirou, shaking with fear, but Jian swung the sword and cut his right hand as easily as a sharp knife cuts a cooked carrot. Shirou screamed in pain while his blood splashed everywhere, including Jian's legs.

'Death hovers over you, Shirou, but it won't come so easily. I will cut you piece by piece if you don't cooperate. And the same thing will happen to your family.'

Shirou couldn't speak; such was the pain he was experiencing. His body and brain were in shock. He was dizzy and losing too much blood.

'Hold out his other hand,' ordered Jian.

'No … No, I will tell you everything. Please don't kill my family.'

'Shirou, you clown! Did you have to lose one of your hands for this? I feel awful already,' Jian said, wiping the blade with a cloth. 'Tell me everything.'

SEVENTEEN

✧

After trekking for nearly three days, Neel had finally arrived at the Indian border. It had been one of the most challenging treks of his entire life. His wounds were still healing and the snow had made it impossible to walk. Not to mention, he had had to avoid all the mountain ridges and navigate in absolute stealth to hide from the drones that patrolled the border areas. He mentally thanked Nushen for the super-helpful bodysuit that aided his disguise and kept him warm.

He started descending from the mountain briskly yet carefully, anxious to set foot on Indian soil. His stomach roiled and his heart raced; he increased his pace and his legs started running on their own volition. Just before he would have come into view, he stopped.

Two Chinese drones were hovering in the sky above the border. *Damn! How do I escape these monsters?* Not only did he have to escape the Chinese drones, he also had to give the ultras on the Indian side, that he himself had built, the slip. He had never thought a day would come when he had to face his own machines outside test environments.

He started analysing the patterns of their movements and saw that the two drones were criss-crossing each other, leaving him a window of less than two minutes to cover a distance of two kilometres and get to the other side. It was practically impossible to do so without getting killed. He needed a camouflage to go to the mountain pass, where he could then run for his life. He looked to the Indian side to see how many ultra-drones were around but, surprisingly, he didn't see any.

He hastily began assembling a camouflage; he knew the drones could detect his bodysuit through advanced sonar sensors. He cut the tree branches and created a mesh in the form of a small dome, placing twigs and leaves on it to create a canopy and covering it with thick snow. From the sky, the drones would see only snow as he would hide inside the dome and push it slowly. He knew it was a gamble but he had no other choice.

He waited until dark and executed his plan, slowly moving towards the border. He had to be slow, as the motion detectors could still pick up on him, and had to erase the trail to avoid creating a line that the machines could see. It took him an hour to cover a kilometre but he thanked his luck for keeping him alive.

However, over the next hour, the winds grew stronger and it became extremely difficult for him to erase his trail in the snow and still hold on to the camouflage. The mountain pass was barely a few steps away when a drone saw a line in the snow and triggered an alarm, firing bullets as it flew towards Neel.

Neel cursed and tossed the dome aside, leaping ahead. He ran as fast as he could and finally reached the mountain pass. The drones fired continuously as he sprinted ahead and slid through a slope across a bend, then started closing in from both sides. There was no way he could escape now. The officers at the drone station had already been alerted and the video analysis triggered a warning that it could be Kalki inside the bodysuit.

When Neel reached the edge of the mountain, he was out in the open and had nowhere to run. He was trying to think of a way to escape when both the drones came to hover right in front of him and he figured they were waiting for orders to kill him. Just when they were about to shoot him, though, a series of bullets took them by surprise. Neel looked back to see an Indian ultra-drone in all its glory. *Oh, thank God!*

'You are trespassing in Indian territory. Return to your side,' the Indian drone warned the Chinese drones, which opened fire, and Neel was caught in the crossfire. He took this opportunity and ran through the gorge as fast as he could. One of the Chinese drones went to follow Neel but the ultra-drone fired a missile and damaged the engine. It fell to the ground with a huge blast. The battle continued with the second drone, giving Neel ample time to escape.

After travelling in the dark for a few hours, he could see a board through the mist. He rubbed it with his hand to reveal—'Indian Territory. 12,325 ft. above sea level.'

'Yes! Yes!' he screamed with joy, like a lost child reunited with his mother. He knelt on the ground and picked up the cold icy soil.

'Mother, I'm back!' he shouted deliriously. 'Thank you for keeping me alive.'

I have to hurry now, he thought. *There's no time to waste.* He started walking briskly then, in some time, running. His stitches still hurt but he didn't care. He fell at times, but he picked himself up. He slid down slopes but climbed back again. He was restless; he was determined. A fire had ignited in him like never before; his mind, body and soul were set ablaze.

As he ran, he thought about the time when he had begun the journey of building his machines—the machines that would change the history of the world.

KALKI'S STORY – GENESIS OF VANAROIDS

———※———

'Arya, tell us more about the Rudras,' Tiger requested, flipping through a book on the history of the Rudras and the scriptures. They sat around a table, drinking coffee and taking a much-needed break.

'What would you like to know?' she asked, sipping her latte.

'Tell me about the origins of Rudras. How did it all began?'

'Well, all I can say is they were followers of Lord Shiva. Infact, it is believed that Rudras were the most elite warriors of Shiva's army. We are not sure about the accuracy of the historical records or details about when they were entrusted with guarding the Scripture of Gods.'

'Who wrote the scriptures?' asked Tiger.

'Unfortunately, I won't be able to tell you unless you become part of the Rudras … It's a fascinating story, the most adventurous I have ever heard! Why was it necessary to write such scriptures and why seek such 'absolute knowledge!' She smiled. 'Again, these are all myths and no concrete proof exists.'

'*The Scripture of the Avatars,*' read Tiger, glancing through a page that listed all the original scriptures of Rudras. 'This sounds fascinating.'

'Oh, yes! It's the ninth scripture that talks about immortality and how to acquire absolute knowledge or enlightenment. From time to time, a handful of people through the ages have attained this stage. We call them the Avatars.'

'Like Ram and Krishna.'

'Yes, they all attained absolute knowledge in their own ways; some were born with it and some had to struggle to attain it. Do you know that there is a prophecy that The Last Avatar is yet to come?'

'In this age?'

'In this or the next. The Last Avatar will be called Kalki.'

They both looked at Neel, who still hadn't said anything.

'What?' asked Neel. 'Sharing a name doesn't mean anything.'

'I wouldn't underestimate what Professor Vati has told you. When she refers to you as the chosen one, perhaps you have the potential to be the one.'

Neel scoffed at the idea.

'Neel, what's bothering you? Why have you been so silent?' asked Arya.

It had been two weeks the team was working with the blade, but Neel had hit a dead-end in building the machine. Vessels and machine parts lay everywhere. He had tried to use the blade to instruct the synthesizer but, for some reason, the output was just not what he had hoped for.

'Because there is nothing to talk. I'm unable to understand the blade. I have read every page of the scripture ten times over and I still don't know how it functions. Look at this.' Neel held out a jug. It looked shaped out and had absolutely no finish.

'Does this look like a jug to you?' he questioned.

'It's a stepping stone,' Tiger chipped in.

'I've tried it a hundred times; this machine hates me. Look around you. It's been two weeks and all I can create is some half-baked stuff. How could I ever build that machine?'

'We have to keep trying, buddy,' Tiger encouraged. 'We have a long way to go, sure, but we have come a long way too.'

'We don't have time, Tiger! That's the problem,' Neel yelled. 'Maybe we should just tell Professor Vati that we're not going to make it. It could take years to get this done. Or worse, it may never happen.'

Arya looked at him for a while.

She walked up to him and put her hand on his shoulder.

'Neel.'

'Yeah,' he said, looking up.

'Let's take a break. I think we have had enough with the blade and the scriptures. Let's get some fresh air.'

'Sure, let's go!' cheered Tiger.

Arya looked at him and signalled him to stay back.

'Err ... I mean, I have some other work at the hostel. Why don't you two go ahead?'

'You sure?' asked Neel.

'Absolutely! See you later.'

They drove to Nandi Hills on the outskirts of Bangalore. On the way, they listened to soothing music, talked about college and had a good time.

They went up the hills and sat at the edge, from where they could see an Anjaneya Temple below. A giant statue of Lord Hanuman stood in the temple complex, breathtaking in its glory and grandeur.

'This is brilliant,' exclaimed Neel. 'What a view!'

'It's stunning,' she agreed, smiling, her hair flowing in the breeze.

'Arya … Can I tell you something?'

'Yep, go ahead.'

'You have rocked my world.'

She laughed.

'You stormed in and changed everything.'

'For good or bad?'

'For good, of course. You're trying so hard to help me reach my true potential. Why?'

'Because I believe in you. I can look in to your soul, Neel, and there is nothing ordinary in there.'

They were silent for a while, enjoying the view and the breeze.

'You know,' Neel started, clearing his throat.

'Yeah?'

'There is a possibility that I may have fallen in love with you.'

She looked at him, surprised but so happy that she couldn't speak for a moment. She smiled and cleared her throat.

'Possibility? It's not confirmed yet, eh?' she asked with an impish smile.

He wanted to respond but before he could utter a word, she leaned in and kissed him. He felt as though he had touched a live wire. The first kiss of his life, and it was with this angel! They kissed for a long time, then pulled back to look at each other and started giggling.

'Is your love confirmed now?' she asked.

He laughed.

'I love you,' he breathed out, looking deep into her eyes.

'I love you too,' she whispered and they kissed again.

They heard the sound of the conch from the temple and pulled apart. Trumpets and drums started playing. She stood up, leading him to a spot where they could see Hanuman's face clearly. Hundreds of devotees stood in front of the giant statue, most holding lamps, and started chanting the Hanuman Chalisa. Their sound reverberated through the hills and reached the skies. She took his hand in hers as goosebumps appeared on their skin; the intense atmosphere filled them with courage and passion.

'When you instruct the blade to forge the machine, what are you visualising?' she asked suddenly, surprising Neel.

'The same thing that we designed; a sleek robot that can fly and fight and do awesome things,' he replied.

Arya took a deep breath.

'That's hardly a vision. You lack inspiration. The blade needs to see your passion, your burning desire, your muse.'

She's right, he thought. He had been trying to build a machine without any clear direction. He then looked at Lord Hanuman and his fearless face amidst a sea of devotees. Sankat Mochan, the destroyer of evil. The god who ends all our sorrows and protects us.

Do you see any trace of panic on his face? He asked himself.

There was none whatsoever. He was the epitome of courage, even in the face of the worst adversities. His enemies dreaded facing him and devotees prayed to him. He was the ultimate fighter who guarded our realm and gave courage to every beating heart.

The Hanuman Chalisa had reached a high pitch; the powerful sound of a conch set ablaze an idea that would change the world.

Do you want to create a robot to protect this country, or a god?

He looked keenly at Hanuman, stunned. A chill went through his spine. He stood with increasing strength and determination as drums and trumpets continued playing in the background.

'Jai Bajrang Bali!' chanted the crowd.

Neel had fire in his eyes.

'I'm going to bring the gods on Earth to protect our country.'

'What?' asked Arya.

'I know what I have to do!'

The next week, Neel rendered the 3D schematics of Lord Hanuman's face on his computer, then, wearing the blade in his hand, moved it to the hologram in the air. They could see Lord Hanuman in his full glory but in a modern avatar, adorned with modern weapons, a futuristic helmet, an impenetrable armour and a long tail that consisted of a number of parts that could separate and join at will. The tail played a multi-functional role in being a weapon with a sphere at the end, as well as a sensor to feed its 'brain' with valuable inputs and stimuli. It could even be used to maintain balance or become an anchor.

Over the past weeks, the trio had worked day and night to build each section of their dream combat machine. All the hard work Neel and Tiger had done in Astras came in handy; they knew exactly how to build a great humanoid robot.

Borrowing from the knowledge of the Rudras, they had created Ultimatium, the strongest alloy on earth. It was lightweight yet strong enough to withstand the radiation from Calamitous.

The machine's body was designed to be able to engage in combat on all terrains—air, sea and land. The flaps at the back; the thrusters on the legs, hands and back; the aerodynamic armour; and the adaptable body gave it the ability to transform into any shape that was best suited for flight, swimming or sprinting on the ground. In the air, it could fly faster than Mach 5 speed.

Arya had created a ground-breaking design for the engine and the weapons payload. The machine packed quite a punch with great firepower and a host of ammunition and weapon tech. She called it the Firegon engine, which resembled a miniature nuclear fusion battery and was truly futuristic.

The machine could probably lift an army truck and throw it aside. Its punch could smash a boulder to smithereens, and it could run up to 200 kilometres per hour by transforming its body to have four limbs, like a cheetah.

The magnetic field created by the Firegon engine proved to be an added advantage, as it could deflect metal parts, bullets and even small missiles. This increased its survival chances and reduced wear and tear on the battlefield.

'Behold the Vanaroid, the mightiest of the mighty machines ever created!' announced Neel.

'Vanaroid ... It's the perfect name,' said Arya, as they looked at the hologram with awe. They could see all the parts and the Firegon engine, which was the heart of the machine.

'It's breathtaking!' exclaimed Tiger. 'Time to give it a thundering voice.'

Tiger had selected a powerful voice after n number of iterations to make it perfect; it had to be the voice of a god.

'Voice module loaded,' he announced.

'Now, the last step: let's trigger the AI,' Arya said, rapidly keying in commands on her system.

'Three ... two ... one ... go!'

They waited with baited breath as the Vanaroid opened his eyes.

'Hello, big guy!' said Neel.

'Hello, Neel,' the Vanaroid replied. 'Arya, Tiger.' The voice was so powerful that it shook the lab.

'Yay!' They jumped with joy.

The AI engine was a brain that was truly revolutionary. It could understand most languages, converse, emote, relate, solve complex problems and even crack jokes. It was adapted to be a complete combat machine with mastery in battlefield formations, martial arts, planning and warfare. It could also improvise and self-learn based on the challenges on the ground.

'I cannot wait to be born,' said the Vanaroid.

They laughed.

'Ready?' Neel asked, looking at Arya and Tiger.

Tiger nodded with determination.

'You can do this!' Arya assured.

Neel held the blade close to his face and closed his eyes. He imagined the powerful face of Lord Hanuman that filled him with immense courage and confidence. At once, he started constructing the Vanaroid in his mind—every single part, atomic structure and feature to the tee. It was nothing but a mind map, a structure that completely defined the machine he wanted to build.

He moved his hands in the air, constructing the Vanaroid and instructing the synthesizer on what he was imagining. He kissed the blade and swung his hands to create infinity, bringing the synthesizer to life. The hearth roared and they stepped back instantly. It made a rumbling sound, making them exchange worried glances as the ground shook and fire gushed out of the hearth.

Neel closed his eyes and focused on the mind map he had created. The synthesizer roared and roared, spitting fire and smoke. Lightning flashes started coming from the metal tower.

Professor Vati came in running.

'What happened? I got an alert about a quake,' she panicked, as the floor and the walls shook. Equipment and weapons started falling all over the lab.

A powerful thunderbolt struck the tower, making all the glasses shatter. Smoke and fire filled the room.

'What have you done?' screamed Vati.

No one replied; their eyes were glued to the mouth of the hearth. Amidst all the fire and smoke, they saw a metallic giant standing with a mace in his hand. They couldn't believe that they had actually done it!

The trio rushed to the hearth and hit the exhaust button, immediately dousing the smoke and fire.

They were spellbound as they looked at what they had forged. The eight-feet tall combat machine stood with a mace, the gada, in his hand. It was a hair-raising experience for everyone.

'It worked! It's perfect!' Arya screamed.

'It's monolithic; it's forged as one machine, with no nuts or bolts!' Neel exclaimed, checking out the exterior.

'The weapons are a part of his body. Look at the gada!' Tiger's jaw dropped. 'Insane!'

They hugged each other, jumping up and down in excitement.

Professor Vati had turned into a statue herself, unable to comprehend what stood in front of her.

'Professor, why don't you take a seat?' joked Tiger.

'Yes, I think I must,' she mumbled and sat down.

They brought the machine out of the hearth.

'Let's install the firmware,' said Arya, plugging the cable into the machine slot to boot the Vanaroid, then loading the AI software into it.

Vanaroid AI Brain setup complete, read the monitor.

Boot sequence starting …

Boot sequence complete. 100 per cent success.

Running diagnostics …

Vanaroid stepped forward and moved his limbs. The diagnostic programme checked each of his parts, weapons and critical functions.

Diagnostics complete. 100 per cent success.

They looked at each other with their hearts in their mouths.

Deploying voice module …

Voice module installation complete. 100 per cent success.

Vanaroid ready to accept voice commands.

'How are you feeling, big boy?' asked Arya.

'I feel powerful,' said Vanaroid. Professor Vati's heart skipped a beat, listening to that voice.

'Demonstrate your power,' Neel instructed, pointing at an artillery gun that looked like an ancient cannon barrel. Vanaroid walked towards the barrel, the floor shaking with his every step.

'Pure iron,' Vanaroid said, analysing the material of the cannon barrel with his sensors. He held the barrel in his hands and broke it into two halves.

'I'm not sure whether you know what you have done here but I can tell you this much: this is history! You have created history,' Vati concluded, still unable to digest the breakthrough.

'Professor,' said Vanaroid, keeping the broken barrel down. 'I'm not going to argue with you on that one.'

They laughed.

'There's no time to waste. Let's conduct the flight trials and run all the tests,' said Neel.

❖

Meanwhile, in Pakistan Occupied Kashmir, a troop of 200 trained mercenaries from the Invisible Hand moved towards the Indian border in a ring formation. While the radioactive chemical, Calamitous, served as the perimeter, the nuclear bomb was strategically positioned in the centre. The mercenaries wore heavy armoured suits to protect them from the radioactive particles they were carrying. The amount of radioactive substance was so great that any living organism within a two-kilometre radius died instantly.

The Indian army commander at the border checkpoint got a call from his Pakistani counterpart.

'Major Vikrant, we are vacating our post. The Invisible Hand is bringing the nuclear weapon surrounded by Calamitous. I cannot risk my soldiers to be exposed. We have to run and I suggest you run too. Good luck!'

The line went dead.

Unnerved, Major Vikrant called his command centre and gave the news.

'Do not abandon your post at any cost, even if we have to burn to ashes,' ordered his superior. 'We are sending in the drones and the air force to protect you. Over and out.'

KALKI'S STORY – JAI JAI BAJRANG BALI

P rofessor Vati entered the cellar with two people wearing hooded robes.

The trio were busy running flight tests on Vanaroid, which was cruising over the Indian ocean and breaching Mach 2 speed.

'Mach 2, baby, Mach 2!' Tiger cheered and they high-fived, although Neel had sensed some instability as it crossed Mach 2.

'Report back to the base,' Neel instructed.

'Are you sure? I was just beginning to enjoy this,' Vanaroid joked.

They chuckled.

'Next time, big guy!' said Neel. 'There is some kind of instability. Come back now.'

'Good morning, team,' greeted Professor Vati.

They turned towards her, wondering who the people in the hoods were.

'Neel, there is someone I want you to meet,' said Professor Vati.

The men in the robes removed their hoods.

'General Ramsey?' Neel gasped.

'Defence Minister Subhash Acharya?' Tiger asked, stunned. They were shocked beyond their wits but Arya just smiled and saluted them.

'Yes, the situation is grave and we don't have time to explain a lot of things,' said Acharya, shaking hands with the trio. He was then the Defence Minister of India, before he went on to become the prime minister in the years to come.

'I don't understand,' said Neel.

'I'm one of the council members of the Rudras. There are nine members in total, including me,' Acharya responded. 'Long story short, I couldn't convince the council to vote in favour of an intervention in the Calamitous terrorist attack. Now, this little experiment that we came up with to bring you into the fold has yielded result.'

'Experiment?' Neel asked.

'Yes, it was our idea to bring you and Tiger in. That was the primary objective of Arya's assignment. She had to ensure that you succeeded and she has delivered. Well done, Arya!'

Neel looked at Arya. 'Arya, is that true?'

Her face had fallen. 'Yes, but—'

'How could you?' he cut in before she could explain.

'Neel,' Ramsey intervened, walking towards him and putting his hands on his shoulders. 'My boy, you have struggled and worked hard your entire life to get to a point where you can protect your country; that time has come. Your genius needed to be channelized but I didn't want you to be corrupted by the Rudras. That's the reason I kept you outside the society.'

'Corrupted? Are you also a part of the Rudras?'

'Yes, I'm very much a part of the Rudras. Over the centuries, a fatigue has crept into our secret society. Our ideas have become stale. It's time for revival; it's time for new blood.'

Everyone was silent.

'Neel,' ventured Acharya. 'We have been observing you for a long time. We recognised your genius when General Ramsey took you in. You are the son this country has been waiting for—I believe in it more than anyone else. We always knew you would become a part of the Rudras, but we had to wait for the right time. When the Calamitous issue came to light, we knew the time was ripe.'

'But we have never met before,' said Neel, trying to fathom the situation.

'Son, you were a month old when I first held you in my arms,' Acharya said.

'Acharya, no!' Ramsey interrupted.

'General, I think it's time he knows.'

'What? Knows what?' Neel asked.

'Your father was part of the Rudras,' revealed Acharya. 'He and I worked shoulder-to-shoulder to protect this country. He was one of the bravest and most decorated commanders our country has ever seen. He sacrificed his life to save the country. He was a hero.'

Neel turned to his grandfather. 'Why didn't you tell me?'

Ramsey didn't respond.

'General Ramsey wanted to protect you. He tried his best to keep you away from any of this because your family has sacrificed enough blood already. But the more you grew, the more you wanted to protect your country. We observed your progress and struggles. I was the one who persuaded him to stop protecting you. We decided to bring you in a few months ago and gave Arya the assignment.'

It was too much for Neel to take. His mind was numb; he sat down in a chair as tears flowed down his cheeks. He couldn't control them. Tiger put his hand on his shoulder to comfort him; Neel held his hand and cried more. Tiger had tears in his eyes too.

Arya came close to him but he said, 'Don't!'

She stopped dead in her tracks, her eyes shining with tears, and moved back.

'Get up, my child!' Ramsey said. 'There will be time to discuss this and get your answers. But now is the time to honour your father. He was a hero; he would never let the enemy win. Honour his legacy. Get up and fight for your country.'

He was a hero. Those words meant everything to Neel. *My father was a hero! I have to fight. I have to continue his legacy.* It was as though he had found a new reason to pursue his vision for the country. He suddenly felt blessed. He wanted to ask so many questions but knew they had to wait.

Neel took a deep breath, got up and hugged his grandfather. It was the first time they had embraced each other.

'Thank you, grandpa. Thank you for being there for me.'

'You are my blood, my pride,' Ramsey said with affection. 'Now, rise, child. Rise to protect this country!'

'I'll do whatever it takes. I will destroy the Invisible Hand,' he vowed.

'Professor Vati, General Ramsey and I belong to a faction in the Rudras that wants to change it intrinsically to be able to better fight our enemy,' Acharya interrupted. 'We may not be able to win in the short-term but we have done several experiments outside of Rudras. You are one of the most successful ones.'

'Sir, I trust that whatever decisions you made were in the best interest of this country. It's not easy to be in your shoes. And the fact is: everything is fair in love and war,' said Neel, looking at Arya. She sighed and looked away.

Acharya nodded in appreciation.

'The need of the hour is to defeat the enemy. Tell me what is needed of us,' Neel added earnestly.

'The enemy is at our gates. They will be crossing over to our side soon, but we will not make it easy for them. Mass evacuation of all border towns is underway and the army is preparing to face them, but countless people are going to fall. Three independent army units trained by the Rudras will be springing a surprise attack to destroy them and dismantle the nuclear bomb. If they fail, I want you to be the last line of defence.'

'Vanaroid is not ready yet,' cautioned Neel.

'We have barely run our first trial and diagnostics are incomplete,' added Tiger.

'Sometimes you need to run before you walk, Tiger. This is your chance to make history,' said Acharya.

There was a loud thud at the other end of the lab, where the aerial exit was located. A plume of dust kicked up everywhere and they looked towards the exit with anticipation. They could hear his footsteps, the tremors reaching their feet. An outline of a god emerged through the dust, Lord Hanuman's visage becoming clearer as he approached.

Acharya inadvertently fell to his knees, folding his hands together. The trio looked at his reaction with astonishment. The previous night, they had added the artificial skin and hair that Tiger had created to complete the machine. The skin could withstand fire, bullets and was frictionless, making it completely aerodynamic.

They knew their machine would evoke a strong response from the public but looking at the defence minister of the country bow down to him made them realise they had created something far greater. It was not the machine he was bowing down to; it was the god. They had created an incarnation of Lord Hanuman!

'Jai Bajrang Bali!' he said.

'I never thought I would see you in flesh and blood in my lifetime,' Acharya uttered, mesmerised, as he looked at Vanaroid.

'How is this possible?' Ramsey wondered. He had never seen anything like this in his entire life and, being a part of the Rudras, he had seen plenty of miracles.

'Mr Acharya, I'm not worthy of being called Lord Hanuman,' Vanaroid spoke in his godly voice. 'I'm merely trying to be his reflection.'

Acharya got back up on his feet and said, 'We are all his reflections, my friend, but you are something else; you are a miracle.'

'How do you know Acharya's name?' asked Ramsey.

'General Ramsey, I'm connected to the internet. I'm learning fast and evolving.'

Acharya turned to Neel. 'Come here, the three of you … You too, Professor Vati.' He looked at them with awe and saluted them for their achievement.

'I have no words. I can only say this—Jai Hind! Jai Hanuman!'

There was an alert on the monitors. General Ramsey hurried to the terminal. 'Dear God! The Invisible Hand just shot down three of our military satellites.'

Acharya's face turned red; Neel could see a bit of fear in his eyes.

'Those satellites were armed to destroy the Calamitous. That was our primary weapon!'

Neel, Tiger and Arya ran to their work station to prep Vanaroid.

'Shoot down their satellites. Blind them!' ordered an angry Acharya.

'What will we shoot? For all we know, they could be using the Pakistani military satellites. We all understand their nexus with ISI and the Pakistani army. It will lead to a full-frontal war,' warned Professor Vati.

Acharya screamed with frustration. 'We will teach these rogues a lesson. We will cut them into pieces!'

Major Vikrant and his platoon were on high alert at the border. He was dreading the moment the enemy would attack, and they didn't keep him waiting for too long. An alarm went off and sirens started ringing.

'Activity on the other side,' reported the analyst sitting in front of the monitor. They could feel the ground shaking as two tanks emerged out of a tunnel no one knew existed. They could see two hundred-odd soldiers in heavy metal armours and around twenty trucks carrying heavy payload, surrounded by tanks and drones to protect them.

General Ramsey established a direct line with Vikrant in the nick of time.

'Do you see the visual, General?'

'Yes,' he acknowledged. 'Get out of there. Now! Abandon the post!' ordered Ramsey.

'But, sir, that's not what I heard from my superior.'

'Major, this is Defence Minister Acharya. I'm authorizing this from the highest level. Run!'

But it was too late; the commander from the Invisible Hand ordered his troop to bring down the shields of the trucks. As the shields lowered, they could see the trucks piled with a purple substance. It was the lethal Calamitous.

'Twenty trucks of Calamitous! God save us!' Professor Vati cried.

In a matter of seconds, Major Vikrant and his soldiers had fallen to the ground, screaming. The radioactive emission from the material corroded the DNA structure of every cell, leaving the person dead in a matter of seconds. All the camera feeds from the post showed soldiers falling like matchsticks. The IAF planes that had been on standby in the air were the next casualty. The pilots were dead and the planes came crashing down, causing huge blasts.

1300 estimated dead, showed the monitor but the number was increasing every millisecond.

Acharya banged his fist on the table. 'In spite of all the intel and heads-up, we still have hundreds dead. Shame on us! Shame on all of us!'

The evacuation was still in progress but the majority were still stuck in the villages. They succumbed instantly, the streets and roads filling up with dead bodies.

7500 estimated dead, showed the monitor.

The Invisible Hand's troop had crossed the border and was marching ahead with zero resistance.

General Ramsey got a call from Army HQ in Delhi. 'General, what are the orders?'

'Ask the defence forces to stand down. We cannot bomb them because they are carrying a nuclear bomb amidst all that Calamitous. I will request for the drones to attack. Wait for my signal,' he ordered.

9700 estimated dead, showed the monitor.

'The numbers are mounting,' worried Acharya. They had tried powerful soundwave blasts and drone attacks, but nothing could stop them.

'All I want at this point is to save millions of lives. If that nuke is blasted, it will be the end of us,' said Ramsey.

'Where is the Vanaroid?' asked Acharya. They walked to the command centre, where the trio were working.

'What's the status?' asked Ramsey.

'Vanaroid to reach in five minutes, cruising at Mach 2 speed,' said Neel, trying to think up a strategy to dismantle the enemy defences and take control of the nuke. 'Ask the Army to get the remaining drones ready. Vanaroid will need some assistance.'

Arya and Tiger were busy analysing diagnostics and setting up the weapon systems as they had sent the machine to combat without conducting any trials whatsoever.

Acharya took General Ramsey aside.

'General, if this experiment fails, be prepared to bomb the nuke and stop them at their current location,' he uttered in a sombre voice.

'It would turn the area into a nuclear desert for decades.'

'Do we have a choice? No one can go near that hideous substance. They could kill millions if they detonate it in a populous area. This is our only option.'

'Do you hear that sound?' asked the Invisible Hand's troop commander.

'Sounds like a supersonic plane approaching,' his subordinate said.

'I don't see anything on the radar. It must be advanced tech,' he opined, just as a thunderbolt hit the ground, sending tremors to their van. Vanaroid had landed with such an impact that soldiers had been flung back with the shockwave. Everyone was alert, trying to figure out what was happening.

'Silence. I can hear something,' said the commander. He tried to operate his systems but none of them were working. 'What happened to the systems?'

'It must have been an EMP blast; all the machines have stopped working and circuitry is burned.'

Indeed, Vanaroid was carrying an EMP blaster, which could send powerful waves to roast any digital machine in its path.

The commander was furious. He put on the helmet of his bodysuit and got down from the van.

A loud sound was coming from the tail of his defence and he turned back. A van carrying mercenaries was thrown up in the air and hit the ground with a blast. There was chaos as everyone ran for cover.

'Who did that?' he screamed on his comm.

'No idea, sir. Our men are all dead there,' said a mercenary from the outer ring of the defence, before he screamed and the line went dead.

'Stop!' yelled the commander. 'There is something out there. Everyone, prepare to engage. Take position.'

Jai jai bajrang bali, tod de dushman ki nali,' a song played nearby.

'Who's playing that? Where is it coming from?' yelled the commander, as the mercenaries looked everywhere.

Back in Bangalore, Tiger was laughing.

Acharya turned to Neel in shock. 'What is that?'

'Vanaroid has a sense of humour,' Neel responded. They could barely suppress their laughter. 'Err … I know it's bad timing. We're still working on the AI.'

In the battlefield, the commander held a loudspeaker and said, 'Whoever you are, come out right now! We have an armed nuclear weapon and we will detonate it if you make one wrong move!'

The music continued to play.

'You think this is funny?'

'I think it's hilarious!' Vanaroid replied, his voice so powerful that they flung back a few steps.

'It's some kind of a giant!' yelled a mercenary.

'Shut up and fire!' commanded the leader. The soldiers started firing at once, aiming where the sound was coming from. They turned when the music started coming from the other side, firing in that direction. After a while, they stopped.

'I'm getting bored of this now. I need some action,' announced the Vanaroid. 'Bring in the rain!' he said and roared. The sound of the roar was so loud that a few soldiers peed in their metallic bodysuits.

With the mace in his hand, Vanaroid jumped out from behind a tree and smashed the mercenaries into pulp, hammering them to the ground. They opened up like soda cans, their blood and guts flowing on the ground. Six Indian drones immediately came in and rained missiles from the top, taking out the outer ring of the defence system. The enemy drones engaged with the Indian drones; a severe dogfight was taking place in the skies.

The mercenaries were scared for their lives. They tried to run and hide but there was nowhere to go.

'What the hell is that?' asked the subordinate.

'It's the monkey god the Indians worship—Hanuman! I have no clue how this is even possible!' answered the commander.

Without an escape, the soldiers started spraying bullets at Vanaroid, which were deflected and hit their own troops. Vanaroid lifted a truck, spun it twice in the air and flung it. The truck rammed through the ground, smashing everything in its way, and cleared a path to the inner circle.

He jumped up and landed next to the van carrying the nuclear weapon. The commander tried firing at him but Vanaroid just looked at him and swung his gada, burying him in the ground with one move. Vanaroid then tore open the top of the van and took out the nuclear weapon.

'What do we do with this, General?' Neel asked Ramsey.

'Ask him to take it to a safe zone. The drones will finish the rest of the enemy troops.'

'Vanaroid, take it to a safe zone.'

'Affirmative,' Vanaroid replied, firing up his thrusters. With the nuclear weapon in his hand, he took off vertically and zoomed up in the air. For the onlookers below, it was a scene straight out of the Ramayana, when Lord Hanuman flew carrying the sanjeevani mountain.

He landed far away in a safe zone and in a matter of minutes, the Indian army reached that location and dismantled the nuclear weapon.

Meanwhile, Vanaroid had returned to the battlefield.

'Remember, no one should be left alive. No eye witnesses,' Neel instructed.

Vanaroid went from truck to truck and killed all the militants.

Acharya and Ramsey looked at the screen with pride. 'Die, you worms! You thugs! The god has come to destroy you,' Acharya said with gritted teeth.

Vanaroid erected the shields for each of the trucks to ensure the Calamitous was covered. However, there was plenty of work remaining. Nearly six trucks had toppled and a high amount of Calamitous had spread across the path.

'General, we have to pull him back. We cannot risk anyone seeing him,' said Neel.

'I'm sure enemy satellites must have already picked up the images,' he said.

'Not really. We hacked all the satellites. There is a complete communication blackout in South Asia right now,' laughed Arya. 'We hacked the Army network as well. Indian drones had picked up the visuals but we wiped them out.'

Acharya and Ramsey heaved a sigh of relief.

They were all ecstatic. Not only had they destroyed the enemy, they had found a hero—the hero of a billion!

'Vanaroid, report back to base station. Great job, big guy!'

'Easy peasy!' said Vanaroid, zooming up into the air.

The next day, sitting in the cellar, the trio watched the news, which showed the nation mourning the death of 9837 people. People had breathed a sigh of relief after the terror attack had been foiled but no one knew how it was done.

'So, do we really become part of Rudras now?' Tiger asked.

'No, Tiger. I cannot relate to their philosophy. To only intervene when an event is apocalyptic—that's heartless to the point of being inhuman. They have an opportunity to save the world, to wipe out diseases and poverty, yet they do nothing. I will never be part of such a cult,' said Neel.

'Neel, think about everything you can accomplish with the knowledge they possess,' Arya interrupted.

'The answer is no. A big no. But we will find a way to work with them as an ally.'

Arya looked at Neel with disapproval but he wouldn't look at her. They hadn't spoken since Acharya had broken the news that her mission had been to recruit Neel and Tiger for the Rudras.

Neel got up and left the cellar; Arya followed him.

'Neel … Neel, wait,' she said, as they entered the university lawns.

'What do you want now?' he growled.

'Please don't be mad at me. I did what was asked of me. It was my duty.'

'Fine, I get that. But why pretend to fall in love?'

She sighed. 'Really? Is that what you think? Look at me,' she pulled him towards her. 'Look into my eyes. You know that I haven't pretended for a single second. I'm crazy about you, Neel.'

He was silent.

'I love you more than anything in this world. You have to believe me. Tell me, do you think I'm lying?' she questioned, her eyes moist.

He knew she wasn't.

'No, but what you did was not fair. It was horrible,' he admonished and pushed her away gently.

'I'm sorry I hurt you, Neel, but I didn't have a choice.'

There was silence for a while as they strolled through the garden.

'Say something, please,' she begged, holding his hand. 'Tell me, how can I make it up to you?'

He thought for a while and smiled.

'I'm sure you know how to make it up to me,' he whispered, looking into her eyes.

She looked incredulously at him and couldn't help but blush, biting back a smile. 'Mr Neel Digvijay Kalki. You've been waiting for that, haven't you?'

'Of course! Is that even a question?'

They giggled, as they came closer and kissed.

EIGHTEEN

Neel touched his lips while he hurried towards the nearest village in Ladakh after escaping the drones. It had been over ten years since that day, but Arya's kiss was so fresh in his mind that he felt it had happened only yesterday.

He saw the village at a distance. It had taken him nearly a day to reach this tiny town in Ladakh called Drokchang. It would be dusk soon and daylight was fading. He entered the town with hopes of finding some shelter and hot food.

He looked everywhere but couldn't find anyone. He went into shops and houses; the village was completely deserted. *Where is everyone?* he thought. *Am I daydreaming?*

'Hello!' he yelled. 'Is anyone there?'

There was no answer.

He kept shouting and running from pillar to post, but there was no response. Not a single soul existed in the place. He was agonisingly disappointed.

'This is a freakin' ghost town!'

In an hour or so, he was able to cover the entire village. Every now and then, he entered an open house to check for electricity; there was none. He tried to find a working phone somewhere, but couldn't. Luckily, he found plenty of packaged food and beverages in the shops. *Why did these people leave everything behind and run?* He had no clue, but he realized he was famished, so he ate and drank to his heart's content. *Food has never tasted so good.*

It was getting dark and increasingly chilly. As he walked the streets, trying to think of what he should do, a sound took him by surprise.

He quickly turned back to see an animal in an attacking stance right in front of him. It looked like a giant wolf with thick black fur, ferocious eyes and razor-sharp teeth ready to rip him apart; it growled as it stared into his eyes. It had a face that could instil fear even in the most fearless heart and Neel couldn't help but admire the creature at the same time. It moved slowly towards him, fiery eyes fixed on his face. Neel realised it was a Tibetan Mastiff, one of the oldest and rarest dog breeds in the world. *A giant beast of a dog,* he thought, and it was looking for a challenge.

On the other end, Neel looked equally menacing with long hair that reached his shoulders and a beard that befitted a warrior who had been in battle for years.

He didn't know what to do. He tried not to look straight into its eyes as he calculated his next moves, for he knew dogs felt challenged and infuriated by a staring contest. *Should I run or climb on to this truck?* He knew it would outrun him without question. His wounds had not healed completely either, so he had to spring a surprise. The dog growled and he could see the whites of its eyes increasing as it prepared to pounce on him.

'Devil, no!' a young lad shouted from behind. 'Come here, it's okay. Come here.'

The dog ran to the boy and stood next to him, barking, though it still held its attacking stance.

Neel heaved a sigh of relief. The boy walked closer; he looked like a local Ladhaki of around ten or eleven years.

'Is that dog from this planet, boy?' asked Neel.

'No, he's not. He is straight from hell. That's why I named him Devil,' replied the young boy. 'He has killed people to protect me before. So, make no mistake, he can kill you too.'

'I'm not going to argue on that. He could probably even kill a tiger.'

'I suppose, yes.'

'I'm not going to hurt you. You can ask Devil to relax.'

'He will relax when he starts trusting you. Who are you?'

'I'm Neel. I was passing through the village when I noticed it's deserted. What happened here? Where is everybody?'

'The town has been evacuated,' the boy said.

'Why?'

'You don't watch the news?'

'No. I was totally cut off from the world, living in the Himalayas for a long time. Tell me,' he asked, putting his knife back in its sheath.

'After the war broke out, the Indian army decided to give away all the disputed land to China in a peace treaty. They didn't want to fight a war on two fronts. They are getting the entire land evacuated for Chinese occupation.'

'War on two fronts?' asked Neel.

'The Indian army is fighting the Pakistani forces. They didn't want another war with China, so they decided it was a small price to pay to keep the bigger enemy at bay,' said the boy, sadness in his eyes.

Neel's heartbeat was increasing; he felt beaten down. Everything had changed in the few days he had spent hiding with Nushen. He blamed himself for what was happening in India. He had sworn to protect his country and he had failed.

'Why are you still here? Why didn't you evacuate?'

'My grandma refused to leave the town. The police tried to force us, but she insisted. She is old and sick; she wants to die in her hometown. I have no other family so I stayed back to take care of her and we hid when they came to evacuate everybody. We are the only ones left in this village.'

Neel thought for a while. 'Take me to her.'

They hurried to a small house at the end of the street. Devil ran ahead of them and pushed the door to get inside. As he entered the cramped house, Neel saw an elderly Ladhaki woman lying on the bed and coughing.

'She is eighty-three and can barely see or hear,' the boy, who had said his name was Nong, told him.

'Can I speak with her?' Neel asked.

'Yes, sure.' He told his grandmother that someone was here to speak with her. The old lady opened her eyes with some effort and squinted at Neel, trying to see who it was. The light was dim; the room was lit only with candles as there was no electricity supply.

Neel sat next to her on the bed and said loudly, 'Grandma, I heard about your condition and reasoning to stay back. But we have to leave now. I can carry you to a safe location. It's dangerous out here.'

Nong translated his words to Ladakhi. The old lady looked at him angrily and spoke, 'This is my country, my village. No one can ask me to leave. I was born here, grew up here, got married and had children here. This is my land and I will die here.'

Neel looked at her wrinkled face and felt ashamed about the situation they were in. She continued to speak in anger but Neel held her hands to comfort her and said, 'You are right. No one has the right to ask you to leave.'

'She wants to know who you are,' said Nong.

'I'm a soldier,' told Neel.

'What type of a soldier are you? The one who will run away like the rest of them or the one who will fight for his motherland?'

Neel fell silent. He got up from the bed and stood by the candles on a table in the corner.

'Son, it's easy to talk, but you are just like the rest of them. Even if you wanted to help, what can one man do? Nothing. Let me die peacefully. My husband died in this bed; I, too, want to take my last breath right here,' the old woman said, coughing. She turned to her grandson and told him to leave the village with the stranger. 'Leave now, my child. You have a long life ahead of you. Go now!'

'No, I'm not leaving you, grandma,' Nong cried, hugging her. Nong reminded Neel of himself as a child, orphaned and helpless. He had vowed to stop any other child from going through what he had; but he had failed.

Neel looked at the burning candles, his eyes observing the flame and its dance to the breeze that sneaked into the room every now and then. Devil stood a little distance away, watching his every move with his menacing eyes.

What will you do, Kalki? asked a voice inside him. *Will you let more children become orphans like you?* He was in turmoil. He banged his fist into the wall. He punched again, his heart, body and soul filled with anger. 'What can one man do?' she had asked. But he wasn't an ordinary man, was he?

No, I am not, he thought firmly. *I'm a destroyer of evil.*

He knew he had to act now. He had to come out of the shadows and become the punisher he had always wanted to be; he had to become the saviour. All his life, he had wanted to remain in the shadows as a faceless entity everyone dreaded, but now he knew times had changed. He had to emerge. *It's time to show your face to the world,* he told himself.

He turned back to the old lady and sat down next to her. 'Thank you for asking me that question, grandma. I'm not the running type. I'm going to stay here and fight for you and your grandson, even if it means I give my life defending your village. I promise.'

When Nong translated it for her, the old lady smiled and said, 'Bless you, my child. May the Lord be with you. May the Lord give you courage and victory.'

'We can never be sure what the universe has in store for us but I will fight till my last breath … Take care of yourself, grandma.' He got up. 'Do you know when the Chinese army is supposed to be here?' he asked Nong.

'According to what everyone said, they will be here tomorrow.'

'Tomorrow? Are you sure?' he asked, alarmed.

'Yes, I'm sure. We've been counting days.'

Neel sat back down, thinking of what he could possibly do; there was no time in hand. 'Do you have a phone around here?'

'Yes, but there is no signal. The mobile phones don't work anymore. No landlines or Internet either.'

'I see.'

'But I know there is a place where you will still get signal. You have to travel three kilometres to a peak where you might get some range. If you don't get it there, you'll have to travel at least twenty kilometres to the next town. There are no working vehicles anywhere and no fuel left. Thieves looted the village last week, after the evacuation, and took everything they could. The only reason we are alive is because of Devil; he ensured that no one dared to come near this area.'

'No wonder the village looks plundered … I'll take my chances; can you tell me how to get to that peak?'

'Devil knows the way; he will take you.'

The dog was all ears. He looked attentively at Nong, then at Neel.

'Do you think that's a good idea?' Neel asked when Devil barked in approval.

'Oh, yes! He knows you are here to help now. He will do anything to protect you, even if he has to give his own life.'

'Okay, then. I need to hurry.'

The boy gave him two phones and a water bottle. Neel strapped the bottle to his back and kept the phones in his pocket, stepping outside with a flashlight.

Devil barked, signalling him to follow, and ran ahead.

'Devil, wait! Devil,' shouted Neel, trying to catch up with the dog. Devil was going uphill, easily dodging trees and not waiting for him to catch up.

'Stop it, you stupid dog!' he yelled, panting for breath and clutching his wounds. Devil came back, barking as though Neel's words had upset him. He even growled a bit. 'All right, I'm sorry. You're not stupid. But can you please go slow? I'm human, remember?' he said, and Devil woofed back with approval.

'Good boy, let's go.' He started running again but limited his speed to match Neel's. 'You're a smart fella, aren't you?' He patted Devil on his back.

It took them over an hour to reach the peak; Devil started barking as soon as they reached.

'Yeah, yeah. Checking, boy.' Neel took the phones out of his pocket, relieved to find decent signal strength.

'Thank heavens there is signal here,' he said, dialling a number. The phone rang for a long while. 'Come on, pick up. Pick up.'

It was a ghost phone number they only used in times of emergency. No one could trace the call except Neel's company. But no one answered and it went to voice mail. He dialled again. He didn't even know what had happened to his team. Where were they? What were they doing? *They must think I'm dead.*

'Hello,' said the voice at the other end of the line. Neel immediately knew who it was and it filled his heart with happiness.

'Hello, Tiger!'

NINETEEN

'**M**y brother! No words can express my happiness right now.' Neel cheered in his mind.

'Bro! Damn, I can't breathe right now, man. Where the hell have you been?' Tiger asked, surprised and overjoyed at the same time.

'In China. I was held captive but I'm back in India now.'

'I can see your location. You're near the border; that's bad news. The Chinese army will be there by morning.'

'Listen, I don't have much time. Remember I used to tell you that there will come a time when the world will need to know who we are?'

'Yes?'

'The time has come.'

'Are you suggesting … But we don't have the time and the crew. The machines are all shutdown. We're under attack; things have changed dramatically since you were here. Everyone is underground and we have lost dozens of our team members. There's a hit on us and we are being hunted down one by one.'

'Who ordered the hit?'

'General Talwar. We have been branded extremists and a threat to the government and the public of India. They stopped just short of calling us a terrorist organisation.'

Neel found it hard to believe that such a day had come. He had spent his entire life protecting his country and being called a terrorist was heartbreaking.

'Where are Agni, Neo and the core team?'

'Everyone is safe. Agni and Neo are with me right now. I had a miraculous escape in Amsterdam and fled from the Netherlands. There was a massive coordinated effort to take me down. Like, the entire World wanted to capture or kill me. The Invisible Hand has placed a bounty of $50 million on my head, can you believe that?'

'These thugs have gone complete rogue. Are you fine now?'

'Yes, I'm fine. I made it back to India two weeks ago; I'm now regrouping and protecting our core team and our facilities.'

'That's good news! Can we mobilize the team right now?'

'Mobilizing the team is impossible right now and the machines cannot be accessed because the Indian army is no longer our ally and routes to Garuda City have been closed. No one is working from there and everything has been shut down as we fear they're being traced. We'll have to go there to physically reboot the machines.'

'You have no time left then.'

'It would take us between six to eight hours to get things back online.'

'I understand. But here's the thing: you need to get here by tomorrow morning or you can come at leisure to take my body back home. You got it?'

'I won't let that happen. I'm coming for you.'

'Godspeed, brother.'

'Godspeed,' said Tiger, unable to control his excitement. He picked up his phone and hit the SOS button.

'General, I'm back,' said Neel, calling General Ramsey next.

There was a brief pause, then a hearty laugh. 'I was waiting for this call, my boy. I knew it was only a matter of time; there is no force in this world that can stop you.'

Neel laughed too. All he wanted was to hug his grandfather but he didn't say the words. 'Times have never been tougher. I was worried about you.'

'Worried about me? Ha!' Ramsey laughed. 'You don't know me or what?'

Neel chuckled. 'I have to admit I kinda missed you, General.'

'Well, that's a first,' he hooted. 'We looked everywhere for you. Where have you been? Where are you now?' Before Neel could even respond, Ramsey jumped in. 'I have a feeling you can't be back just like that. There must be a storm coming with you.'

Hidden deep inside the dense forests of the Western Ghats was the facility called Garuda City, where Neel's company, the Astras, manufactured the drones in a joint venture with the Indian government. Because it was meant to be a top-secret facility, Acharya's government had given them a hundred square acres near the Dandeli Wildlife Sanctuary on the edge of River Kali in Karnataka. It was adjacent to another government facility where part of India's nuclear missile arsenal was kept.

Garuda was a state-of-the-art facility that had hundreds of underground floors, with labs and manufacturing centres that were straight out of the future. It was Neel's brainchild. They had produced hundreds of ultra-drones here and a variety of futuristic technology, including Vanaroids and other next-generation combat machines.

The facility, which was more like a city, had once housed four thousand scientists, manufacturing personnel, weapons experts and PhD students, along with Neel's core team. It had also contained the School of War, an education centre where the brightest minds in India were trained in various areas of modern warfare.

The facility was now empty. After the death of PM Acharya, General Ramsey, along with Astras' core team, had evacuated the facility in less than a day's time. There had been no time to waste and they couldn't have taken any risk.

When Tiger came back, he had tried to regroup the core team and started planning a strategy to counter the rising threat of the Indian High Command. He was now a hundred kilometres away from Garuda with Agni and Neo, his trusted team members.

'How do we get to Garuda without being killed?'

'It's not going to be easy; that area is now completely guarded by the Indian army because of the Nuclear arsenal facility,' said Agni, who was the elite combat specialist in the group and Tiger's partner on the field.

'It's impossible to get there. We only have a few hours left and we are a hundred kilometres away,' added Neo, the computer whiz-kid of the core team.

'Blasted timing!' yelled Tiger.

'There must be something we can do?' Agni asked.

'Nothing. We shut Garuda down completely so that even if the army reaches the facility, they won't be able to make out what's beneath the surface. We can't access it remotely until someone goes there and reboots the main control programme,' said Neo.

'Can you get me a chopper or a plane?' Tiger asked.

'You won't be able to make it close enough to the facility without getting shot down by the army,' replied Agni.

Just then, he got a call on his cell phone. 'General Ramsey?'

'How are you, hellboy?' General Ramsey greeted.

'General! Oh, thank God. I was wondering how to contact you. We have a situation here.'

'I know. A stealth fighter jet is on its way to your location. It will pick you up and discreetly drop you to Garuda. No one will suspect an army jet. There's no time to waste. Get ready to shake the world.'

'Woohoo! Let's rock and roll, baby!' cheered Tiger.

Neel dialled another number after speaking to General Ramsey. While it was ringing, Devil stood next to him, rubbing against his legs and sniffing around him. Neel knew he was still trying to analyse him. He patted his head, stroking his fur. 'Thank you, Devil. Your service to this country won't go unnoticed.'

Devil woofed softly and rubbed his face against Neel's hands. *Strange beast*, thought Neel.

'Heena Khan here,' said the voice at the other end.

'Heena … It's me.'

'Is that—it can't be true. You're alive? Everybody said you were dead.'

'I was, but I'm back from the dead.'

'You vanished when the country needed you the most. You know what they did? My father got killed in a terrorist attack! Did you hear me? My dad is no more! You're responsible for all this, Kalki, you!' she sobbed.

'I'm sorry, I know that I'm guilty. You're right, this is all my mistake.'

'Your sorry won't help. And yes, it is your mistake! You failed. You have no right to be called the saviour of our country if you vanish when people need you the most. How dare you! Who will bring back my father?'

Neel was silent. Her words came out like lashes.

'Do you know what has happened to India since you vanished? People are living in fear. People are dying in thousands. No city or town is safe anymore. There are terrorist attacks everywhere. There is corruption everywhere and no one has faith in the Indian High Command. Everything you wanted to accomplish for India has gone down the drain.'

'I know and I'm here to fix it.'

'We need Kalki. This country needs Kalki.'

Heena Khan was one of the most influential television news anchors in India. She was the most controversial, yet the most followed; the most hated, yet somehow the most loved. Everything about her was extreme. Her news show was one of the most watched television shows globally.

Over the years, Kalki had given her top-secret information about defence and international affairs, so much so that she owed Kalki a great deal for her success. She knew Kalki was a powerful man with no face and no existence; he was a vigilante out to serve justice his own way. She knew Kalki didn't need money, fame or credit but wanted to use the media to remove roadblocks for India and protect the citizens.

When the Pakistani army had accused India of triggering the cross-border exchange of fire, Kalki had provided the footage captured by the drones his company had deployed on the border, which clearly showed Pakistan's army firing bullets at a silent Indian border checkpoint. It had left Pakistan red-faced and put tremendous pressure on them to stop their cheap tactics to annoy India.

On another occasion, Kalki had exposed a scam in the defence procurement sector that had led to the resignation of the then Defence Ministry of India and the arrest of top businessmen in India and the US. Later that year, he had told her that the Chinese nuclear submarine was moving around the Andaman and Nicobar Islands, the footage of which had almost triggered another war with China. No one knew how Heena Khan managed to get her hands on such information and footage, not even her own channel.

'What do you want in return?' Heena had asked Neel several times. She had neither met him nor seen him. All their conversations had taken place over the phone or the net.

'The reward is in the exposure of the information itself. You owe me nothing.'

'There must be something I can do for you.'

'Someday, I'll ask you for a favour,' Kalki had said as an afterthought.

'Anything for you. I'll wait for that day.'

Today when she heard Kalki on the call, she felt euphoric, but angry that he hadn't been there to protect her family.

'Do you remember I had told you that one day I would ask you for a favour?' Kalki asked over the phone.

'Of course, I remember.'

'It's time.'

'What do you want?'

'It's time the world knows who Kalki is.'

TWENTY

A gent Chang walked into Jian's chamber in Beijing. 'General, Nushen has taken the bait. She has disguised herself as a middle-aged woman and entered the spa to meet Meifen.'

'Excellent,' Jain said with anticipation. 'Bring up the visual. Where is she right now?'

'She is alone in the steam room with Meifen. We have our eyes and ears inside. Here's the feed.' Chang brought it up on the screen.

'Meifen, it's me,' Nushen said, entering the steam room.

Meifen was sitting in a corner. When she went closer, she realized she was crying.

'What happened?' Nushen asked, worried.

She cried harder.

'If you don't tell me what has happened, how will I help you?'

'I'm sorry, Nushen. I'm really sorry,' she sobbed.

'Why?'

'He threatened to kill my family; I couldn't do anything. I'm so sorry.'

Nushen stood up, alarmed. 'How did he know I approached you?'

'Agent Shirou tipped him off.'

'Agent Shirou?' She froze.

'They tortured him and cut his hand. He gave up all the information and told them how you used me to spy on him.'

'What! Damn you, Jian!'

'He said he would kill my family if I didn't send you a distress message. I couldn't go against him, Nushen. You don't know him; he is a monster. He always gets what he wants.'

'Your family is safe. They are far away from his reach; I already ensured that.'

'You don't know him the way I do. He would have found them eventually.'

She had used Meifen a hundred times over the years and had trusted her blindly. *This is not happening*, she thought.

She took out her phone to call for backup but there was no signal, even when she moved out of the room. 'The signals are jammed!'

'They will be waiting for you outside. Forgive me …'

'My men checked this place before; it was clean. How are you sure?' questioned Nushen. She had done her recce of the place before she entered the building and her men had given her a green signal.

'Goddess, they brought me here. They're outside. Run. Save yourself.'

'You've done nothing wrong! I will save you, promise.' She rammed out of the door to the dressing room.

She tried calling her men for help again, but didn't get any signal, even near the window. *Bloody hell! Definitely a mobile signal jammer.*

She hurriedly put her clothes back on and opened the door of the changing room, when she saw two agents aiming their guns at her outside.

'You are under arrest, Madam Nushen. Put your hands up in the air and get down on your knees.'

'I think there is a misunderstanding. I'm not Nushen. My name is Shei Lin,' she said in Mandarin, acting surprised. She looked nothing like Nushen with her disguise on.

'Put your hands up in the air and get down on your knees. Please, madam. Do it now!' urged the agents.

'This is a big mistake,' she kept saying and got down on her knees. 'I'm telling you my name is Shei Lin.'

'Put your hands up in the air, please,' warned one agent, coming forward to handcuff her. When he closed in, she twisted his wrists to grab his gun and threw it aside. She swiftly took out her gun and shot the other agent with it. The bullet hit him between his eyes and he dropped dead. She turned to her left when two more agents started shooting at her and held the first agent as cover, who was shot several times.

'Why are they shooting at her?' asked Jian.

'General, those are just tranquillizing bullets. They won't harm her.'

By then, she had taken both the agents down in two clean shots. She removed two tear gas canisters from her bag and threw them on either side. When they hit the ground, smoke started emanating from them and filled the corridors. The smoke detectors rang and the sprinklers were activated.

How did I screw this up? She cursed herself for getting into this situation. Jian had outwitted her, but she was not a rookie; she knew very well how to get out of a botched-up mission.

She looked for an outlet and went through the fire escape to the basement, hurriedly removing her disguise and throwing her jacket away.

'Did we lose her?' asked Jian.

'Don't you worry, General. There is no way she can escape.'

There was not a soul in the basement. *This doesn't look good,* she thought, running to her car and into the driver's seat. She drove as fast as she could and was out of the building within a few seconds, but stopped when she reached the exit. She couldn't believe what she saw; the road was empty and the building was surrounded by police and rapid response teams.

'Madam, surrender yourself or we will be forced to shoot you,' the cop announced in the loudspeaker. 'There's nowhere to run. Get out of the car and put your hands up in the air.'

How do I reach out to my men? she thought. She had her trusted agents waiting outside in case something went wrong but her radio and phone both weren't working.

Her phone rang suddenly.

'Goddess, this is Jian,' said the voice on the phone, when she answered it. She was trying to analyse weak areas that she could punch her car through, but it was completely barricaded. There was no escape.

'Nushen, I know you are upset with me but I'm not the bad guy. Cooperate with the cops and they will escort you to me. You are not being taken prisoner. You will come home a queen—my queen.'

'You can only dream of making me your queen, you bastard. I would rather die here than surrender,' she said in a stern but calm voice.

He chuckled. 'Goddess, I would never let anyone harm you. No one will put a finger on you, including myself. It's my promise. Come to me; let's talk this out. Don't fight me.'

'Don't try to sweet talk me. I'm not a child. You sound ridiculous.' She turned her car around.

'What are you going to do?' he asked.

'You'll see,' she said, just as a missile cruised in and blasted the barricade. The vans and cars went up in the air and fell aside, burning.

Thank you, Shen! She knew her brother had come to her rescue. Three more rockets came in, rapidly taking out most of the police cover and reducing everything to ashes.

She hit the accelerator and zoomed through the fire.

The cops, the Chinese intelligence wing and the special forces team were all chasing Nushen as she sped away in her car. The choppers were chasing her and armed soldiers were everywhere, waiting to pull the trigger. Fortunately for her, the car was bulletproof and fully loaded with guns, ammunition and communication equipment. It's just the comm channels that were dead.

She made it into the express way and pushed the gas to the max. No one was shooting at her on Jian's orders and she used it to her advantage.

She was hoping to somehow disappear between one of the flyovers where they didn't have much visibility but looked ahead and saw police vans blocking the road on the flyover.

She cursed when she noticed tire busters, trying to hit the brakes, but it was too late; her tires tore and the car lost balance because of her speed, crashing into the police vans waiting on the flyover.

She was hit on her head, even as the airbags inflated instantly upon impact. The windows shattered. She could feel blood dripping from her nose and head as she struggled to cut herself from the seatbelts with her knife.

'Madam, raise your hands up in the air. You have nowhere to run,' the cop announced.

'You don't go down easy, do you, Goddess?' Jian muttered, watching the live feed.

Nushen managed to get out of the car with great difficulty and looked around in despair. She was surrounded by cops and bleeding from her head and nose. Her vision became blurry; she could barely walk.

She looked across the flyover, trying to assess whether she could make the jump from the bridge. She decided to take her chances, slim as they were.

'Don't shoot. I give up. I'm coming in,' she said, walking towards them slowly.

'Stay where you are and don't move. Get down on your knees now!' warned the cop. Before he could even finish his sentence, she leapt and ran towards the edge to jump.

'Take her down,' ordered Jian.

'Fire!' said Agent Chang.

The sniper shot her leg just before she could reach the edge. She fell to the ground, unconscious.

TWENTY ONE

The cops walked in and stood in attention. Jian then witnessed the moment he had always imagined in his head. Nushen was escorted inside in chains, held by four muscular guards. Not that she resisted; she didn't have the strength after being shot by a tranquiliser. She had been given medical attention and intravenous drugs to bring her back to normal, but her head still hurt.

She looked up at Jian, wanting to kill him but having neither the energy nor the liberty.

'Welcome, my queen. Welcome to your rightful palace,' said Jian, walking closer to her. 'Why is she in chains? Who put her in chains?' he roared.

'Stop the drama, Jian. You very well know you would be dead if I wasn't in chains,' she mumbled, still in a drugged state.

He got upset. He held her hair tightly and kissed her lips forcefully; she pushed her face aside and spat on his face. 'I will kill you, son of a bitch! How dare you!'

He cleaned his face and slapped Nushen. 'Don't make me do that again, Goddess. I don't want to hurt you,' he said, controlling himself. 'All I want is for you to be mine. I will make you my queen.'

'On my death bed, you will. Not when I'm alive,' she retorted.

'Oh, don't be so mad. Let me cheer you up,' he said. They dragged Meifen to Jian; Nushen looked at her guiltily.

'You wanted to set her free, didn't you? That's what you told her when you recruited her. Did you think you were smarter than me?'

'Jian … listen to me. You have me now, don't you? Let her go.'

'Let her go?'

'Yes, let her go. I request you.'

'Dare I not oblige you when you request something for the first time? That's not possible. You are my empress and your wish is my command,' said Jian, turning toward Meifen.

'Master is very happy with your service. I will set you free. You can do whatever you want now.'

Meifen couldn't believe what she was hearing. She didn't have the nerve to walk away.

'Go on, you are free. You have earned it!'

'Thank you, master. Thank you!' she cried, tears in her eyes, and turned around. Before she could take another step, he took a knife and cut her throat open. She collapsed to the ground instantly.

'No! No, Meifen!' Nushen cried, falling down to hold her. 'Why would you kill her?'

'You asked me to set her free and I did. Death is the ultimate freedom. Next time, choose your words carefully,' he laughed.

'You're a monster!'

'Nushen, you are losing your game, aren't you? Do you know why you are in this situation? Because you started trusting people. Inspite of being backstabbed by your faithful dogs during the coup, you still trusted Meifen and Shirou. And what did they do for you? They betrayed you.'

Nushen looked at him with heavy eyes.

'If I had let her live, she could have betrayed me some day. I don't spare anyone. I eliminate every threat immediately; the same way I'm going to eliminate Shen and your latest fling, Kalki, in front of your eyes.'

'I'm going to kill you, Jian.'

'My Goddess, you killed me with your divine face and that heavenly body the day I saw you. Now, I intend to make you my wife and my queen and have you bear my progeny,' he said, touching her belly.

'Let me loose, you coward, and then we can talk,' she snarled, gritting her teeth.

'I will tame you, my queen. But before we do that,' he signalled Agent Tu. 'Get her ready for the wedding and the night I have patiently been waiting for.'

'With pleasure, General,' Agent Tu replied.

Before Nushen, could resist, she was given a sedative shot on her neck. She closed her eyes and was taken away for wedding preparations.

In a discreet building on the suburbs of Beijing, a dejected Shen entered the basement with three of his trusted soldiers. He cursed himself for not being able to save Nushen, but he knew it had been impossible, given the circumstances.

They entered the elevator, which took them down ten floors below the basement and came to a stop in a huge room that opened into what looked like the future. Everything there was generations ahead in terms of technology, amenities and comfort. There was something peculiar about the people who were busy working inside. They all had glowing porcelain skin, blonde shiny hair, tall and athletic build, and beauty that was godly. Hidden from the world, this place—called the Cradle—was indeed the cradle of the *Homo Supernus*. Shen and Nushen had achieved the impossible and the Cradle bore testimony to that.

When Shen entered, they stopped working and walked towards him. They called themselves The White Knights—a hundred of them, all trained and efficient like Nushen and Shen. They were the super-soldiers; they stood in line and saluted Shen.

'At ease,' he said. 'General Jian has taken Nushen hostage. We have to bring her back, even if it means burning Beijing to the ground. Prepare for war.'

TWENTY TWO

※

The first rays of the sun hit the cold misty mountains. The Ladakh valley was deadly silent and the wind howled occasionally to wake up the lone man and his dog, sleeping at the edge of the mountain.

After trekking back to the village, Neel had gone straight to the deserted hotel, located at the edge of the village, from where the slope started. He could see a great distance into the valley from the front of the hotel. He hadn't slept all night, for he didn't know when the Chinese army would arrive, and had fixed the circuitry of the solar power batteries to light up the entire hotel.

He had spent the night watching various news channels to catch up on what he had missed in the last few weeks.

Through the night, Heena Khan had dared to run a special show about the treaty IHC had reached with China and the consequences it had on the population that lived along the border. Footage and stories showed the populace from these towns and villages migrating towards mainland India. It was estimated that half a million people had been uprooted because of the treaty and there was an uproar in India. Various groups and institutions across India had protested the move, making it difficult for the army and the police to maintain law and order. People had taken to social media to protest, and the world blamed China for being opportunistic when India was at war with Pakistan. The UN had tried to mediate between the countries to bring back peace but it hadn't been successful.

Why did the Indian High Command accept this peace treaty? Neel wondered. *Something doesn't add up.*

A news item showed that after he had taken oath as the president, General Jian had put forth an agenda to annexe all the lands that had been usurped by China's neighbours. As a part of that agenda, a Chinese delegation had arrived in New Delhi to put forward a proposal, telling India to either give them back their part of Leh, Ladakh and Arunachal Pradesh or face the wrath of the Chinese army. Because India was already at war with Pakistan, and because of the Chinese nuclear shield, China had the advantage.

The Indian delegation had negotiated hard but acceded to giving up part of Leh and Ladakh to maintain peace with China. They had managed to retain Arunachal Pradesh, with China legally agreeing that it was India's land.

The news showed General Talwar arguing that India could not sustain a two-front war and the price of 0.026 per cent of the land was negligible compared to the damage war could cause. 'We have promised jobs and lands to all the families that have been uprooted. It's the responsibility of the IHC to ensure everything is smoothly settled. Settlement camps have been opened in the industrial city of Baddi in Himachal, and we have ample opportunities for jobs and farming in the area.'

Heena further showcased a debate of the think tank in the Indian community. 'China is asking 0.026 per cent of our land right now, but tomorrow it will come back for Arunachal Pradesh. Besides the agreement, what is the guarantee that Arunachal Pradesh is safe?' asked a senior security expert. Similarly, the world had reacted strongly and had pressurized China to step back. General Jian had turned a blind eye; he issued a notice stating that it was an internal matter between India and China and no one should interfere, mentioning that it had been an unsettled dispute for centuries between the neighbouring countries that was now settled amicably.

In recent months, India had lost countless lives in the border areas because of terrorist attacks, civil unrest and the war with Pakistan. Shortage of food and medicine had further aggravated the situation; some experts felt this peace treaty was a boon, given the circumstances.

On the other hand, after the bombing in New York and London, USA and UK, along with the NATO allies, had attacked the Invisible Hand's strongholds in Iraq, Syria, Afghanistan and tribal Pakistan. Russia and China had stayed away from that conflict. The coalition troops had destroyed several of Master Zar's key assets and strongholds in the past few weeks but it was far from over. The bombings across the world continued and killed millions of people. The attacks wouldn't stop, no matter how hard anyone tried. World War Three had begun.

All this left a bitter taste in Neel's mouth. His eyes burned with anger. *General Talwar, you traitor! Why are you doing this? What's your story?* He didn't know how, but he knew it was the Invisible Hand that had ensured he reached that level. That was their modus operandi—instating their key people in every country to eventually become dictators. He vowed to unearth the truth and put an end to this.

He spent the rest of the night outside, sleeping at the edge of the mountain and waiting for sunrise.

The dog barked and ran around in circles. 'Devil, what is it?' asked Neel, struggling to open his eyes. It was already morning. He hastily followed Devil to see two drones hovering above them; they were from the news channel Nation24x7, where Heena Khan was the chief editor. The drones had 'PRESS' written in big bold words that would be visible for everyone below, just so no one struck them down.

Right on time, thought Neel. Heena had kept her promise. *And why wouldn't she? This is probably the story of the century.*

Devil was standing in his attacking posture. 'Easy, Devil. These aren't enemy drones. They are the press.' He seemed to ease his stance. Neel went inside the hotel and saw that Heena was doing a special show with live coverage of the area that would be occupied by the Chinese army. They showed footage of the beautiful valley and the town that was now deserted.

'As you can see, the police department and the border security force have evacuated the entire town. It's a sad situation that we are giving away a part of our motherland to China on a platter. The entire nation is shocked with this attitude of the new rule in India. Since when did we become such a spineless nation that we cannot fight for our sovereignty? No matter how small or big the land is, half a million lives are at stake here today. And what has the army told us so far? Nothing, except that they cannot hold the line on two fronts. What were we doing all these years? Why didn't we prepare for a such a day? Did the army become complacent over the years with the emergence of Kalki and the Astras group?

'Let's take a short break and we will be back with the live coverage of the Chinese occupation in Ladakh. Stay tuned,' she told the viewers as someone else took over.

She stepped out of the set and saw Trivedi, the channel head, staring angrily at her. 'What are you doing? We have a direct order from the IHC not to say anything against them. Do you want us to be hanged? The country is in emergency, for God's sake. They call it a media gag for a reason.'

Before she could reply, Heena's phone rang. It was from Pradeep Das, the PR head of the Indian High Command.

'Talk of the devil!' She showed the screen to Trivedi.

'Answer the call and tell them we will be watchful. And don't fight with them like last time. I have a channel to run and investors and employees to take care of. Understood?'

Heena nodded and took the call.

'What are you doing, Heena?' Pradeep asked without wasting time on pleasantries.

'Sir, we are just showing live coverage of the Chinese occupation of India. Is there a problem with that?'

'How did you get wind of this? How do you know the ground zero?'

'That's my job, sir.'

'Don't instigate people on this issue. The army cannot fight wars with all our neighbours, you know it. We don't want to take China head on. It will lead to mass destruction and the lives of millions of people will be at risk. Do you understand? If you show or say anything inappropriate, I'll shut you down.'

'That sounds more like a threat than a directive.'

'Yes. And I'm stating the truth of what will happen to you and your channel. I have the powers to shut you down and lock you in jail forever. Don't forget that the country is under the rule of IHC; I have sweeping powers to arrest and neutralise anyone who we think is against the peace and safety of this nation.'

Heena didn't have time to fight with him. 'Sir, we will just show what is going on, nothing more. I'm sure the country deserves to see this much. Now, if you may allow, I need to get back on air.'

'I'll be watching you,' Pradeep warned and hung up.

Trivedi looked at her in frustration. 'Not now!' Heena interrupted whatever he was about to say and walked in. She saw her secretary and something struck her.

'Mohan, come here. Do me a favour. Share the feed with all the other channels. They won't be able to send their drones to ground zero any time soon. Let this be the day when all the media channels unite for the good of the country,' she said.

'Are you sure?'

'Oh, yes, I have never been so sure. Do it.'

He was about to walk away when she added, 'Another thing. Seal all the doors and don't let anyone inside. Get backup power ready; the transmission shouldn't be cut at any cost. They will come to arrest me, but make it extremely difficult for them to reach me.'

He looked worried but ran towards the transmission room.

It was nearly 8.30 a.m. when Neel looked at the broken clock on the wall. 'Where are you, Tiger? Come on,' he muttered under his breath. He was restless.

Devil barked and ran outside again. 'Don't! Come back in here,' he said, as he saw the television screen showing the Chinese drones approaching the town.

Drokchang would be the first town they would encounter after crossing the border. They showed footage of a giant Chinese hovercraft landing near the border, trucks and battle tanks driving out of it.

'What kind of technology is this? We've never seen such a hovercraft before. It doesn't look like standard Chinese aircraft. Looks straight out of a Star Wars movie,' Heena commented.

It was a considerable force; an entire battalion of tanks, anti-missile bombers, communication equipment and heavy-duty excavation machines. Two more such hovercrafts landed and hundreds of soldiers marched out.

'These are not normal soldiers,' said the security expert, Amit Ponappa, who was sitting next to Heena. 'This is something else. This is the next-generation army equipped with advance bodysuits. China is showing off its muscle. They are sending a signal that this new army can defeat any enemy in the world. Moreover, this is just the sweeper battalion that is here to weed out any threat and clean the area before the actual army comes in.'

Neel looked at the screen. *What are those excavation machines? What are the Chinese planning to do in Ladakh? Whatever it is they are planning, I will never let them succeed.*

He took a deep breath and closed his eyes. He then picked up a ten-foot pole he had attached the Indian flag to. He had managed to find it the previous night; the flag almost dilapidated and torn around the edges.

He wore his trademark Kalki mask, a makeshift one he had created the night before. Then he went outside the hotel with Devil, standing at the edge of the mountain slope that led to a valley. He could be seen on the horizon far and wide; the road stretched out for miles in front of him.

There was no one in sight, though he knew they would be on the horizon anytime now. There was no sign of Tiger; he hadn't given them enough time. They weren't prepared and, moreover, the entire team was underground because of the witch-hunt against them. *How could they come? I can't be foolish.*

The Nation24x7 drone happened to spot Kalki and Devil. 'Can you close in, please?' Heena asked on the live broadcast, and the drones zoomed in on Kalki. The wind was blowing fast, kicking up the dust. In the midst of it, the camera picked up the vision of a tall man with a bread, holding a long pole with a fluttering Indian flag. A giant doglike creature stood next to him.

'What is that?' squeaked Heena, trying her best to sound natural, but the view of a lone man with an Indian flag, standing with a beast of a dog beside him, was nothing short of awe-inspiring.

The audience across the world was stunned. A deadly silence spread across the nation; everyone stopped whatever they were doing and glued themselves to the screens.

'We have some activity on the ground. I cannot believe my eyes. There is a man standing at the edge of a mountain with an unusually big dog, holding an Indian flag. The Chinese army will be at that spot within minutes. Who is this man?' Heena asked live on-air.

The drone zoomed in; while one part of the screen showed Kalki, the other showed the Chinese battalion moving towards the town.

'The entire area has been cleared by the BSF and police forces, yet there stands a man who looks like he wants to encounter the Chinese Army all by himself. Look at his face; am I the only one terrified here?'

'No. I am equally terrified right now. He looks determined to disrupt something. Either he is insane or he is brave to the point he's going to face an army alone,'

Ponappa pointed out. 'Hang on a minute! The man is wearing a mask,' he added. 'Is that—is that Kalki?'

'That's not possible! I can't believe my eyes; I think it's Kalki!' shrieked Heena. 'Look at his mask—the messiah is back! We have to confirm whether it's really him.'

She looked up to the camera, addressing the viewers.

'Dear viewers, there is someone at the border of our country right this moment with a death wish written on his face and a dog next to him that can scare the wits out of anyone. This crazy man cannot be anyone but Kalki. He has saved our country countless times and, when the world thought he was dead, he is back again to prove everyone wrong. But ... he is standing there alone. What is he planning to do? Can we send in a probe to him?' she asked the drone operator.

'Yes, we can. Sending in the probe now,' came the reply.

'Kalki is back,' read the news ticker on the screen of all channels. The nation stood on its feet, excitement filling their hearts but anxiety churning their guts.

Two spherical mini-drones ejected from one of the drones and flew down to Neel. Devil tried to jump and attack the mini-drone, barking aggressively and missing it by inches.

'No, Devil. They won't harm us. Easy, boy, relax,' said Neel, patting him on its back. The probe could pick up every word and relay it across the globe.

'We at least know the name of the dog now,' said Heena. 'It's called Devil; what an appropriate name for the magnificent canine.'

One of the probes came closer and opened a screen, showing Heena.

'Hello, Kalki! I'm Heena Khan from the Nation24x7 news channel.'

'Hello, Heena,' Neel growled in a grave voice.

'Apologies, but just to confirm … are you Kalki? *The* Kalki?' she enquired.

'Yes, I'm Kalki.'

The entire country cheered as one.

'Master Zar, the supremo of the Invisible Hand, had announced that you were killed by his group. Everyone thought you were dead. Where were you when the nation needed you the most?'

Before Neel could answer the question, he saw the first Chinese army truck approaching.

'Devil, get ready. It's time for some action.'

Heena hurriedly asked, 'Can you wear our mike so we can talk? It's attached to the drone below the screen.' Neel took the mike, which had a camera attached to it, and wore it around his ears. The drones moved back above him. The viewers could now see what Neel was seeing.

The battalion was approaching slowly. He could see nearly twenty-odd tanks and trucks with troops, accompanied by drones hovering around them. *This is a seriously upgraded army,* he thought.

And then they stopped.

'We have a visual on the ground, sir,' the Chinese major reported to his senior.

'Say what? We were assured that there would be no one on the ground,' he said, looking at the screen in his vehicle.

'Sir, of course a few rats would remain. We are here to sweep the ground, aren't we?'

'You're right, what's the fun without any friction? Send in your drones and check what's going on,' ordered the senior. Two drones moved ahead and a satellite zoomed in on the area.

In the meantime, Heena asked the question again, 'Kalki, where were you? The country wants to know!'

The news was currently trending on every social network, news channel and radio on the globe.

'I was betrayed by a few of our own countrymen and captured by the Invisible Hand. I was later handed over to the Chinese Intelligence Agency and would be dead by now if it wasn't for one person from China, who believed it was important for me to escape and save the world from General Jian's tyranny.' The wind blew fiercely as he continued to speak, his long wavy hair flowing behind him. 'I'm Kalki and I'm not dead. I'm here to stop the Chinese army from occupying my motherland.'

Heena cleared her throat and said, 'Sir, I cannot explain how relieved we are to see you alive. There are celebrations going on in the streets of India as we speak. But are you aware that a treaty signed by the IHC agrees to give away the land you are standing on to China?'

'I don't give a damn about the treaty or the IHC or that freak called General Jian. This is my country and any enemy who sets foot on this land will be destroyed.'

The viewers were stunned; he looked menacing and determined.

'What are you going to do, Kalki? You seem to be standing alone against a formidable enemy.'

'I will do what is necessary. I will protect my country or die protecting it.'

'Who exactly are you, Kalki? Apart from the fact that you are always there when the country needs you, we don't know anything about you.'

He was silent.

'This is the first time you have ever come on live television. Why fight in the shadows?' she persisted.

'Who am I? Why do I want to fight in the shadows? These are epic questions that don't have short answers, but I'll try to answer them because I want to tell the people of India that they are not alone. I want to tell them that we will not be defeated. I won't let that happen.'

They listened as the words fell out of the man like a war cry.

'My name is Neel Digvijay Kalki,' he said, and removed his mask. For the first time, the nation saw who Kalki really was. He threw the mask aside and continued, 'I'm many things but, first and foremost, I am a son of Mother India; a son who is not afraid to sacrifice his life a hundred times to defend this country. I'm the proud son of a soldier who sacrificed his life to protect this country. I'm the grandson of General Ramsey, a great servant of India and the advisor to the late Prime Minister Acharya. I'm the founder of the Astras group, the company that made the drones that guard India's borders. The weapons, the armour, the radar and the robots that our military uses are built by my group.

'I'm an orphan; I lost my parents and family members to war and terrorism very early in my childhood. All through my life, I have fought to ensure no other child goes through what I have. My life is all about protecting this country and punishing our enemies—internal or external. I know there are people right now who would be upset at seeing me here today, especially General Talwar of India, General Jian of China and the Invisible Hand's Master Zar.'

There was a hush in the studio and the streets. They had heard conflicting stories about Kalki, the Astras and the boon or the threat they were to the nation and the world. Every week, every month, they had heard stories about how Kalki had protected his country and his people. But this was the first time they witnessed him in flesh and blood.

Neel continued, 'I had to stay in the shadows because you cannot defeat someone you cannot see. I wanted no fame, money or power. I wanted to be a silent warrior, a guardian protecting Bharat Mata. Soon, I became a soldier who would punish our enemies if they dare look at our mother. I'm the man who enemies have tried to eliminate a hundred times but who refuses to die. I'm a man who gives them nightmares … I'm basically just bad news for them.'

He shouted the next part, 'Today, it was important for me to step out of the shadows. I had to give my countrymen the confidence that we will defeat the enemy. Make no mistake, we will restore democracy and we will punish those responsible for killing PM Acharya and our leadership.'

'Sir, you have to see this,' Pradeep said to General Talwar in New Delhi, hurrying to the TV screen.

'That pest! Why is he still alive?' roared Talwar.

Chinese drones came in close to stream the video live to the Chinese command centre. It was broadcasted to the screen in General Jian's chamber, where he was in a meeting.

'Son of a bitch!' Jian yelled. Everyone sat silently in the room.

'Why doesn't he die? Why? What does it take to kill this one man?' he screamed. No one dared to look at him.

'Goddess, what have you done? You traitor,' he snarled and pushed a table aside, which rammed into the wall with a thud. 'And now he is challenging us with that dog by his side? What is he thinking?'

'It must be a trick to confuse us, a strategy to throw us off guard,' Agent Chang said. 'There is no way he can stop us. He wants the sympathy of the world with him. If we crush him, we become the villains in the eyes of the world. If we don't, we become pussies who don't have the courage to remove a man who stood against our entire battalion.'

In New Delhi, General Talwar watched people chant Kalki's name and place his pictures on a pedestal of gods.

He received a call on the intercom.

'General, the RAW chief Rathore is here with the Russian hacker,' his secretary informed.

'Send them in.'

'Tell me you have some good news,' he said when they came in.

'Sergey has done the impossible. He has cracked the security device that Kalki's company had designed,' announced Rathore.

'Are you sure?' asked Talwar, getting up instantly.

'Yes,' Sergey confirmed in a heavy Russian accent. 'As I told you the last time, the Rift had nine levels of game play, or rifts, that work as security layers. It would have been impossible for anyone to crack it but they committed one mistake.'

'What mistake?'

'How do I explain to you … Okay. So, in laymen terms, the creator of the device kept one door open that, I think, could be used by him to break in, if required, and I found that loophole. We could extract all the files because of it. It total, we have 417 files.'

'Can I see those files? What are they?'

'They are all encrypted. It will take us a week to decrypt them but we will crack it,' Sergey assured.

'But he decrypted one file and it gave us information on a secret facility called the Garuda City,' said Rathore.

'Garuda? Do we have the location?'

'Yes, we do.'

Talwar's excitement knew no bounds.

'Prepare to attack in full force. But keep it very discreet. No one should know about it, even Pradhan.'

'Yes, sir.'

'Don't make any mistakes this time. While the Chinese kill that foolish Kalki on the border today, you will bring me all the machines and information they possess. Give the orders for attack!'

Neel continued speaking on the screen, 'It pains me to see that today I have to stand alone to fight an enemy at our doorstep. I have strong reasons to believe the IHC is under the influence of the Invisible Hand; I don't know what they are planning together but I know it's not in the best interest of this country. The Invisible Hand is a strategic weapon of General Jian and together they have vowed to take India back to an era of slavery. But no, sir, that's not going to happen because we will not be the puppets or victims in this game. I won't compromise the integrity of our motherland, even if it means I have to sacrifice my life today.'

General Ramsey saw the live-stream on his phone. He was ecstatic to see him in flesh and blood, but concerned that he was standing up against an entire battalion.

He looked up at the flag he held and stressed, 'Today, I'm going to die for my country. Yes, you heard me right. I will either die protecting my country or I will be successful in sending the Chinese back to their side. Let my death be a reminder for all of you that we will not succumb without a fight. We will give our blood and soul to protect this nation.'

Such was the power in his voice; such was the tension at that time; such was mood of the nation, that all they needed was a leader who could show them a way. And the nation had found one.

'Kill him, kill him,' Jian yelled. 'I don't care what the world thinks. Let's finish this maniac; he is our biggest problem. We'll deal with everything else later on. I need the Weapons of Gods. I need Shambala. He cannot ruin our plans.'

'General, it would look cowardly on our part to kill one man standing in front of our army. The world is watching us.'

'He is openly challenging our authority. He is calling me a freak! If we keep silent, the world will think I'm a coward,' snarled Jian. 'Take him out. Teach that dog how to bow to Jian!'

The wind suddenly stopped; there was perfect silence in the valley all of a sudden, as though the gods had stopped breathing to watch what was about to happen.

'Kalki,' said Heena. 'I have no words to describe my feelings right now, sir. The entire nation is standing with you today. You are not alone; the very spirit of this nation is standing with you. I salute you, Kalki. May the gods intervene and help you today. The prayers of the entire nation are with you.'

Neel took a deep breath. 'Jai Hind!' he roared, tightening his grip over the flag to fill himself with the courage he needed to face his death. His heartbeat had reached a fever pitch.

'Jai Hind, sir!' said Heena.

Neel took the mic out and threw it aside.

Pradhan walked hurriedly into General Talwar's chamber.

'General, there are going to be protests all over the country! If Kalki dies, people will burn things down. You are playing with fire.'

'Stop it, Pradhan! I don't care. I will give a shoot at sight order to eliminate the protests.'

'Take my suggestion, General. Call off the treaty with China. You still have time. Ask them to back off immediately.'

Talwar laughed.

'Have you lost your mind, Pradhan? Call it off to save Kalki?'

'No, for the sake of this nation, General. It will lead to a revolution.'

'I'm not backing off and that's final,' he yelled.

The Chinese trucks and drones started moving forward, announcing from their speakers for anyone in the area to move out. They came to a distance of about two miles away from the village and stopped. They announced once more, 'You are standing in Chinese territory. We request you to move back immediately. I repeat, move back immediately.'

'Brace yourself, Devil,' said Neel. The dog barked and took up his attack stance.

'What is he going to do? Kill us all with that flag?' the commander of the Chinese battalion scoffed.

His subordinate laughed. 'Perhaps he is counting on the dog.'

'Don't be foolish. No one in his right mind would do this. Be careful, this could be a trap,' said another soldier.

'He's right. But I don't see anything on the radar or our satellite images or our drones,' said the subordinate.

'Move back immediately or we will open fire. I repeat, we will open fire.' Neel didn't move an inch.

All the screens in India—the billboards, the malls, the televisions screens at homes, schools, and even the prisons—showed it live. People thronged the nearby screens or glued themselves to their mobile phones to watch the streaming video.

Watching the television, the soldiers in the Indian army broke into chaos. 'What are we doing here when a lone man is fighting our war?' asked an angry soldier. They felt frustrated that they had orders to do nothing. The nation had taken such a heavy toll recently that all they wanted was to fight the enemy.

'Fire a warning shot. Hundred meters away. I'm sure he will shit his pants and run. Let's have some fun before we kill him,' the Chinese commander ordered.

A Chinese tank came forward and raised its barrel at Neel. The audience watched with bated breath; they closed their eyes and prayed hopelessly.

Neel clenched his fist around the flag.

'Fire!' said the commander.

The rocket came out with a thumping sound. Neel could see it coming towards him with great speed. He held the flag and didn't bat an eyelid when it hit the ground a hundred meters ahead of him. The impact shook the earth, kicking the soil high up in the air so there was no visibility, and causing the birds to fly in alarm. The camera drones circled around but couldn't catch any view of Neel or Devil. There was pin-drop silence across the country, like a spell had been cast to take away the vocal cords of humanity.

It took a while for the dust to settle. They could see the flag still fluttering in the air and it raised hope in their hearts. Finally, they saw the man and dog standing exactly where they had been before.

'Is that all you got?' Kalki yelled, his words reverberating. 'Come on, you cowards!'

People erupted into cheers on seeing him alive.

'Fifty meters. Fire!' ordered the commander.

They fired another missile and, this time, it was too close to Kalki. The impact was so enormous that it threw Kalki and Devil off the ground; they went flying back by twenty meters. There was no way to survive that blast.

'Confirm whether the target is neutralised,' said the commander.

Yet again, they waited for the dust and smoke to settle. The nation sat at the edge of their seats, some crying, some banging their fists on the table, some throwing chairs around, some ranting away on social media and a majority praying to God to help Kalki.

There was no movement on the screen.

'This is the end of India,' Heena breathed out.

TWENTY THREE

The dust settled in a few minutes and they couldn't see the flag. The camera drone finally spotted Kalki lying face down on the ground, still holding the flag. He looked unconscious. His clothes were in tatters and blood spread over the ground around him.

'Come on, Kalki. Wake up,' said Heena. 'Don't die on us. India needs you.'

General Ramsey kept his eyes on the screen, watching with dread. 'Dear universe, be on his side today. I beg you,' he said out aloud.

A masked vigilante who people thought was dead had come back to awaken a decaying nation. India, at that moment, was united; people of every walk of life, every religion, every stratum, became one to pray for this stranger who was standing up alone against the enemy.

Devil limped towards Kalki and barked. The dog was wounded and bleeding. He barked again and again, trying to wake him up.

'This is undoubtedly one of the worst days in the history of India. Out of a billion and a half people, only one man has the balls to fight for the country and he is now lying immobile with no one except a dog trying to come to his rescue. What has happened to us? When did we become a country of such spineless people?' Heena went on, forgetting that she was facing an imminent arrest after the show. Loud noises came from outside and her assistant came running.

'The police are here, Heena, what do we do?' he asked, live for the entire nation to see. 'They want us to shut the transmission.'

'Don't open the door. We will not stop this transmission today, even if they shoot me down,' declared Heena. She turned towards the camera. 'Dear viewers and citizens of India, let's not give in to the atrocities of the IHC. Let's stand up and fight alongside Kalki. I urge all the other television channels to continue showing the broadcast of what's going on in Ladakh right now. My blood is boiling, isn't yours? Are we just going to sit and do nothing? Each one of us must ponder over this.'

The scene of a dog pulling a dead man by his collar enraged the youth in the country; a revolution had already begun in their minds. The war, the emergency, the inaction of the army and the inability of the police force to control the unabating law and order problems had taken a heavy toll on everyone. Kalki had come at a poignant juncture to stir a storm in the souls of the youth.

The enemy trucks were waiting to confirm whether he was dead. 'All clear, sir. The target doesn't seem to have moved for a while. No signs of life,' said his subordinate.

'The show is over! Let's get back to work,' the commander replied.

The trucks and tanks started moving again.

Devil managed to turn him around and licked his face but he remained unconscious. He continued to bark with vigour. Blood continued to flow through his wounds but there was no movement whatsoever.

You are the hope against hope. You are the pillar on which this nation is learning to stand back up. Draw strength from the heartbeats of a billion people and rise. He heard Arya's voice in his mind.

'I don't have the strength.' He managed a breath.

Your limitations are in your mind; they are not real. You're limitless.

He opened his eyes and took a deep breath.

Rise and show them you are not easy to kill. Rise!

And he sat up, mustering all his courage. His body had almost given up but he gathered all the energy that was left in him and tried to get up.

'Wait a minute. There is some movement. He's moving! Kalki is alive,' Heena reported with excitement. He struggled to get up, pushing up on his hands before he fell down again. He didn't give up; he fixed the flagpole on the ground and got up with its support.

'Sir, he is back,' said the Chinese subordinate.

'Kill him! Fire directly,' the Chinese commander ordered, frustrated.

Kalki kissed the flag and held it high. The nation cheered with every step he took towards the enemy but they knew he wouldn't survive the next impact.

'Bharat Mata ki Jai!' he roared with all the energy left in him.

'Enough of this nonsense. Fire!' said the commander, and they fired directly at Neel. The rocket came in hot but exploded mid-air. There was something different this time. The thunder had gained ten times more volume, making everyone close their ears. There was no dust and Kalki stood holding his flag.

'What was that? What just happened?' asked the Chinese commander, worried.

'What just happened?' Heena wondered on-air.

'No idea,' said Ponappa.

They saw Kalki and the dog standing in the same position. *Right on time, Tiger*, Kalki thought and thanked the universe. *Let the show begin.*

The Chinese checked the radar but nothing was visible anywhere.

'How did we miss the target?'

'No idea, sir.'

'Don't miss this time. Fire another one!' said the commander.

They fired again and the missile moved swiftly towards Kalki. However, the it was intercepted by a smaller, and much faster, missile and exploded mid-air.

'What is going on?' said the Chinese commander. 'Is this some trap by the Indian army?' he said, dialling his superior at HQ.

'Sir, an unknown party is intercepting our missiles,' he spoke into the receiver.

One of the news camera drones went close to Kalki.

Neel took a mic from the drone and spoke, 'My dear brothers and sisters of India, till now you have only seen our defence forces taking a beating. You have seen our country being ravaged by ruthless dictators of enemy nations. You have seen the Chinese battalion trying to kill a lone man. But now you will see how India can respond. You will see the gods descend to Earth to defend us. I bow before Mother India and vow to slaughter every enemy who has ever set foot on our soil. Welcome to my show!'

The audience looked at each other in confusion. 'The gods will defend our country?' Heena asked, baffled, just before powerful lightning bolt flashed in the sky. A thunderbolt hit the ground with an earth-shattering sound and created a quake that shook the enemy tanks and trucks.

The impact kicked up dust and, before it could settle, five more gigantic thunderbolts struck the earth, causing tremors that shook the valley.

'What is going on?' asked the Chinese commander, his mouth wide open.

'I don't know, sir. That lightning came out of nowhere!' mouthed the commander.

'Something just crash landed on Earth,' said the subordinate, alert.

When the dust settled, people couldn't believe their eyes. They saw nine giants walking out of the dust to stand beside Neel. In one hand, they held their gadas, the power mace; in the other, the Indian flag.

'Is this for real or am I daydreaming?' Heena said in disbelief.

'What are those?' Ponappa asked, dumbfounded.

The giants were like nothing anybody had seen before; they sent a chill down the spines of the enemy battalion.

'Move back! Move back!' the commander said. 'Take positions!'

The world was spellbound. It was a scene straight out of a sci-fi movie.

The giants held up their flags simultaneously and stuck the sharp end into the ground, erecting nine poles with the Indian tricolour fluttering high up in the air.

'There is something familiar about them,' Heena mumbled.

When the drone closed in, they saw the faces of the giants.

'Dear God!'

'Is that Lord Hanuman?' Ponappa gasped.

Everyone saw the Vanaroids in their full glory, each one different in shape, size, character and visage. They had weapons loaded on their torsos, shoulders and backs. They looked menacing, yet they were the gods; they had only one thing on their mind—to tear down the enemy.

'I never thought I would say this, but I think what we are seeing is the Lord Hanuman and his vanar sena,' Heena uttered.

'The gods have indeed descended on the earth!' said Ponappa, his mouth wide open.

'Jai Bajrang Bali!' screamed Kalki. The Vanaroids roared, the sound creating tremors in the valley. It was as though a hundred lions had roared simultaneously.

The enemy battalion flung back; they didn't know what they were up against.

'Jai Bajrang Bali!' chanted the entire country, rejoicing at the appearance of Lord Hanuman.

Kalki held the tricolour high.

'Vanar Sena! Destroy the enemy!' he cried out, his war cry echoing in the valley.

To be continued...

SCRIPTURE OF GODS

※

SCRIPTURE OF AYUR (LIFE OR VITAL POWER)

The first scripture is based on medicine and life sciences. One would be amazed at the advanced knowledge our ancestors had achieved. From genetics to microbiology to vaccinations, they had known more about the human body and brain than what our current society has discovered in the last few centuries.

This scripture contains a treatise on yoga and the benefits of meditation for healing, using both extrinsic and intrinsic streams of energy. Over the centuries, knowledge of this original scripture passed on through the ancient education system through the sages, even contributing to the vedas. The practice of Ayurveda emerged centuries later with the knowledge of this original scripture.

Further, it is believed that the technique of making medicine and vaccinations emerged from this scripture. The ancient texts such as *Charaka Samhita*, *Sushrata Samhita* and even *Kama Sutra* are believed to have been derived from the knowledge of this original scripture.

This voluminous scripture details how the human body can tap into different sources of natural energy including the Sun, moon and cosmic rays to survive for years without food or water. It also shows a path to enhance human strength and attain superhuman physical abilities.

Lastly, it talks about a technique to enhance human lifespan by hundreds of years. One of the Rudras' forefathers invented a technique to rejuvenate body cells by throwing out toxins and increase longevity. When these toxins flush out, they leave a blue tinge on the skin over the decades making the Rudras look blue naturally.

SCRIPTURE OF BODHI SHAKTI (AWAKENED POWER OF THE MIND)

The second scripture deals with mind powers, communication, mind-reading – accessing dreams and telepathy. However, not everyone is gifted with a mind that can master mind-reading. Moreover, telepathy is the most difficult skill to learn. Few possess the power to even attempt it successfully.

This illuminative scripture contains a treatise on controlling matter with your mind, both living and non-living. Only a few people in the history of the Rudras have succeeded in mastering this art.

Human brain can send waves. You can amplify these waves and direct them to do whatever you want. You can change the frequency and wavelength to be able to communicate with almost anything.

Furthermore, this scripture explains how to enhance mental powers and attain unthinkable psionic abilities that people would consider paranormal. These powers include astral projection, apportation, clairvoyance, hydrokinesis, pyrokinesis, levitation, remote viewing, altering perception and so on. People often confused this with magic and art of trickery.

Most powerful forms of mind powers include altering the reality and the laws of nature itself. Only the Avatars had the power to manifest this power, hence being called the Gods, the one who can manifest miracles.

SCRIPTURE OF THE IMMORTAL YODDHA
(GREAT WARRIOR)

This legendary scripture contains nine volumes of dissertation and tutorial on warfare, both physiological and psychological. They teach principles of complex martial art techniques that include attaining superhuman strength and paranormal abilities to control the *pancha mahabhuta* (five great elements of nature), which are *bhūmi* (earth), *jala* (water), *agni* (fire), *vayu* (airwind) and *vyom* or *shunya* (space or zero).

For example, how to kill someone by a mere touch by reversing the pulse of their body or how to make your body into a weapon or how to levitate while fighting an enemy.

Known as the most lethal teachings of martial arts ever known to humanity, it is believed that the warriors who master these texts become invincible and immortal, as death itself cannot defeat them.

SCRIPTURE OF RASAYANA (ALCHEMY)

The great scripture of Rasayana is about Alchemy and the science of metamorphosis or transmutation of metals. It talks about the technology of making powerful and complex Yantras (machines) and Astras (weapons) that are unheard of, even defying the laws of nature.

The *Weapons of Gods* were forged by the forefathers using the knowledge in the scriptures. These yantras and astras are believed to have the power of destroying the universe, let alone Earth. The *Weapons of Gods* were hidden in the city of Shambala but was lost in time to humanity. It is believed to be hidden somewhere deep within the Himalayas in the vicinity of Mount Kailash.

SCRIPTURE OF SURYA (SUN)

This scripture talks about light and how to control and utilise it. Light is the source of all our energy and our ancestors were clever to exploit its powers for both our body and matter. *Weapons of Gods* enhanced the speed of light. We can do wonders when we break the absolute velocity and that's what some of these mega-weapons do.

SCRIPTURE OF YUGAS (TIME)

This scripture contains a discourse on how to attain omnipresence – a power to simultaneously be present or move back and forth in past, present and future. Also, a power to travel between the multiverse or the parallel universes that exist from eternity to eternity. Further, it explains what is time, space and space-time continuum and achieve teleportation, time travel, and space travel.

It also delves into the eternal cycle of time and the four yugas – Satya Yuga, Treta Yuga, Dwapara Yuga and Kali Yuga.

SCRIPTURE OF VIMANA (AVIATION)

This technological scripture is about avionics, the science of flight, and also talks about how to create anti-gravity, build advanced space crafts and aircrafts, travel at the speed of light, use the power sources of nature to propel engines infinitely and create machines that can even enter the core of a burning star.

SCRIPTURE OF PRALAYA (DESTRUCTION)

Known as the book of the destruction, this scripture delves into anthropology, the science of civilizations, the evolution, politics, economics and predictions of the rise and fall of societies. As cycles of birth, destruction and rebirth of civilizations take place, a pattern emerges through these cycles and the volumes of this scripture dissect key factors of this process and teach how to navigate through these challenges and keep humanity from becoming extinct – this ultimately becomes a core responsibility of the Rudras society.

SCRIPTURE OF AVATARS

And the last but not the least, the ninth scripture contains a treatise on how to acquire Absolute Knowledge or Enlightenment. From time to time, a handful of people through the ages have attained this stage. We call them the Avatars. Like Rama and Krishna, they all attained Absolute Knowledge in their own ways; some were born with it and some had to struggle to attain it.

This scripture has not been read or understood by anyone in centuries, for the one who understands it will be the next avatar.

AUTHOR'S NOTE

I was always fascinated with the prophecy of Kalki, the 10th and last avatar of God. As predicted by the ancient Hindu *puranas* and epics, his birth will end the age of darkness on Earth. It is said that Kalki the Destroyer will be all powerful, and merciless towards evil.

But what if this God incarnate was born mortal?

It's true that fiction follows facts. Intrigued by this idea, when I further researched ancient Indian secret societies, I was captivated by what I discovered – myths and legends of mysterious stealth groups that were created to protect the ancient wisdom of our forefathers. This laid the foundation for *The Rudras* in my book.

I take pride in India's history and knowledge that our ancient ancestors possessed. Sadly, most of that knowledge was lost to wars and invasions. But what if we are wrong? What if this knowledge was not destroyed but hidden? What if this was done so that it couldn't be used for evil?

And what if there was a deeper agenda? What if our forefathers wanted to secretly pass on the omnipotent knowledge and cryptic message to the prophesized last avatar? This premise formed the basis of this trilogy, which is written on a fabric of mythology woven with threads of science-fiction and the tense geopolitical equations that truly surround us today.

I first hit upon the idea on 12th December 2010 and it kept me wide awake for a few nights. It has taken me nearly eight years of research, writing, rewriting and practically living this book – a journey to create the true Indian superhero; Kalki, the last avatar, in flesh and blood.

I feel blessed to have had this vision and have loved every bit of this creative journey. I hope you enjoy this rollercoaster ride!

ACKNOWLEDGEMENTS

The eight years I spent writing *The Last Avatar* were a defining chapter of my life, one filled with excitement but also a lot of hard work. The canvas of the trilogy was so huge that it took me considerable time to narrow down the plot and create my characters. Moreover, everything had to be based on a well-researched premise. I couldn't have accomplished this without few exceptional people who stood beside me through the journey.

I will have to start by thanking my pillar of strength, my reality check, my wife Sonia Sharma, who read unending drafts and provided invaluable suggestions to help me create the Kalki universe. Writing this book meant taking away time from my family; it wasn't easy and I couldn't have done this without you. Thank you, Sonia!

My mother Vijaya Mudagal and father Dr Gurappa Mudagal, whose blessings and constant guidance kept me going. They are more eager than anyone else to read this book. Mom, Dad, I hope you find it worth the wait!

I thank my agent, Kanishka Gupta, who continues to believe in me and my work. The book wouldn't have seen the light of the day without you.

I am excited to be working with a great publishing house, HarperCollins India, which has put all its weight behind the book. Thank you, Manasi Subramaniam for commissioning this book and Arcopol Chowdary for being my guiding light in the publishing industry.

A very special thanks to my editor, Swati Daftuar, who believed in my vision and worked relentlessly to help me chisel the book to a new level. I'm fortunate to have found you. Thank you, Swati!

I cannot forget to thank my team at my company GoodWorkLabs who helped me with the graphics for the Vanaroids, as well as with creating the Age of Kalki website, marketing the book and a million other things. You are a wonderful team!

Lastly, my work is built on top of the works of the giants, who scripted the ancient Indian epics and *puranas*. I bow to them for blessing me with this story.